RULES

Desire, Oklahoma 4

Leah Brooke

MENAGE AMOUR

Siren Publishing, Inc.
www.SirenPublishing.com

A SIREN PUBLISHING BOOK
IMPRINT: Ménage Amour

RULES OF DESIRE
Copyright © 2010 by Leah Brooke

ISBN-10: 1-60601-755-1
ISBN-13: 978-1-60601-755-5

First Printing: February 2010

Cover design by Jinger Heaston
All cover art and logo copyright © 2010 by Siren Publishing, Inc.

ALL RIGHTS RESERVED: This literary work may not be reproduced or transmitted in any form or by any means, including electronic or photographic reproduction, in whole or in part, without express written permission.

All characters and events in this book are fictitious. Any resemblance to actual persons living or dead is strictly coincidental.

Printed in the U.S.A.

PUBLISHER
Siren Publishing, Inc.
www.SirenPublishing.com

DEDICATION

To my supportive readers.
Thanks for all the wonderful emails.

RULES OF DESIRE

Desire, Oklahoma 4

LEAH BROOKE
Copyright © 2010

Chapter One

Erin Robinson looked around the beautifully decorated restaurant and couldn't help but appreciate all the hard work that had gone into the party. She knew Ethan Sullivan and Brandon Weston, who owned the restaurant and adjoining hotel, had spent all week getting it ready for tonight.

Twinkling lights glittered from the ceiling, creating a romantic but festive atmosphere. Poinsettias had been placed everywhere, small ones, huge ones, and every size in between. A huge tree covered with gold ornaments stood in the middle of the buffet area so that it could be seen from all sides. Erin had noticed the strategically placed bunches of mistletoe earlier and carefully avoided them. She knew they would be well appreciated tonight and used often, but not by her. As she looked around, several people smiled or waved. She smiled back politely, feeling completely out of place. She knew she'd never really belong here.

Although she lived here now and knew most of the people at the party, Erin didn't consider herself one of the locals. She'd moved to Desire a few months ago when her baby sister, Rachel, had gotten pregnant. Erin had tried to get her sister to come live with her in Houston, but Rachel had a thriving business here and two men that she loved, and wouldn't budge. So Erin had quit her job as secretary to the vice president of a big oil company, bought half of Rachel's lingerie store and moved to Desire. She'd missed her baby sister so much. And it was only a matter of time before Rachel would need her.

Erin's gaze slid to where Rachel and Boone Jackson, one of her sister's *two* husbands, slow danced. Rachel looked beautiful in her dark green maternity gown, looking ridiculously happy as she and Boone carried on an intimate conversation on the dance floor. The love Boone and his brother Chase felt for her sister showed in every look, every touch, and if Erin could wish for anything, it would be that Rachel's marriage could last.

Boone looked brawny and overwhelmingly masculine next to her petite sister, his head bent attentively, listening to whatever Rachel said, his big hands holding her gently. Erin noticed that one of his hands occasionally slid over Rachel's swollen abdomen as though reminding himself that all was well with the baby.

Several weeks ago, they'd had a slight scare with Rachel's pregnancy. They'd all been terrified that she would lose the baby, but thankfully everything had worked out just fine. But the fear still remained. Boone, Chase and Erin hovered, always on the alert. She knew they drove Rachel crazy at times but she'd been taking care of her baby sister almost half her life and couldn't stop now.

She would continue to do so and stay in Desire, ready to pick up the pieces when Rachel's relationship with Boone and Chase fell apart.

Erin watched as Chase moved to the dance floor and after a few words with his brother, took his turn dancing with Rachel. Chase stood almost as tall as his brother and was just as large. Both men worked in construction and their bodies showed the effects of it. She'd never expected them to be so solicitous and gentle with her sister. But they were. They'd become even more so since learning that Rachel carried their child. She couldn't help but smile as Rachel laughed up at whatever Chase said to her and allowed herself to be enfolded in his arms to dance again.

How in the hell did her sister juggle two husbands?

Her gaze slid involuntarily once again to where Jared, Duncan, and Reese Preston sat on the other side of the room. Every time she looked over, she found at least one of them staring at her. This time, Duncan's eyes met hers from across the room, and yet another unwelcome jolt of lust slammed into her. His eyes held hers for several long moments before she could finally drag hers away.

Those heated glances from the Preston brothers kept her on edge and she did her best to avoid them. She hadn't been entirely successful. Of their own volition, her gaze slid toward them with annoying regularity. She could admit only to herself that she'd known the whereabouts of each of them since she'd walked through the door.

Needing to get away from temptation, Erin finished her drink and moved to the bar for another. The men standing at the bar could literally take a woman's breath away. Because of the very essence of the town, most of the men here just exuded sex appeal.

To say that Desire, Oklahoma was an unusual town would be putting it mildly. When she'd first arrived, Rachel's men had taken great pains to explain just how Desire differed from everywhere else. The men in Desire protected and coddled all of the women, absolutely adored them and did everything in their power to keep them safe and happy. They also thought nothing of turning their woman over their knees and spanking her if she did anything to risk her health or safety. Erin still struggled to understand why the women put up with that part.

The fact that Dom/sub and ménage relationships were the norm here had at first put her off. Considering Desire a town where the residents only thought of sex had her scrambling to figure out how to talk Rachel into leaving. Whenever she brought it up, Rachel refused. Boone and Chase got mad as hell.

Michael Keegan and John Dalton who owned the only bar in town, appropriately named The Bar, had volunteered their services tonight. They, along with another four of Desire's bachelors smiled as she approached the bar. Logan James owned the leather store and Beau Parrish owned the adult toy store.

Ryder and Dillon owned the garage in town and she'd heard that their partnership extended beyond the business. They wanted a woman to share that they could spend their lives with.

She just didn't get it.

It truly amazed her how these relationships worked here. The men and women looked so happy, more so than she had ever seen before. She just couldn't understand why. One man would make her nuts. Why on earth would anyone want to put up with more than one?

She knew it was none of her business, but she couldn't help being intrigued. She'd only come tonight because Rachel told her it would be expected. When she lived in Houston she had to attend many parties because of her job. During those parties the men had eyed other women behind their wives' backs and the women complained about the men while making catty remarks and setting up liaisons with other married men. She'd never even seen a hint of that since she'd moved here. She could honestly say that she'd never met a happier group of people in her life. It made her nervous as hell and reinforced her belief that she'd never fit in here.

The single men at the bar laughed and joked and all four men looked up, moving aside to create a space for her as she approached.

"Hello, Erin," Ryder drawled. "You look beautiful tonight. Where are your men?"

Erin blinked, suddenly wobbly, and leaned against the bar. "I don't have any men." They all smiled at her, flirting lightly, but none of the men in this town ever became obnoxious with it. For that she was grateful.

Logan lifted a brow. "But I thought—" He pursed his lips. "Never mind. You look ravishing, as usual. What would you like to drink?"

"I've got it." One of the extra bartenders who had gotten Erin's margarita earlier came forward with a glass. The woman wore thick makeup and Erin noticed that she couldn't seem to take her eyes off the men. "She's been drinking the virgin margaritas that Michael made for Rachel. Hi. I'm Patty."

Erin smiled politely. "Hi. I'm Erin. Do you live here?"

Patty giggled, sounding a little hoarse. "No. Mr. Sullivan asked me to help out tonight."

Michael stared at Patty oddly before turning back to Erin. "How do you like it? It's one of my specialties."

Erin thanked the woman and took a sip. It had gotten warm in here and she'd become really thirsty. "It's very good." She took another sip. "I usually don't care much for mixed drinks, but I like this."

Beau grinned at her. "When are you coming into my store? I have a lot of nice toys that I'd be happy to show you."

Erin's face burned and a giggle escaped before she could prevent it. Beau's wicked grin could make any woman's heart beat faster. Movie star gorgeous and thickly muscled, he had a slight Cajun accent that she knew drove the women wild. "I don't trust you enough to go to your store. I've heard stories about you and your toys." Erin clamped her mouth shut as her face burned even hotter. What the hell was she doing? She didn't flirt!

She looked up at Michael suspiciously. "Are you sure there's no alcohol in here?"

Michael shook his head. "None. I wouldn't lie about that, and I know Rachel's drinking it. I wouldn't dream of giving alcohol to a pregnant woman. Believe me, if I served alcohol to unsuspecting women in Desire, I'd be hung by my toes in the middle of Main Street."

The men chuckled, agreeing. Still thirsty, she finished her margarita, then asked for a glass of water.

The men gave her all their attention. Other places a woman might be ignored or would have been made to feel in the way, but not here. In Desire when a woman came near, all attention went to her. It would take a while before she would be used to it, if ever.

Feeling the beginning of a headache coming on, she decided to go outside for a bit. It had gotten even warmer in here with all these people and she needed some air. Another quick glance assured her she could slip away without Jared, Duncan, or Reese seeing her.

She'd started to walk away when Patty called her back. "When I saw you'd finished yours I fixed you another."

The men all looked at Patty oddly again. Not wanting her to get into trouble just for fixing a drink Erin didn't really want, she accepted it, thanking her for her thoughtfulness.

Excusing herself, she moved toward the terrace doors that had remained closed against the chilly night. Right now she welcomed the cold and she needed a few minutes alone. Walking out onto the brick terrace, she breathed in the frigid air and felt her head begin to clear a little. Sipping the icy drink, she avoided as much of the salty rim as possible. The salt just made her thirstier. She decided that for the rest of the night she would switch to water.

Wandering briefly around the terrace, it didn't take long before she started to feel the cold and moved closer to the wall, not quite ready to go in yet. The brick wall would afford some protection from the breeze. From here she could also study the people inside unobserved.

When she'd first come to Desire, she'd been totally unprepared for what she'd found. She didn't understand how these relationships could possibly work, but for some reason they did here. Whenever she got the chance, she observed them, trying to figure them out. One of the newest ménage relationships in town stood right in front of her.

Jesse Erickson stood with her husband, Rio, his arm around her waist as they spoke to her sister and brother-in-law, Nat and Jake Langley. Rio caressed Jesse as they stood talking, his big hand moving slowly up and down her back.

Jesse had come to town several months ago to visit her sister, Nat, and had decided to stay.

Rules of Desire 11

From what she'd heard, Clay and Rio Erickson, brothers who'd grown up here, had gone nuts over Jesse from the start and had set out to claim her. Both men were chauvinistic and headstrong. Erin had no idea how Jesse could stand it.

Jesse appeared to be very happy. She looked beautiful as always, her slim figure shown to perfection in the long column of red she wore. The strapless dress appeared to invite her husbands to touch and kiss her exposed shoulders all night. Clay came over and held something to Jesse's mouth, feeding it to her. The love on his face as he gazed at Jesse warmed something inside her. Before coming to Desire, she'd never seen so many men completely enthralled by their wives. As she watched, Clay dropped a kiss on Jesse's lips, then one of her exposed shoulders before walking away.

Jesse had been married to the men for several months. All three seemed extremely happy now, but Erin couldn't help but wonder how long it could last.

Jake and Nat looked happy. They had been married a number of years. Jake, known as a dominant or Master didn't share his wife. That made more sense to Erin. Not that she wanted a man who would try to dominate her. She couldn't even imagine herself trying to live that way. Erin pursed her lips as she thought about it. No. She could never let a man try to rule her. She couldn't stand one who was a pushover either. No. She wouldn't be able to put up with any of them for long.

Her gaze slid to Gracie Sanderson as she danced with one of her *three* husbands. The four of them owned the diner in town and seemed to bicker all the time, but anyone could see how much they all loved each other.

Gracie laughed as Finn whirled her around. She had also been married for several years and had two grown daughters. Erin couldn't understand how a marriage like that could have lasted so long. She had to admit, though, they all seemed happy. Go figure.

Her gaze involuntarily slid to Isabel Preston. Isabel also had three husbands and had been married the longest of anyone in town. Everyone could see that her husbands, brothers, absolutely adored her and she them. Isabel and her husbands owned the grocery store and had three grown sons.

Jared, Duncan, and Reese Preston apparently wanted to live the way their parents did, wanting a woman they could share. Erin had the uneasy feeling that she had become the woman they had set their sights on.

Jared, Duncan, and Reese made custom furniture. That's how she first met them. Her coffee table had been damaged in the move here and she'd gone to them to buy a new one.

Reese had been at the store and somehow had not only sold her a coffee table, but had talked her into going out to dinner with him.

Erin hadn't had a lot of sexual experiences and had been unprepared for the need that had raged through her whenever she spent time with him.

She'd met Jared, Reese's oldest brother, when Boone and Chase had ordered furniture made for the new baby. She'd been anxious to meet Reese's older brother along with the rest of his family.

More serious and quieter than Reese, Jared had a commanding presence she hadn't expected. When they'd shaken hands, she'd felt the same delicious tingle she had when Reese touched her. She'd pulled away quickly, embarrassed that she'd had such a reaction to him. She dated his brother, for God's sake!

No longer trusting her feelings, and feeling guilty as hell, she'd stopped dating Reese.

Duncan had been the one to really throw her off kilter. She'd met him at the club, of all places.

Club Desire, a BDSM club in town, was owned by Blade Royal, Royce Harley, and King Taylor. The men from Desire met there for a variety of reasons that Erin didn't want to think about. They hung out there quite a bit and offered each other support regarding the lifestyles they lived.

Erin had gone along when Kelly, Blade's new wife, had helped Rachel sneak in. Boone and Chase had been fighting their need for her sister and had gone to the club to avoid her. Rachel wouldn't tolerate that and had talked Erin into sneaking into the club with her.

Jared, Duncan, and Reese had been playing cards with Boone and Chase when they'd walked in. She'd carefully avoided looking at them. Instead she'd strained to see who'd been making all the noise on the other side of the room. Erin couldn't believe it when she saw Law and Zach Tyler, two more of Desire's men who liked to share, in the corner with their hands all over a naked woman. She'd made some flip remark to Rachel, asking about having sex with two men.

Before she could react, a steel band had wrapped around her waist from behind and a hand had covered her eyes. The hot wall of muscle against her back had caused a riot of sensation to shoot through her. Her body tightened in need, her breasts swelling, hot where they'd rested on the arm wrapped around her. She'd been amazed to feel her panties dampen. A low voice at her ear had made her tremble even more. "How would you like to find out what it's like with three men?"

Her body's overwhelming response to his whispered words had shaken her to the core and it had taken every ounce of self control not to let it show. Not until they got outside and the hand over her eyes had been removed did she get her first close up look at Duncan, who still had her pulled firmly back against him.

Just as handsome and compelling as his brothers, Duncan had an intensity that hadn't been leashed as tightly as Jared's. He also didn't have Reese's carefree attitude. Direct and volatile, Duncan made her hot as hell.

Erin carefully avoided all three of them now as much as possible, unable to get over the tumultuous effect each had on her.

"There you are."

Erin spun at Jared's voice. She'd been so lost in her thoughts that she hadn't heard him come outside.

He looked so tall and handsome in his tux, breathtaking in fact, but she knew he looked every bit as good in jeans and a t-shirt. She could only imagine how good he would look in nothing at all. She'd seen the rather impressive bulge in his jeans several times and her mouth had watered every damned time.

On top of that, he looked good enough to eat, especially with that sexy as hell scar on his cheek. It wasn't only the looks that got to her, though. He had a presence that she found impossible to ignore, and gave off vibes that bombarded her system, sexual vibes, making her even hungrier for him. His eyes glittered as he moved closer, the hazel green mesmerizing her as the power of his gaze slammed into her, making her shiver.

He frowned. "You're cold."

"No. I just—" She broke off when she felt his hands close over her arms. Thankful that he'd blamed her shiver on the cold, she shrugged. Now that she'd been pulled from her thoughts, she actually did start to feel the cold.

"You're half frozen!"

He took off his jacket and bundled her into it. "What are you doing out here? Duncan, Reese, and I have been looking all over for you. Come on. Let's get you inside where it's warm."

She couldn't help pulling the jacket tightly around her. It still carried the heat from his body along with his own unique scent. His arm around her waist held the delicious feeling closer as he propelled her back into the restaurant. She cursed the fact that the jacket kept her from feeling the touch of his hand on her hip more directly.

What the hell was she thinking? She didn't want to feel anything from any of them more directly. Did she? She took another sip of her drink wondering how much longer she could resist them.

When Jared started to lead her to his table, she paused unsteadily. "I've been sitting with—"

"Rachel, Boone, and Chase will know where you are. Come on. Let's get you warmed up."

Erin allowed Jared to lead her to the table he and his brothers shared with Hunter and Remington Ross. It should be illegal for a town to have this many gorgeous men running loose. The two men looked as forbidding as ever but looked up and smiled faintly at her approach. Both always looked so serious, seldom smiling. Combined with their muscular, hard-packed bodies, and quiet intensity, they had women clamoring to get close to them. She loved to watch, amused at the women's efforts. She didn't see Duncan or Reese, but she knew they would be joining them soon. If the men sitting at this table couldn't warm her, nothing could. Suddenly, sitting here sounded like fun.

Hunter inclined his head toward her. "I see you finally found her. Your brothers are still looking. Hi, Erin."

Erin took a seat, returning their smiles. "I didn't realize a search party had been sent out." She put a hand to her forehead. She'd gotten awfully warm again and it started to make her feel woozy.

She looked up to see Duncan and Reese approach from different directions.

Reese sat down next to her and looked up at Jared. "Where'd you find her?"

Jared sat on her other side and Duncan took a seat next to him. "She was alone on the terrace. She's half frozen."

Duncan reached for her hands, frowning when he felt them, wrapping his around them and rubbing gently. "Have you eaten?" His gaze moved over her. When she felt it on her breasts, felt her nipples pebble, she pulled her hands free and closed Jared's jacket tighter around herself. When she shook her head, he smiled at her. "I'll get you a plate. Maybe some hot food will help warm you up."

She watched Duncan as he moved away, admiring his broad shoulders and fluid grace. Imagining how smoothly he would move as he stroked his length into her, she squeezed her thighs together. Damn, her insides quivered just thinking about it. When she realized she'd been staring, she hurriedly turned her attention to the two men across from her. "Ethan and Brandon did a good job with the food.

Everything looks delicious. That chicken looks good."

Remington nodded. "It is. Would you like to try some?" He offered her a forkful.

She opened her mouth, allowing him to feed it to her and hummed her appreciation. "It *is* good!" Everything suddenly seemed wonderful. She began to relax and leaned back in her seat, tapping her foot to the music.

Reese glared at Remington and stood. "I'll go get some for you."

Rem's lips twitched as he continued eating. "So why did you go out to the terrace? It's cold outside."

Erin smiled and leaned toward him, whispering conspiratorially. "I needed some air and my feet hurt." She leaned back and smiled as he chuckled. "Men outnumber the women here. Most of the women are married and their dance partners don't like to share. The single ones, like me, are in high demand."

Hunter and Remington laughed. Jared chuckled at her expression, then frowned. "Do your feet still hurt? Put them up here."

Erin blinked. "No. They're fine now."

She jumped when Jared reached for her foot. "Really, Jared, they're—"

"Look at these shoes. I don't know how you can even walk—your feet are freezing!"

Erin tried hard not to show her reaction to having her feet lifted to his lap. He quickly unbuckled her high-heeled sandals and wrapped his hot hands around them. When his thumbs stroked her arch, the tingling sensation went all the way to her slit.

"Jesus! Your feet are like ice."

Wrapped in his big hands, her feet looked small and pale. She tried unsuccessfully to pull them away as he began to massage them. "Jared. That's not necessary."

"Not necessary? Your feet are ice cold."

She had to admit her feet had begun to warm. Struggling against the erotic feelings his touch inspired, she tried again to pull away. He didn't let her. Instead, he turned his chair to face her and settled her feet between his thighs. He continued to rub them as he and the Ross brothers spoke. With her feet being massaged by Jared, she'd long since lost track of the conversation.

If she even flexed her foot, she knew she would come in contact with the bulge in his dress pants. It took tremendous effort to keep her feet still. She wanted so badly to touch him, press against that impressive bulge and feel it grow. "Your scar makes you look like a pirate. Very sexy."

She smiled as seductively as she knew how, ignoring the way his eyes narrowed at her. She *could* flirt. Imagine that.

"Clay asked me earlier if I knew if Erin liked Missy."

Hearing her name, Erin turned to Hunter. "Who?"

Hunter chuckled. "Missy is a beautiful chestnut filly."

Jared spoke to Hunter but his eyes stayed on her. "Erin hasn't seen Missy yet. I was hoping to talk her into coming out to the ranch to meet her."

Erin blinked at him, her head spinning. Their masculine sexiness made her dizzy. "I'm supposed to come to your ranch to meet a horse?" Had she missed something?

Duncan appeared and leaned over to put a plate on the table in front of her. "Erin's coming out to meet Missy?"

Reese took the seat next to her and put another plate of food in front of her.

Erin looked at him incredulously. "I hope you don't think I can eat all of that."

Reese shrugged. "We don't know what you like yet, so we got you a little of everything."

Erin decided to ignore the 'yet' and thanked them before looking at Jared. "May I please have my feet back now? I can't eat like this." She slapped her hand over her mouth as a giggle escaped.

Jared frowned at her again and rubbed her feet one more time before releasing them. "At least they don't feel frozen anymore."

Erin bit her lips. They had started to get numb. "Thank you. I should give you your jacket back." She started to remove it, fumbling with it but with a hand on her shoulder, he stopped her.

"Keep it on. You're still cold. I'm going to go get a plate. Would you like another drink?"

She nodded and grinned. "Yes, please. I'm awfully thirsty."

He took her glass, downing the remains of it and lifting a brow. "Michael's virgin margarita?"

Nodding, she giggled. It seemed awfully intimate for him to drink out of her glass that way. It made her think of other intimacies. No, she wouldn't think about that. No matter how much she wanted him and his brothers, she couldn't go there. She just couldn't remember why. Mentally shrugging, she smiled up at him. "I'm not a big drinker."

Duncan stood. "I'll get it. I need another anyway. Anyone else?"

When Jared and Duncan left the table, Reese gestured toward her food. "Eat before it gets cold." He leaned close and whispered in her ear. "I've missed you like hell, sweetheart."

Erin looked up at him, startled by the admission, but unable to deny the warm glow that went through her. He smiled at her tenderly and she felt her face grow warm as she turned to her plate. "Me, too. I'm sorry I had to stop seeing you."

"Would you start seeing me again?"

Erin averted her gaze, staring down at her plate. "I can't. I'm sorry." Why did it hurt so much to say that?

Reese watched that she started eating and picked up his own fork. "Did I hear you say you would go riding with us?"

Erin almost choked on her food. "Riding? I've never been riding in my life."

Reese nodded. "We know. Rachel told us. You'll like it. Missy is very gentle."

She looked up to see Hunter and Remington nod their agreement. "Reese, I never said anything about riding. Hunter asked if I'd met

Missy, and Jared told me that Missy is a horse. A chestnut filly, I believe he said." Erin had no idea what that meant. They all seemed to be privy to a language she knew nothing about.

Reese nodded and reached over to stroke her hair. "My brothers and I have always had a fondness for chestnuts."

Before Erin could ask what he'd meant by that, Duncan rejoined them. He leaned over her to put her drink on the table in front of her, running a hand over her hair as he moved away. Involuntarily, she leaned into his caress before she could stop herself. She straightened hurriedly and stabbed another piece of chicken, frowning when it proved difficult.

Not believing she'd actually done that, she avoided Duncan's gaze as he took his seat next to Jared's. Damn, they all looked so handsome and their tuxedos did nothing to hide their fabulous builds. She *really* wanted them naked.

Reese turned to her. "So do you want to come over tomorrow to meet Missy?"

Erin took a sip of her drink, unsurprised to see that her hand shook. The intense attention Duncan and Reese gave her made her shaky. She'd gotten too hot again and pushed Jared's jacket off her shoulder.

Reese reached out to help her, eyeing her intently. "Are you okay, sweetheart?"

She saw the concern in his eyes and she couldn't imagine what worried him. "I'm wonderful. Isn't the music great? You look very handsome in your tux, do you know that?" She bit her lip to keep a giggle from escaping. She sure had the giggles tonight.

"Thank you, honey. Are you sure you're all right?"

"I'm fine. Isn't this a great party?"

Duncan watched warily, his eyes also narrowed, making him look like a dangerous rogue. His bad boy good looks and cocky grin aroused her so much she squirmed in her seat. She'd bet her half of the lingerie store he would be fantastic in bed. Ever since he'd pulled her against him at the club that night, she'd wanted him badly. Remembering the bulge in his jeans as he held her firmly against him, she shuddered. Damn, her panties had gotten soaked.

Then why did she feel like she should avoid him? Confused, she decided she'd think about it later.

It had been a long time since Erin had been in a situation that unnerved her. Known in Houston as being able to handle anything thrown at her, she found herself in unfamiliar territory with these men. That alone gave her a reason to avoid them. Maybe that's what bothered her.

Thinking about it made her dizzy. She wondered what would happen if they knew how they made her feel. It would be fun to find out.

"You're all so sexy, you make me dizzy when I'm with you." She giggled again before she could prevent it.

"Something wrong, love?"

Jared's voice had her snapping her head around and eyeing him as he took his seat next to her. Why did he call her 'love'? They barely knew each other. "No. Nothing."

Uncomfortably aware of the men's scrutiny, Erin tried to avoid their gazes and divided her attention between the Ross brothers and the food that she only picked at. She couldn't prevent another giggle that escaped. When Hunter and Remington excused themselves, Erin found herself alone with the three men.

"Have you had any alcohol tonight?"

Erin turned at Jared's question. She started laughing, finding it hilarious. "Nope. Need my wits tonight. That's why I'm drinking the virgin margaritas. So I can deal with the three of you. I should go back to my table. I'm awfully thirsty. Maybe I should get some water."

Without a word, Reese poured her a glass from the pitcher on the table and placed it in front of her.

"Thanks." Erin drank greedily before gesturing toward the dance floor. "Everyone seems to be having a good time."

Jared nodded. "Yes. There have been a lot of good changes since the last Christmas party. Three good marriages."

When Erin turned toward him, propping her chin on her hand to stare at him, he smiled at her and continued. "Boone and Chase used to make an appearance, probably just because they knew it was expected. They'd sit at the bar and have a couple of beers, talk to a few of us and leave. Now they're here with their new wife and a baby on the way and having a great time."

Erin glanced over to where Boone escorted Rachel back to their table. "I should get back to them." She reached for her shoes.

Jared stopped her with a hand on her arm. "They know where you are. Finish eating, love."

She pushed her plate away, the sight of the food making her nauseous. "I'm finished eating. I'd better—"

"Good." Jared pushed his own plate back and stood. "Come and dance with me. They're playing slow songs now so it won't hurt your feet. Leave your shoes off. I promise not to step on your toes."

He stood and helped her to her feet when she swayed. She knew she would have looked ridiculous refusing him. It was only a dance, and she really wanted him to hold her. He held her with one hand at her waist and the other clasped hers and held it to his chest.

It startled her that without her shoes, she only came up to his shoulder. "You're bigger than I thought."

He stared at her thoughtfully as he moved. He danced gracefully, making her shudder every time her nipples brushed against his chest. Her breath caught and she glanced up at him. He met her gaze innocently and she couldn't mention it in case he hadn't noticed. When she got bumped from behind, he hurriedly gathered her close and turned with her in his arms. She had to bite her lip to keep from gasping when she not only felt her nipples move against his chest, but also the evidence of his arousal. The spin had made her feel even dizzier.

Feeling his lips on her hair, she closed her eyes in bliss. Until Reese, it had been years since she'd been held like this and she'd never felt as desired as she did with Jared and his brothers. Wondering what it would feel like to be the center of attention the way the woman at the club had been that night with Law and Zach, she sighed. Leaning against him, she wished their clothes would just disappear. Erin giggled as she thought about everyone's clothing magically disappearing.

No! She couldn't do this.

Why not? Damn it, she'd forgotten again.

Stiffening, she pulled back. Jared allowed her a few inches, his hand firming on the small of her back. She couldn't help but watch, mesmerized as he drew her hand to his lips and brushed a kiss on her knuckles.

"Relax, love. I just want to hold you."

"You call me love." Erin looked up at him, then higher to the twinkling lights. When that made her dizzy, she closed her eyes and lowered her head to his chest. Finally she looked back up at Jared again to find him staring at her, frowning.

"I do." Inclining his head, he watched her intently.

"I like it." She giggled, shivering again when his eyes narrowed. Leaning close, she whispered, "But don't tell anybody."

God, she just wanted to lean into him, lay her head on his chest and feel his arms wrap around her. Just then they turned and she saw Reese approaching, smiling at her tenderly. She stiffened in Jared's arms. How could she respond to Jared this way when she had the hots for his brother?

"Can I cut in?"

Erin couldn't meet Reese's eyes. She no longer felt like dancing but after the way she'd stopped seeing him with no explanation, she couldn't very well shun him like that. He deserved better. And she owed him an apology.

She closed her eyes as Jared touched his lips to her forehead.

He passed her to his brother, murmuring something under his breath.

She went into Reese's arms feeling the now familiar warm, tingling sensation that she used to feel only with him. Knowing she also felt it for his brothers added another layer of guilt. She looked up to find him watching her, his eyes warm and tender and it made her feel worse. "Reese, I'm so sorry I stopped going out with you and never even told you why."

"Tell me now."

"I, well, I heard that you and your brothers, you know, um, share."

He nodded, smiling gently. "That's right."

She leaned close, lowering her voice. "Well, I can't do that. It's not right that I have the hots for your brothers, too." *Did she just say that out loud?*

"Why not?"

If he'd sounded sarcastic, she could have blown him off with a scathing remark, but he'd sounded interested and curious. She let out a sigh. "I just can't. I can't go from one man to another like that." She giggled again. "Besides, I'm not a seduct...um...seductress."

"You sound as though we would be willing to share you with the whole world."

"That's what it would feel like to me. I know that I sound presume...uh...presumptu—I mean, your brothers probably don't even like me."

"They do."

"Hell, I don't even know if *you* like me that way."

"I do."

"But I thought that it would be better just not to get involved with someone who wanted a relationship like that, when I know that it's something that I could never do. I didn't even tell anyone that I was seeing you and—"

"I know."

"When Rachel asked me if I knew you and your brothers I lied to her."

"I know."

"Because I didn't know how to tell her without sounding like I don't approve of her re…uh…marriage. I do, I mean as long as she's happy. I just don't see how it can work." Erin bit her lip afraid she'd already said too much. She looked up at him and saw his eyes twinkle in amusement. Suddenly she remembered what he'd said. "No! You and your brothers can't be interested in me that way." What would it be like to have all three of them to herself, naked and aroused? She wondered if they'd be willing to have sex with no strings. Wouldn't that be something? Maybe tonight. Already aroused, she wanted badly to feel one of them between her thighs.

"I'm afraid we are." Duncan moved in behind her. "I'd like to know just why you don't see how your sister's marriage will work."

She found herself spun into Duncan's waiting arms and felt Reese kiss her shoulder before walking away chuckling. The spin had made her dizzy again and she grabbed onto Duncan to keep her balance.

"I'm waiting." Duncan raised a brow at her continued silence.

"You're really handsome." She sighed and leaned against him. "You make me so hot." She leaned her head back and looked up at the lights. "They look so pretty."

He gripped her chin and tilted her face back to his. "What the hell's wrong with you tonight? I want an answer. Why don't you think your sister's marriage will work?"

He put her hackles up enough that she told him. "I don't understand how you can share a woman. I mean, if you really care about her, wouldn't you want her for yourself? And how could a relationship like that work without anyone getting jealous? If I had to share a man with another woman, I'd be ready to kill her." She clapped a hand over her mouth. *Had she said that out loud, too?* Funny, her lips felt numb.

Duncan regarded her thoughtfully. "Come on. We'll talk together. Lesson one in making a relationship like this work. All major conversations and decisions are shared."

Duncan led Erin back to the table, frowning when she stumbled. Meeting his brothers' inquiring looks, he steadied her. "Where are Hunter and Rem?"

Jared's lips twitched. "They left. I'm surprised they stayed as long as they did. What's going on?"

Duncan seated Erin. "Erin has some issues that need to be discussed and I told her that all major discussions and decisions had to be shared. She has some major issues with men sharing a woman. She doesn't think it can work."

Jared frowned. "But Rachel—"

Duncan sat back and crossed his arms over his chest. "She doesn't hold out much hope for them, I'm afraid."

Erin glared at him. "Big mouth."

Duncan grinned. "Lesson two. My brothers and I have no secrets from each other, especially regarding our woman."

"I'm not your damned woman. Stop saying that."

Jared leaned forward. "Do Rachel, Boone, and Chase know you feel this way?"

"No! And I don't want them to. I want them to be happy for as long as they can."

Duncan looked at his brothers before staring back at Erin. "Erin wonders how anyone could share a woman if they love her. She thinks that a man who loves a woman would want her all to himself."

Jared nodded. "That's true in a lot of cases, but not with us. We grew up in a house with three fathers. My mother is probably the happiest woman you'll ever meet. There has always been someone for her to talk to, always someone to spend time with her. I can't speak of my mother's sexual experience, of course, but in a relationship where there's more than one man, most women are completely satisfied."

He leaned forward and stroked her arm. "If I was making love with you, I may be so caught up in it that I would miss something, not see that you didn't like a certain touch or that you needed more attention elsewhere. There are also places that I can't reach from certain positions, and I only have two hands."

Erin's face burned, but could see that he was taking her question seriously. Unwillingly intrigued, she forced herself to face him as he continued, propping her chin on her palm. Her mind clouded and she fought to clear it.

"My fathers share the responsibilities, the work, and the worries. They had each other to talk to about problems instead of dumping things on my mother when she was busy with us." He sat back, taking a sip of his drink. "Our fathers don't have to worry so much and at least one is always available, making for a happy wife and happy children. A woman who doesn't have to worry because she has more than one man who takes care of things and is sexually satisfied, again, with more than one man to meet her needs is a happy woman. A happy woman makes the whole house a happy place to be."

Duncan nodded. "Sharing a woman with my brothers, I would have someone who understands exactly what I'm going through because they are in exactly the same boat. If our woman needed to make love, or talk, or just wanted to be held, we would make sure that at least one of us was available. There wouldn't be a 'Sorry, I have to finish this table tonight, so I don't have time to talk to you,' or 'Sorry I can't help the kids with their math homework while you're feeding the baby.'"

Erin saw that they had obviously given this a lot of thought. "But don't you get jealous?"

Reese shook his head. "We wouldn't let a woman play one of us against the others. We had a woman like that and got rid of her in a hurry. We would all want to spend time with her together and separately and we would all have to respect each other's time. Doesn't Rachel seem happy to you?"

Erin's glance slid to where her sister sat with her husbands. "Yes," she admitted. "At least for now. I see what you're saying though. You've given me a lot to think about. But, as good as you make it sound, I can't go from one man to another that way."

Jared eyed her thoughtfully. "Why don't you think about what we've talked about and we'll talk more tomorrow. Come out to the house and meet Missy and we'll go for a ride."

"I don't think—"

"You want to relieve your mind about your sister, don't you? We can talk some more where there's more privacy. Take time to think about it tonight, and we can talk about any other of your concerns tomorrow while we're riding."

Erin did want to talk to them more. They'd gone a long way in making her feel better about Rachel's marriage. And just seeing the others so happy tonight had already made her feel better. But she didn't want them to get the wrong idea. Maybe tomorrow she could convince them to have sex without a relationship. She had needs, dark needs she carefully kept hidden. She'd bet they could fulfill them. Maybe she should ask them tonight. They all looked at her expectantly and she realized they were waiting for an answer about riding.

"As long as you understand that it's just riding. I can't have a relationship like Rachel's, not that you asked but just to let you know up front. I just think that we should have that understood from the beginning. I know you didn't ask for more but—"

Duncan grinned. "I've already found out that she rambles when she gets nervous."

Reese put an arm around her and pulled her against him. "So you'll come riding with us tomorrow?"

Erin nodded and immediately regretted it. She didn't like the rambling comment and wanted to say something to him but suddenly she didn't feel well at all. "I can drive over—"

Jared shook his head. "No. One of us will pick you up at noon. Come on. Let's dance again before we have to take you home."

"But I came with—"

"Boone and Chase are taking Rachel home now." He gestured to where the three of them approached. "She's yawning. Poor thing." Duncan smiled as Rachel and her husbands walked up to their table. "Hey, honey, tired?"

Rachel smiled tiredly. "I was fine a little while ago. All of a sudden, I'm exhausted. I'll probably be asleep before we even get home. Are you ready, Erin?"

"Sure, I—"

* * * *

Jared stood and kissed Rachel's forehead. "I wanted another dance with her. We'll take her home. Go home and go to sleep, sweetheart. Let your men take care of you."

Rachel giggled. "Boone and Chase end up carrying me everywhere. I keep falling asleep on them."

Boone wrapped his arms around her from behind, rubbing a hand over where their baby grew. "We'll carry you everywhere gladly, baby."

"You say that now. Wait until I weigh a ton."

Boone looked down at her lovingly. "You're not going to weigh a ton, Rachel. You look beautiful. Come on. You and junior need your sleep."

"Everybody should go to bed." Erin nodded happily and giggled. She stopped, putting a hand to her stomach, before slumping against Reese.

Jared looked over at Erin and frowned again. She hadn't been acting like herself ever since he'd found her on the terrace. He looked over at Boone to see him watching his sister-in-law with narrowed eyes.

Boone scowled. "How the hell much did she have to drink tonight?"

"I was about to ask you the same question." Jared lowered his voice and watched Erin suspiciously. "She's had nothing but two virgin margaritas since she's been with us. Did somebody spike it?"

Boone's eyes went wide. "I hope not. Rachel's been drinking it all night." He looked over his shoulder at his brother. "Chase, stay with Rachel. I'm going to go talk to Michael and John."

Duncan stood. "I'll go with him."

Jared helped Rachel into the seat next to her sister and rubbed her shoulder. "We'll take care of her, sweetheart. Don't worry." They all worried about Rachel's blood pressure and no one wanted her upset.

Rachel eyed her sister worriedly. "She hardly ever drinks. Only when she's really depressed. I've never seen her like this."

Jared rubbed Erin's shoulder as she lay heavily on Reese, her eyes closed. He looked up at Boone's approach. "Well?"

Boone's face looked tight with anger as he moved to kneel between the two women. "The mix seems fine, but one of the bartenders disappeared. A woman told Michael and John that Brandon had sent her and told Brandon that Michael and John had hired her. John said that the woman appeared to like Erin and served her drinks all night. She's the one who fixed the drink when Duncan went up earlier. Duncan went to get the sheriff. We've got to get both of them to the hospital. We think the woman spiked Erin's drink with something. I don't want to take the chance that she spiked Rachel's."

Just then, the music stopped as a stone-faced Brandon stood on a chair. "Ladies and gentlemen, we may have a problem."

Jared tuned him out as Ace Tyler, the town sheriff, came to the table and went straight to Erin. Gripping her chin, he forced her to open her eyes. Jared watched in fear as the sheriff felt her pulse and turned to them. "You'd better get her to the hospital fast. Follow me. She'll probably pass out. She may be sick, make sure she doesn't drown on her own vomit."

He moved to Rachel and looked her over. "I don't think you've had anything but go just to be sure."

"Oh, my God! Erin, the baby!"

Ace smiled gently. "It'll be fine now."

Jared could see the temper in Ace's eyes as he stood and knew that the sheriff had moved beyond furious.

"Follow me. Hurry. I think she's been drugged. Let's get her in your truck and I'll put her in the recovery position. You're going to have to hold her in that position until we get her to the hospital."

A white-faced Reese picked Erin up and they all raced outside to their cars. Reese lay her on her side, listening as Ace explained to him how to make sure her mouth was down and her airway open before racing to his own car. Jared jumped in the driver's seat and followed Ace, sirens screaming all the way to the hospital, alternately cursing and praying the entire time.

Chapter Two

Jared, Duncan, and Reese all paced in the waiting room impatiently. Ace stood next to them, watching them grimly. Jared had never seen Ace so coldly furious before. His own fury threatened to erupt, but the stark terror that kept growing inside threatened to bring him to his knees. He would spew later. Right now he had to hold onto hope that Erin would be all right.

The waiting was killing him.

Duncan kicked a chair. "We sat there with her for hours. Hours! And the whole time she was being drugged, *poisoned*, and we did nothing to stop it. Hell, I even brought her a drink that had been drugged! If I ever get my hands on that fucking bartender—"

Ace put a hand on his shoulder. "I know how you feel. But you and your brothers leave this to me. No one is going to get away with doing shit like this in Desire."

Several other men poured into the waiting room with their women, all wearing anxious expressions.

The sheriff moved toward them. "The doctors here are aware of the situation and I want as many as possible tested."

Blade Royal hurried into the waiting room, his wife Kelly's arm gripped firmly in his. "I want her tested. She drank it, too."

Ace nodded. "There's a sign-in sheet set up. Sign her in and have a seat. Is she showing any symptoms?"

Blade, pale and obviously shaken, shook his head, pulling his wife closer. "Not yet."

Ace nodded. "Good." He smiled at Kelly. "Have a seat. Erin's in bad shape and Rachel's pregnant. The nurse will test everyone but we're sending in people showing symptoms first. If there's any chance that you're pregnant, tell the nurse."

Kelly gripped Blade's arm and, if it were possible, Blade paled even more. Half dragging, half carrying her, Blade rushed Kelly to the nurse's station.

They all looked up as Boone and Chase escorted Rachel out.

Jared grimaced at how frightened Rachel looked. "How is she?"

Boone ran his hand over Rachel's hair. "She's fine, thank God. What's going on with Erin?"

Jared looked pointedly at Rachel and smiled reassuringly. "The doctor's with her. She'll be fine. We'll take care of her."

When the nurse came out, they all but pounced on her. If they didn't tell him something soon, Jared would go back there with or without permission.

"The doctor is still with the other young woman, Erin Robinson."

Jared fought to breathe as fear tightened his gut. "Is she okay?"

The nurse regarded him for a moment. "Are you a relative, sir?"

Jared bared his teeth and started to speak, but Ace put a hand on his arm to stop him.

"He's her fiancé. These men brought her in and will be taking responsibility for her."

When Rachel, Chase and Boone approached, the nurse nodded, addressing all of them. "She's very ill. The doctor is still with her and will be out to talk with you soon." She paused. "Sheriff, he especially wants to speak to you. I need to get back to testing these people."

The waiting room had filled with citizens of Desire, one by one going in to get tested. Many came to speak to Jared and his brothers and to offer support.

"Ill?" Rachel asked shakily. She gripped Boone and Chase's arms tightly. "How ill? I want to see her. I need to be back there with her."

Boone pulled Rachel close to his chest. "You will, baby." Over her head, Boone's face tightened with anger and concern. When he met Jared's eyes questioningly, Jared nodded.

Jared touched Rachel's hair. "We'll take care of her, honey. I don't want you to worry."

When she looked up at him tearfully, it nearly broke his heart. "Why would somebody do this to Erin?"

He wanted to know the same thing. "We'll find out what happened and why. I promise."

They looked up as Dr. Hansen came in, lifting a hand in greeting as he rushed to the back. Desire's town doctor would be furious at this, and Jared felt better just knowing that he'd come. With him here, there would be quick action and they would get all the information they needed.

Jared watched the sheriff move away to take a call. He tried to smile as he watched Duncan lean down to reassure Rachel. He couldn't stand to see the women so upset, especially the woman who he hoped would become his sister-in-law. Her blood pressure problems with her pregnancy had already given everyone enough of a scare.

Duncan kissed her forehead. "Don't you worry, honey. You just relax and take care of our future niece or nephew."

Rachel smiled through her tears. "I knew it." She sniffed and turned her face into Boone's chest, crying softly.

When Jared saw Ace finish his call, he strode purposely toward him. "Any word on the bartender?"

Ace's features appeared to be carved in stone. He looked anxiously over to where Hope Sanderson and her sister Charity came out from being tested. Gracie and her husbands jumped up when they saw their daughters.

Hope smiled at them reassuringly before approaching Ace. "We're fine." She looked up at Jared. "I really hope Erin's okay. Please let me know if you need anything."

Jared thanked her, noticing that some of Ace's tension drained, but the sheriff still looked mad as hell.

Ace blew out a breath, rubbing a hand down his face. "Nobody knew the bartender. So far the only person that's been affected is Erin. I don't even know what the hell she put in Erin's drink. I'm guessing it was one of the date rape drugs. As soon as I talk to the doctor I'm going back out there. My deputies, Linc and Rafe are already there. Brandon and Ethan had security cameras installed all over the restaurant, everywhere except the privacy booths. We're going to see what we can learn from them. I want to print out some pictures of this woman and put them into the computer. I want this bitch."

Jared fought to tamp down his rage. "You're not the only one."

"You and your brothers leave this to me."

"Yeah, just like you would if it was your woman lying in there."

Ace's gaze slid to where Hope stood talking to the group of women who lived in Desire, before turning back to Jared. "Damn it, Jared. I'm the law. You and your brothers just take care of Erin."

Duncan and Reese walked up to them and looked up at Jared questioningly. Jared turned back to Ace. "You'd better find this bitch before we do."

Dr. Hansen came out and headed straight for them. "Sheriff, I need to talk to you."

"Doc." Ace gestured to Jared and his brothers. "Jared, Duncan, and Reese are Erin's men."

Dr. Hansen smiled faintly. "Good, she's going to need someone to look after her." His gaze slid to Chase. "I want you to keep an eye on Rachel. Her blood pressure is slightly elevated."

Chase nodded grimly. "Thanks, Doc."

The doctor waited until Rachel and Boone hurried over before he continued. "Erin's very ill. Someone drugged her."

Rachel's eyes went wide. "Someone really did drug her? I hoped that it was a mistake. What did they drug her with? Will she be okay? I want to see her."

Dr. Hansen frowned at her. "We're admitting her. If everything goes well, she can go home tomorrow as long as someone is going to be with her. I'll let you see her in a while, but if you don't calm down, I'm going to admit you and sedate you."

He turned back to Ace. "It was gamma-hydroxybutyrate, Ace. GHB."

Jared frowned and turned to the doctor. "Isn't that—?"

"Liquid Ecstasy," Ace finished grimly. "Who the hell thinks they're going to get away with drugging a woman in Desire?"

Jared's stomach churned. "How is Erin, Doc?"

Dr. Hansen sighed. "She's been violently ill. She's been medicated to counteract the effects of the drug. She'll be watched closely tonight. The greatest risks right now are convulsions, respiratory problems, and the very real possibility that she could be sick again while she's unconscious and drown. The good news is that she hadn't slipped into a coma. Most GHB drugs are homemade mixes. But it's a drug that's used to treat narcolepsy. It takes quite a bit to knock someone out. My guess is that she had a little in each drink all night. It would have been too salty to drink all at once. I'm surprised she didn't taste it. It ruins the taste of most drinks."

Duncan scrubbed a hand over his face. "She was drinking virgin margaritas. There was salt on the rim."

Reese turned pain-filled eyes to the doctor. "She kept saying she was thirsty."

Jared put an arm on Reese's shoulder. "We'll stay with her." Worry and anger warred within him. He had to put aside the anger for now. Erin needed him. She needed him and his brothers to take care of her. He would deal with the anger later.

Dr. Hansen nodded. "I figured you would. The nurse will come out for you and give you instructions. Someone will have to stay awake all night to watch her."

Michael, John, Brandon, and Ethan rushed into the room and headed straight for them. The anger and strain on their faces matched that of everyone else.

John spoke first. "How many and how bad?"

Duncan's jaw clenched. "Just one so far. Erin appears to have been her target."

When Rachel whimpered, Boone put an arm around her and led her to the row of seats.

"Target?" Brandon asked incredulously. "Who the hell would target Erin?"

Reese stopped pacing. "That's what we're going to find out."

Ace shook his head. "That's what *I'm* going to find out." Your job is to take care of your woman and watch out for her until I can figure out what the hell is going on. I don't know if this is an isolated incident or if this woman is out to get Erin for some reason. I need you to keep an eye on her so that I can find out."

Chase slid a glance to where Boone settled Rachel on his lap. "Boone and I want to be in on this. She's our sister-in-law."

Jared gestured to where Boone held Rachel. "You have enough to deal with right now. I promise you, we'll take care of her."

John nodded in agreement. "Michael and I will work with Ace. You two take care of your women. They're our first priority. We stood next to that fucking bitch all night and watched as she served Erin a fucking spiked drink and didn't notice it. How could we have all missed it?" His eyes slid over each of the men. "We're so sorry. It never should have happened."

Ethan raked a hand through his hair. "It happened at our fucking restaurant, and at our fucking Christmas party. We feel like shit. I don't know what to say, but we won't stop until we find the woman who did this." He looked at Ace. "As soon as you're done here, come back to the restaurant. Devlin Monroe from the security company is going to meet us there to go over the tapes. I think your two deputies are already there." His face hardened. "We're getting too fucking soft. This is the third time in less than a year that our women have been attacked. We're going to have to have a meeting to talk about this."

Michael nodded. "Good idea. We're going back to the restaurant with you. Maybe we'll see something that might help, and I know

Ace has questions for us. We already gave a sample of the mix to the doctor. We have the rest of it ready for you." He looked at each of them, his jaw clenched in anger. "I made the mix. I want this fucking bitch."

Jared watched the doorway, waiting for the nurse to come out. "Right now I can't think about anything but Erin."

Clay, Blade, and Jake joined them. Clay put a hand on his shoulder. "Any word on Erin?"

"No, we're still waiting. All we know is that she's been drugged. Liquid Ecstasy. They've given her an antidote and they're admitting her. We're staying with her until she's released. Doc said she could have slipped into a coma. We're just grateful that she didn't."

Clay smiled faintly. "Thank God for that. Rio and I will stop at your place and take care of the horses."

Jared rubbed the back of his neck, frustrated and anxious to get to Erin. "Jim and Bud should take care of that. They're really good about that kind of thing." Where the hell was that nurse?

Clay nodded. "We'll stop by anyway to make sure. If you need anything, *anything*, give us a call."

Jake turned to Chase. "Nat's going to help Rachel and their new employee, Marissa Mallery out at the store. Tell Erin not to worry about a thing."

Duncan turned from where he'd also been watching the doorway the nurse had disappeared through. "Thanks. We don't need Rachel overburdened either."

"We all help each other here, you know that." Jake frowned. "I would love to get my hands on that bartender."

Reese grabbed Jared's arm. "Didn't you finish Erin's drink at the table?"

Jared nodded. "Yeah, but it was only a sip and I'm a lot bigger than she is."

Ace's head whipped around and he grabbed Jared's arm, leading him to the nurse. "I want you to get tested anyway."

The nurse came through the doorway just then and looked startled at Ace's expression. "I came out to get the men who'll be staying with Ms. Robinson. She's resting now."

Jared nodded impatiently. "You can test me after I see Erin." He and his brothers followed the nurse to Erin's room. Walking through the door, he rushed to her side, his insides clenching in fear. "She's as white as the sheet."

All three of them approached her, reaching out to touch her, needing the contact.

Reese looked scared to death as he stood looking down at her. Duncan's face tightened with fury, his eyes colder than Jared had ever seen them.

Jared touched her fingers, grimacing at the IV that pierced her skin, and wanted to howl his rage and helplessness. They hadn't taken very good care of the woman they had every intention of claiming for their own. "I could easily kill the person that did this to her." Jared looked down at her, his heart in his throat, silently promising to get her through this.

* * * *

Erin grimaced at the terrible taste in her mouth. Her head felt like it weighed a ton as she turned it on the pillow.

"Are you all right, baby?"

Erin forced her eyelids open to see Duncan standing next to her and holding her hand as Jared and Reese approached. Jared moved to the other side of the bed while Reese sat next to her legs. She looked around to see that she lay in a hospital bed. Frowning, she tried to remember how she'd gotten here. She remembered being really sick, but nothing else.

"Am I in the hospital?"

Jared touched her cheek. "You are."

"Why? What happened?"

Jared's hand moved over her hair. "What do you remember?"

Looking from one to the other, Erin thought about the previous evening. "We went to the Christmas party. I went on the terrace and you came to get me. We went inside and sat at the table." She rubbed her forehead as her memory blurred. "Somebody brought me food." She shook her head and regretted it when it made her dizzy. "We talked. I don't know. I remember talking about leaving. Then…I don't know. I was sick."

Duncan sighed tiredly. "You don't remember how you got here, do you?"

Erin rubbed her forehead. "Sure I do." Struggling to bring last night into focus only made her head hurt. She looked up at Jared fearfully. "Why can't I remember?"

Jared's jaw tightened. "Somebody, the bartender we think, drugged your drink with GHB, a date rape drug."

He gently lifted her against his chest. She leaned into him, gripping his shirt. She had no idea what had happened, but she was scared and Jared felt warm and solid. And she trusted them. She didn't stop to wonder why. She just did. A sudden thought occurred to her and she scrambled from his embrace. "Where's Rachel? Oh, my God. The baby! Did they drug Rachel?"

Duncan blocked her attempt to get out of bed. "Rachel's fine. No one but you was drugged. She's been frantic about you. Dr. Hansen made her go home."

Erin pushed the sheet aside. "I have to get up. I have to—" Startled that she felt so weak, she reached for Duncan when she swayed.

Duncan lifted her legs back onto the bed and tucked the covers around them. "You have to stay right where you are until the doctor comes in and discharges you. Then you're coming home with us."

Erin blinked. "No. I'm not." It scared the hell out of her that it came out weakly and she fell back against the pillows, all of her energy gone.

Reese rubbed her thigh through the blanket and she tried to ignore the heat from his light caress that made her skin tingle even in her weakened state. "You're staying with us until we can figure out what's going on. We think the bartender drugged you, but we don't know for sure and we don't know why."

"I thought men used date rape drugs to knock a woman out so that he could have sex with her without her consent. Who would have done that to me? If I was sitting with you three, wouldn't you have been the only people there with a motive to drug me?"

Jared lifted his head, his eyes cold. "Do you think *we* drugged you?"

Erin sighed. "Of course not. But no one has any reason to drug me."

Duncan's jaw clenched. "Someone did. You're staying with us until we figure this out."

Erin shook her head, immediately regretting it. "I can just go back to my apartment."

Duncan leaned over her. "The doctor won't even release you unless you have someone with you that can watch out for you."

She tried to sit up. "But I'm fine."

Duncan raised a brow as she fell back onto the pillow weakly. "Ace also wants you guarded. The time he has to spend watching out for you is time taken away from finding the person who did this."

"Fine, then I can stay with Rachel."

"Rachel's blood pressure already went up and the doctor threatened to sedate her. Boone and Chase have their hands full just watching out for her."

Jared gripped her chin. "Do you really want to put your pregnant sister in the line of fire if someone is out to do you harm?"

Damn it. "But we hardly know each other. I don't think I'm in danger, I mean, I'm new here. I haven't been here long enough to make enemies. But even if I am, why would you bring me to your house and put yourselves in danger? No, I'm better on my own."

Jared's grip on her chin firmed and he dropped a kiss on her dry lips. "You know why. For the same reason you've managed to avoid us. We want you, Erin, and we think that you want us and have been fighting it."

She met his eyes, wanting to drown in them as he regarded her tenderly. "It could never work. I'm not that kind of person. I prefer to be on my own."

"Well I guess we'll all have the time to find out if it'll work. And you're not going to be alone ever again."

She didn't have a chance to answer before the nurse walked in, quickly followed by the doctor.

After the doctor pronounced her fit enough to leave, warning the men to keep an eye on her, he discharged her.

Reese made a face. "We'll eat at home. The food here is terrible. Ace has already called and he's got some questions for you. I told him to meet us there. I figured you'd be anxious to get out of here."

They headed back to Desire in Duncan's truck. She leaned heavily against Reese in the back seat, more exhausted than she could ever remember being. Once she got some rest, she'd be fine. Then she could do whatever the hell she wanted to do no matter what they said.

Enfolded in Reese's arms, Erin thought about what the doctor had said before discharging her. He'd only released her after a litany of instructions to the men, telling her that he knew she would be better off at home with them. He told her that everyone had been anxious to get her back to Desire where she could be guarded closely. Not being used to such attention, Erin couldn't believe the unreality of the situation. It all had to be some sort of mix up. No one in town had any reason to drug her. "If I'm going to be staying with you tonight, I want to stop at my apartment and get some things."

Reese smoothed her hair. "Let's get you home first. One of us can stay with you—"

"No. I don't want you pawing through my underwear. I'll get my own things."

Reese laughed. "Someday soon we're going to paw through your underwear while you're wearing them. Just relax and let us take care of everything."

Exhausted, she appreciated his solidness and how good it felt to be held against him. Leaning on him the way she did, she felt his heat, his strength. The strong arms wrapped around her made her feel safe and warm. She'd never experienced this kind of comfort before and she couldn't believe how amazing it felt. Just being held with no ulterior motive other than to provide comfort. She suspected that his embrace somehow comforted both of them.

She would allow it, if just for a little while.

Jared turned in the passenger seat, smiling at her tenderly. "We'll take you home first and get something to eat. As sick as you've been, you've got to be hungry. Then we'll get your things."

As soon as they got to the house, Duncan and Reese took her into the kitchen while Jared excused himself to go to his office and make some phone calls. Reese seated her, ordering her to stay put while they fixed breakfast.

Erin watched the men while she looked around. She couldn't believe the size of the kitchen. The table could easily seat a dozen people. "Did you guys make this table?"

Duncan turned from where he was scrambling eggs in a large bowl. "Yeah, we needed one that would seat all of us. We've always known that we would share a woman. When you add children to that, we knew we'd need a lot of room at the table."

Erin nodded, trying very hard to ignore the rush of warmth it gave her to imagine herself in that role. She could never live that way, but she found it hard to deny the attraction she felt for these men. Not that she would ever do anything about it. But she couldn't help wondering what it would be like to be loved by these three strong, masculine men. Men she actually liked and respected. She cleared her throat. "The table is beautiful. Big, but beautiful. The house is great."

Reese leaned down to kiss her forehead as he started setting the table. "We'll show you around later. We want you to be comfortable here. Consider this your home."

They had just started to put the food on the table when Jared came back into the room and took the seat next to her. "I called Boone and told him that we brought you home. I called Ace and told him the same thing. He'll be over later to question you about last night." He piled scrambled eggs on her plate and offered her the bacon.

Duncan poured her a glass of juice. "You need to eat something and drink plenty of liquids today."

"I heard the doctor."

When all three of them looked up at her tone, she sighed. "I'm sorry. I know you're just trying to help. I'm really grateful for your help. I'm tired, hungry, and grouchy. Just ignore me."

Jared leaned over and kissed her full on the lips before she could stop him. "It's okay, love. The doctor warned us you'd be irritable." He grinned, winking at her. "Make that more irritable that usual. You're not going to be yourself for a few days. Eat and then you can go lie down on the sofa until we get home."

Erin opened her mouth, about to say something bitchy about his bossiness, and then thought better of it. Nodding, she resumed eating. She really was bitchy today. They refilled her juice glass several times. She couldn't seem to get enough of it.

It had been decided that Duncan would stay with her while Jared and Reese went to her apartment to get her things.

After the others left, Duncan led her to the sofa in the living room. "Come here, baby."

Erin sat on the sofa with Duncan, eyeing him warily. When he did no more than settle on the other end and start looking for something she would want to watch on television, she relaxed. They ended up finding a black-and-white movie that Erin liked. Before she knew it, her eyes had started to close.

* * * *

Duncan patted his thigh. "Come here, baby. I want you close." He helped a drowsy Erin settle her head on his thigh and pushed her hair back so that he could see her face. Pulling the afghan from the back of the sofa over her, he watched her eyes close and felt her breathing even out. Turning the volume down, Duncan just watched her sleep.

They finally had her in their house. Now they could prove to her just how good they could be together. First though, they had to get her to trust them. Erin only appeared to trust Rachel, and to some extent Boone and Chase. She watched everyone warily as though braced for…something. He didn't know what.

He considered it a major victory that she would trust him enough to sleep curled next to him. They were on the sofa and both fully clothed, but it was a start.

He ran his hands through her hair, loving the silky feel as it flowed through his fingers. He couldn't wait to see it across their pillow as he and his brothers slept next to her after making love to her.

Damn, she was a little firecracker. He'd bet she used that smart mouth and in-your-face attitude to cover a lot of insecurities. They'd have to find out what they were and get her to trust them before they would be able to get really close to her.

Erin had a tough shell and she didn't take crap from anyone. Inside she was as soft as a marshmallow and struggled to hide it. A damned near irresistible combination for them. They needed a woman who could stand up to them but not one so hard that she lost her femininity.

Added to that, they all got hard every time they got anywhere near her. The chemistry between them blew him away and the challenge of making her purr set his teeth on edge. Christ, he wanted her.

They'd come to respect her, hell, they *liked* her. She never bored them and the conversations they'd had with her kept them all on their toes.

Duncan stroked her cheek as she moaned in her sleep, crooning to her until she settled once again. An overwhelming feeling of protectiveness washed over him as he looked down at her. Anyone who wanted to hurt her would have to go through them to do so.

Possessively, he also swore that he would happily disassemble any man who tried to take her from them. She'd led them on a merry chase, but now that circumstances had brought her to live under their roof, he knew he and his brothers would do whatever they had to in order to keep her there.

He glanced up at the clock. Jared and Reese had been gone quite a while. He'd thought they would have been back by now. He continued to watch the movie, waiting for them and playing with Erin's hair as she slept. Another hour went by before he heard his brothers come in.

His brows shot up when he saw them. Both had dirt and what looked like blood on their shirts. "What the hell happened to you?" Erin shifted on his lap and he cursed himself when he saw that he'd woken her.

"I'm sorry, baby."

* * * *

Erin sat up groggily and looked up at Jared and Reese. "Why are you all dirty? Is that blood?" Scrambling from the sofa, she tripped on the afghan that had been thrown over her.

Jared caught her. "We're fine, love. It's just a few scratches."

Erin lifted his shirt and saw the scratches and dried blood on his chest. "You're scratched up all over. Your arms, too." She moved to Reese. "You, too. What the hell happened?" She looked at Duncan who'd risen to stand next to her. "Get me a first aid kit."

Jared shook his head. "No." When he pulled her tightly to his chest, her pulse leapt. "A shower will take care of it. Ace is on his way. Someone cut the supports on the stairs to your apartment. The stairs collapsed when we tried to climb them."

Incredulous, Erin gaped at them. "What? Are you kidding?" Shaking her head, she stared at them in horror. They could have been badly hurt. "Maybe they were just old and the wood had rotted."

Reese came to her and pulled her close, wrapping his arms around her. "No, honey. Ace looked at them and even called Boone to inspect them. Someone cut them deliberately. We had to get a ladder to get to your apartment." Reese's hands roamed over her back soothingly when she trembled.

She backed away, needing to put some distance between them. This entire situation had gotten out of hand. If only she didn't feel so groggy, she could make sense of it. Moving to the window, she turned to face them. "Why would someone do that?"

Reese sighed heavily. "We don't know yet, but if you had gone up those stairs in the condition you were in last night, you would have been seriously hurt, maybe killed."

Jared cursed under his breath. "And no one would have ever known you'd been drugged. Ace said last night how important it was to get everyone tested right away. By the time someone found you today the drug probably wouldn't have even shown up."

When they heard a car pull up, Reese pulled her away from the window as Jared went to look out. "It's Ace. He has some questions for you, love."

Erin nodded and moved reluctantly out of Reese's embrace. "I'll go make some fresh coffee."

"I can do it."

"No." Erin waved him away. "It'll give me something to do for a few minutes. I need to think." Erin went into the kitchen and started the coffee. She knew where they kept everything from watching them earlier.

Why the hell would someone want to hurt her? She'd only recently come to town and hadn't argued or fought with anyone. It didn't make any sense. Wondering if this had all been some kind of mistake, she got the mugs down from the cupboard and stared out the window.

She could hear the low murmurs in the other room and knew they were talking about her. The sheriff would have questions for her, and she honestly didn't know what she could tell him. Bracing when she heard them approach, she turned back to the coffee.

Once they'd all come into the kitchen, Erin sat and faced the sheriff. "I don't know what I can tell you. It all feels like some kind of a bad dream. I don't understand any of this."

The sheriff smiled at her tenderly. "I know, honey. But I have to get as much information as I can. I need to figure out why someone would want to hurt you."

"But I'm new here! I know a lot of people now, but I'm not really close to anyone but Rachel. What could I have done to make someone dislike me so much?"

"That's what we need to find out. It could be any number of things. According to Rachel, Boone got you a drink as soon as you got there. Did you notice anything wrong with it?"

Erin shrugged. "I usually don't drink anything like that but since Boone had taken the trouble to get it for me, I drank it. He told me it was a virgin margarita. Rachel likes margaritas and Michael made them especially for her. But I think a lot of people were drinking them."

"How do you know that Michael made the mix?"

Erin blinked. "I don't know. Someone might have told me." She frowned as she tried to remember. "I don't remember. I hate this. I hate that I can't remember parts of last night. It makes me feel helpless and I can't stand it." She reached out to grip Jared's hand, pulling back at the last minute.

When Jared reached over and took her hand in his, she smiled gratefully. "I'm sorry. I'm not usually such a wimp, but I don't like that some of what happened last night is gone."

Jared smiled back, his eyes tender. "We're here for you, love. You have nothing to fear. Anyone that wants to hurt you will have to go through all three of us in order to do it."

Erin shook her head. "No. I don't want anyone hurt because of me." She looked at the sheriff. "Maybe I should leave town for a few days."

All four men shook their heads. Ace leaned forward. "What if she followed you? What if you got hurt and no one knew it? No. I need you to stay right where you are."

Duncan smoothed her hair. "You're not going to work, either."

"What? I can't leave Rachel there by herself."

Jared squeezed her hand. "Marissa is there helping Rachel. Nat is also working in the store. Jesse and Kelly are helping when they can. The store is fine and one of the men is there at all times."

Erin groaned. "All this trouble because of me."

Reese touched her shoulder. "None of this is your fault."

Ace opened his notebook. "We have to figure out whose fault it is. And to do that, I need some answers. If you didn't usually drink anything like that, why did you get another one?"

Erin sighed. "When I went to the bar I had the glass in my hand. The woman behind the bar saw it and smiled, and she got me another. She disappeared before I had the chance to say anything. So I drank it. I was really thirsty and got some water. When I was about to walk away, she gave me another margarita." She shrugged. "The men all looked at her strangely when she did that and I didn't want her to get in trouble for fixing me a drink I hadn't ordered. So I took it. That's the drink I had when Jared found me."

When Ace's face tightened angrily, Erin asked. "What?"

"GHB has a salty taste. It ruins the taste of most drinks. That's why she gave you another margarita. With the rim salted, you wouldn't have noticed the salty taste. We think that was the first two drinks she'd drugged."

Duncan shoved back his chair and stood. "That makes the drink I got her the third."

Erin clenched Jared's hand tighter.

"She handed you this drink?" Ace asked, writing furiously in his notebook.

Erin nodded. "Yes, I thought it was so nice of her when she made it so fast when there were other people there. Several men were standing around."

Duncan cursed. "Yeah, real nice."

"What did she look like? I have her on video and the other's descriptions, but I want your take on her." Ace asked, looking up from his notebook.

Erin closed her eyes as she tried to remember. "Blonde, a lot of makeup." She frowned. "I don't remember what color her eyes were. But she was big."

Ace's brows went up. "Big?"

"Yes. I don't know what kind of shoes she was wearing so I can't tell you how tall she is. Last night she was taller than me but not as tall as Michael and John. I couldn't see her feet to know if she wore high heels or not, but I remember thinking that she looked big. You know, like too muscular. She was wearing a turtleneck. Yes, I remember that she was wearing a turtleneck because I looked to see if she had an Adam's apple. I thought it may have been a man."

Dead silence filled the room. "What? Did I say something wrong?"

Ace shook his head. "I'm going to go back over that tape again." He looked at her. "Did you leave a boyfriend when you came to Desire?"

Erin shook her head. "I didn't date very often. The only person I've gone out with in the last year besides Reese is Jacob. But there's never been anything between us."

"Did he want there to be something between you?"

Erin shook her head. "Maybe at first, but when he realized I didn't want anything beyond friendship, he was okay with that."

"I'll need Jacob's last name and address."

"But that's silly. Jacob wouldn't hurt a fly."

Duncan slammed his cup down on the counter. "Somebody drugged you and cut the stairs to your apartment, Erin. Somebody's trying to hurt you. Everybody's a suspect."

Erin stood and moved to the kitchen window, wrapping her arms around her middle. "That's ridiculous. You're not a suspect." She hadn't been prepared for Duncan's reaction. He came over and grabbed her arms, lifting her to her toes. "Of course I am! I even handed you one of the spiked drinks."

He released her so abruptly she had to grab the counter for support as he stormed out of the room.

"Come here, love."

Stunned by Duncan's outburst, she docilely allowed Jared to pull her onto his lap as he spoke to the sheriff. "Ask your questions, Ace. We need to find out who's doing this."

Erin watched the doorway that Duncan had disappeared through as she absently answered the rest of the sheriff's questions. She allowed Jared to hold her on his lap the entire time, and she leaned against him, absorbing his strength. Just for now. By tomorrow she would feel more like herself and be able to figure something out.

She kept glancing at the doorway. Duncan had looked tortured by the fact that he had given her one of the drinks that had been drugged and she hated that he blamed himself. By the time the sheriff had finished questioning her, she felt worn out. Nevertheless, when Jared and Reese led Ace out, she went in search of Duncan.

Chapter Three

Erin found Duncan in the workshop out back. The door stood open and she went inside, watching silently as he worked on a table. His expression looked grim as he sanded the piece and although she knew next to nothing about working with wood, he appeared to be using more force than necessary. Her heart lurched at his expression. She couldn't stand that he blamed himself for what had happened to her.

"Duncan?"

He looked up and her pulse quickened at the way his eyes lit up, before he averted them. "Yes, baby? Come on in."

She walked into the barn, glancing at several works in progress. "Wow. You guys certainly make a lot of furniture."

He smiled faintly, his smile not reaching his eyes. "We're lucky. A lot of people like our furniture and keep us busy. What are you doing out here? Where are Jared and Reese?" He came forward and kissed her hair before moving back to the table.

"They're inside. I just wanted to talk to you." She still hadn't gotten used to the way they reached out to touch her every time she came near. Unused to physical contact, it disconcerted her each and every time they did it. She cleared her throat. "You know that it's not your fault that I was drugged, don't you?" She jumped, startled when Duncan picked up a hammer and threw it across the room with enough force to put a hole in the far wall.

He turned to her, his face a mask of fury. "I handed you a drink that could have potentially killed you, Erin. How the hell am I supposed to feel about that?"

The misery on his face pulled at her. Not questioning why, Erin walked up to him and put a hand on his chest, feeling the play of sleek muscles as his arms came around her. "You and your brothers took care of me. You got me to the hospital and you brought me home with you. I'm very grateful—"

His lips thinned as he scowled down at her. "Fuck that! Do you think I want your fucking gratitude?"

Taken aback, Erin caressed his tight jaw. "How can I not be grateful? You saved my life."

Before she could blink, he pulled her close and covered her mouth with his. Fire raced through her as he tightened his hold, crushing her against his chest. His hand cupped the back of her head, holding it in place as his mouth ravaged hers. His tongue swept through her mouth like lightning, furious and powerful.

The effects of his kiss rippled through her entire body. Her senses reeled, making her dizzy as his heat and strength surrounded her. Her nipples pebbled almost painfully, throbbing as they brushed against his hard chest. Her pussy clenched desolately, her clit swelling as moisture soaked her panties.

His hands on her buttocks tightened as he lifted her and, without thought, she wrapped her legs around his hips. Feeling the evidence of his own desire as his steely length pushed insistently against her center, she tried to push herself closer, moaning her frustration that their clothing prevented it.

When he lifted his head, she stared at him, dazed, as she involuntarily rubbed herself against him. His lips twitched as he looked down at her, his eyes blazing with need. "Now do you have an idea of what we want from you?"

Erin caressed his face, running her thumb over his firm bottom lip. It took several seconds before she could form a coherent thought. When her mind finally cleared, her own desires shook her. In her experience, men like Duncan didn't exist. He was everything she desired in a man.

Rules of Desire 53

The problem was that so were his brothers. "Duncan, I can't be what you and your brothers need. You have no idea how much I want to. But I want all of you so much."

"Erin! Erin damn it, where are you?"

She flinched at the sound of Jared's panicked voice screaming her name.

Duncan's eyes never left hers. "She's in here with me!"

A few seconds later Jared and Reese flew through the door, both releasing a relieved sigh when they saw her.

Jared came closer and ran a hand over her hair. It didn't appear to faze him that Duncan held her with her legs still wrapped around him. "You need to let us know where you're going, love. One of us needs to be with you at all times." He moved in behind her and nuzzled a sensitive place on her neck that surprised a cry from her. "Hmm, I found a soft spot."

She'd never thought of her neck as an erogenous zone before. She ignored his chuckle, arching to give him better access.

"My brothers and I are going to have a lot of fun finding all the places that give you pleasure."

Reese looked back over his shoulder from his position beside them. "I think we should take this inside. I don't like being out here exposed like this with her."

Duncan rubbed his lips over hers. "Good idea. Erin doesn't think she can be what we need. Let's take her inside and show her just how wrong she is about that."

She still had her legs wrapped around Duncan as he carried her inside. Flanked by Jared and Reese, he carried her straight to the bedroom. He lowered her onto the bed, covering her body with his. He took her mouth possessively, making it his, his deep, drugging kisses making her lightheaded.

Her pussy clenched repeatedly as she arched into him, trying to rub against him, needing more. She'd never felt such need before. With Reese, she'd come close but had never allowed him to get her into this position. Duncan's hard body pressed hers into the mattress. When he lifted his head, she saw that both Jared and Reese lay on the bed beside her.

Jared gripped her chin and turned her to face him. "You're like a cat, rubbing all over Duncan and trying to get closer. You even purr. I want to hear you purr some more. I've never heard anything so sexy."

Erin fisted her hands in Jared's hair as his lips moved over hers. She felt her jeans and socks being removed as lust licked at her hungrily.

When Jared raised his head, she lifted her gaze to his. The need in his eyes drew her in and she knew right then, she could refuse them nothing.

She wanted this. Needed it. She was a grown woman and there was nothing wrong with finding pleasure with them. But she had to make them understand it could be nothing more than that.

She licked her lips, trembling as Jared's eyes followed the movement and blazed even hotter. She traced the sexy scar on his cheek. "I want you so much, but it can't be any more than that. Please try to understand."

"Why not, love? Why can't it be more?" He traced a finger over her lips, making them tingle. "You know how much you mean to us, don't you? This isn't just sex for us."

Erin shook her head, not wanting to talk, but she had to be honest up front. "That's the problem. I need it to be. I can't be like Rachel, like Jesse. I can't be with more than one man. But I want you, all of you, so much. Please."

Jared's lips curved as he turned his head and playfully bit her finger. "We'll just have to change your mind about that." He reached for the hem of her shirt and pulled it over her head.

Lying between Jared and Reese as Duncan moved over her, Erin had trouble believing this was really happening. She wanted each of them desperately. The need she had for all three of them together threatened to overwhelm her.

Duncan unfastened her bra and stripped it away. "Jesus, you're beautiful."

"I don't know if I can handle this."

"We'll go slow, baby."

Erin gasped at the feel of his mouth on her nipple and began to twist restlessly.

Reese began to suck and nibble at her other breast. "Not too slow."

It felt so surreal to have more than one man pleasuring her. It felt so erotic, so naughty. Never had she felt so vulnerable, and her nakedness only increased the sensation. At the same time, she felt more powerful and desired than ever before. Need like she'd never experienced raced through her. The pull on her nipples caused her pussy to clench frantically. She needed to be filled. Her clit felt huge, swollen and sensitive and she whimpered as she tried to rub herself on Duncan.

"Ohhh! Please." Why didn't they hurry? Men usually rushed through sex but Jared, Duncan, and Reese just continued to play with her.

Jared chuckled as he rubbed a hand over her abdomen. "Already, my love? Don't worry, we'll take good care of you."

Duncan lifted himself off of her, moving to take Jared's place as Jared moved from beside her to settle himself between her legs. She shook in earnest when she felt her panties being removed. When Jared lifted her knees and shouldered his way between her thighs, she moaned, gasping when she felt Duncan's teeth on her nipple.

The first touch of Jared's tongue on her slit had her crying out desperately. "It's too much. I can't." She gripped Duncan and Reese's hair to pull them away.

Both untangled her hands from their hair and pressed them to the mattress beside her head. Reese lifted his mouth from her breast. "Sure you can, sweetheart. We've only just begun. Just lay back and let us take care of you."

Jared's tongue poked into her and she moaned harshly. No one had ever done this to her before. Oh, God. It felt amazing!

Duncan lifted his head, watching what Jared did to her for several long moments. When he looked back at her, his eyes blazed. "Jared's enjoying the taste of you, baby. I can't wait to get my mouth on that pussy. Do you like that, baby? Do you like having your pussy licked?"

"I've never—Ohhh! God, it feels incredible!" How could it turn her on so much that they watched as their brother did this to her?

Duncan's brows went up. "No one has ever licked that sweet little pussy before?"

Erin shook her head. "I don't do things like this. Sex is hard and fast and over."

Duncan chuckled. "Sometimes. But we like to play. Since you've never had a mouth on your pussy, can I assume that you've never had a cock in your ass either?"

Erin looked up at Duncan in disbelief, just as Jared clamped his lips over her clit. "Ohhh! What did you do? Ahhh!" The most indescribable feeling washed over her and she grabbed onto Reese and Duncan desperately. Oh, my God! She'd had orgasms before but she'd never felt anything like this. Ever.

Her mind went blank as the world spun all around her. Pleasure radiated through her, curling her toes and making her feel as though someone had touched her with a live wire.

The intensity of it scared the hell out of her.

Jared moved over her and lowered his mouth to hers. She tasted herself on him, something she'd never done before and didn't think she would like. But within seconds she tasted nothing but him. His tongue danced erotically with hers and swept through her mouth, and she arched into him, trying to get closer. Feeling completely swept away, she gripped him, frantically trying to hold on to something solid, exchanging her grip to Reese when Jared moved slightly away to roll on a condom.

Rules of Desire

She stilled when she felt the head of Jared's cock poised at her slick opening and held her breath as he began to push into her. Hard hands on her buttocks lifted her, seemingly effortlessly, which caused her a moment's panic and her eyes flew open.

Jared stared down at her, his eyes glittering darkly, but he kept his voice low. "I've got you, love."

Reese caressed her cheek. "Everything's okay, sweetheart. We all want you so much."

She shuddered as Jared pressed into her, wrapping her legs around him to pull him close.

He resisted her efforts, taking his time and entering her slowly. She moaned her frustration as he stroked shallowly into her, going a little deeper with each stroke. It felt so unreal and incredibly intimate to feel Duncan and Reese, not only watching, but participating as their brother made love to her. As though from a distance, she realized she'd become far too aroused to care. Amazed at her own response, she struggled just to keep up. Not used to being so out of control, she felt the stirring of panic as she fought to center herself.

Jared sunk his fingers into her hair, his eyes gentle. "You're very tight, love. Being inside you feels better than anything I've ever felt." When she cried out at a deeper thrust, he murmured to her tenderly. Duncan and Reese caressed her thighs and arms, praising her as she took Jared's thick length into her body.

Duncan nuzzled her jaw. "You look so beautiful, all flushed and pink. I love seeing you caught up in it. You turn me inside out."

Reese nibbled at her neck. "You're so soft, like warm silk."

Jared continued his slow, mind numbing strokes until he finally worked his cock all the way inside her. He began stroking faster, going deeper with each stroke, stretching her deliciously until she felt him touch her womb. At some unspoken communication, Duncan moved away. Jared rolled her until she sat astride him and Reese and Duncan quickly moved back in.

With his eyes on hers, he spoke to his brothers. "She's so hot and tight."

Reese's hands stayed busy on her breasts, his hands and mouth hot and hungry on her nipples. "You are so responsive."

Slightly uncomfortable with all the attention, Erin closed her eyes again. Making love in the dark and under the covers hadn't felt nearly as intimate as having three men look at and touch her all over in broad daylight. The cock filling her touched something inside her that had never been touched, something that had her clenching around him and fighting to hold off her orgasm. She couldn't let go. She couldn't allow herself to become that helpless, especially with all of them watching. She'd seriously underestimated just how strongly they would affect her. How could she have known?

Jared's hands firmed on her hips, slowing his strokes. She opened her eyes and looked down to see that need had tightened his features harshly. "It's like fucking a hot, soft glove. You feel so good, love. Even better than I imagined."

Her hands fisted on his chest, the play of muscles beneath the velvety skin exciting her even more. "It's too much. I can't—Ohhh!" Cries ripped from her throat before she even knew they were there. Teetering on the edge of something so big it scared her, Erin fought it with everything she had.

Reese's mouth covered hers as he pulled at her nipples, swallowing her cries. The tug at her nipples sent sensation straight to her clit and pussy, eliciting even more cries. He raised his head, his eyes glittering with need. "Our little darlin' likes that. Does it feel good, honey? I can't wait to get inside that soft pussy."

"I don't…I can't…" Erin felt Jared nudge a spot inside her and she caught her breath as he did it again and again. "What are you—Oh, God! Ahhh!" She couldn't stop clenching on him and she went over, not able to hold back any longer.

Jared groaned harshly, surging into her deeply. "Jesus!"

Erin could feel his cock pulse inside her and she gripped his forearms tightly as the waves of pleasure kept washing over her.

Aware of all three of them watching her, she squeezed her eyes closed, struggling to gather control of herself once again. Bit by bit the waves of pleasure began to die down. She'd never even imagined she could feel that way. Her body still rippled as she frantically gulped in air.

As her cries diminished, Reese's mouth covered hers again. One of his hands roamed over her back as the other palmed a breast, his calloused palm creating a magnificent friction on her nipple.

Duncan's hands moved over her belly and bottom, his lips moving from her breast to her shoulder and back again. Already weakened, she had no defense against the arousal that started to build once again.

Jared lifted her from his length and moved from beneath her, startling her once again with his strength. Used to men who lived in suits left her completely unprepared for men like Jared, Duncan, and Reese. When Reese lifted his head, Jared took his place beside her. Cupping her jaw to hold her in place, he covered her mouth with his own.

She pulled from Jared's kiss, gripping his arm. "Please. I can't come anymore. Reese and Duncan can take me but don't worry about making me come again."

Jared tightened his grip and nipped her bottom lip, making it sting. "If you weren't new to this and it wasn't our first time together, I would turn you over my lap and spank your ass for that remark."

The matter-of-fact way he'd said that made it sound all the more ominous. She turned away and looked over to see that Reese had undressed and reclined on the pillows at the head of the bed. His cock pointed toward his stomach, hard and angry looking, even larger than she had imagined when it had brushed against her all those times. As she watched, he wrapped his hand around his thick length and began a slow, mesmerizing stroke. The purplish head had a drop of pre-cum on the tip, and suddenly she felt ravenous for the taste of him.

"Come here, sweetheart. I want to feel your mouth on my cock."

With a last hesitant look at Jared, she bent and moved toward

Reese on her hands and knees. She'd wanted him so badly for so long and the sight of him propped against the headboard and stroking his thick cock had to be the most erotic thing she'd ever seen. Even though she knew she wouldn't be able to come again, she wanted to give him pleasure. "I've never done this before. Tell me if I do something wrong." Holding onto his rock-hard thighs, she took his cock inside her mouth.

He hissed at the first touch of her tongue over his thick shaft. When she sucked gently, he groaned. "You've never, oh, fuck. Oh, that mouth, fuck. Slow down, honey or I'm gonna come too soon."

She felt the bed shift as Jared moved away. Duncan knelt beside her, running his hands over her back as she sucked Reese's cock. Jared returned, his hands sliding to her breasts, cupping them and running his thumbs over her nipples. Kneeling beside her, Jared kept one hand over her breast while the other moved to slide slowly up and down her back. She had no idea how they could do this to her. Amazed that her arousal began to grow again, she tightened her grip on Reese's thighs. She couldn't lose control that way again. Already her clit throbbed with the need to be touched and her now empty pussy clenched helplessly, just begged to be filled.

Naked flesh touched the back of her thighs. A firm grip lifted her bottom higher. It had to be Duncan. His rough hands moved over her bottom, moving closer and closer to her center. With Reese filling her mouth, his hands in her hair and both Jared and Duncan using their hands to arouse her, she didn't stand a chance. When Duncan touched her puckered opening, she stiffened and couldn't hold back a whimper.

"Easy, baby. We can't take your ass until it's been stretched."

She whimpered again in her throat, fearing the unknown, fearing the loss of control again. Reese tightened his hold on her hair. "It's okay, honey. No one will do anything to you that won't feel good. Jesus, your mouth is fantastic."

Jared urged her on, his voice penetrating the fog and sending her even higher. "Let go, Erin. We know how passionate you are. Let go so we can make you feel good. We'll take good care of you, love. You just have to trust us. We're not going to let you hold onto that control with us, Erin."

Duncan's hands continued their journey and worked their way between her legs. When a thick finger slid into her drenched pussy, she couldn't keep from rocking her hips. "You like that, huh, baby. You are so damned hot."

Hearing the rip of foil, she arched toward him. When she felt the head of his cock at her opening, she groaned and pushed back, needing him to fill her. Desperate sounds of need burst from her throat again as he pushed into her, stretching her again with his thickness. The thick head of his cock pushed relentlessly into her, so slowly she couldn't stand it. She bucked frantically, trying to get him to move faster, but he stilled her with his grip on her hips. "Easy, baby. I'm going to fuck you nice and deep but you've got me too fucking hot. I want it to last."

She felt Jared's lips on her back and arched, the indescribable feeling of having all three of them touching her sending her senses soaring again. She could never have imagined feeling this way. Her entire world had been reduced to what they did to her, where they touched. The combined scents and voices of her lovers intoxicated her, driving her higher.

Reese pulled her hair to one side, and she felt Jared's fingers caress her cheek as he leaned toward her, his lips moving over her shoulder and she knew he watched as she sucked his brother's length into her mouth.

"You are incredibly beautiful, love. We're never going to let you go now."

Duncan's thrusts stilled and she felt a coldness against her anus. She bucked, trying to lift up but found herself held in place by Reese's hands in her hair and Jared's hand flattening on her back.

Duncan groaned. "Relax your bottom, baby. I just want to stretch you a little. I won't hurt you."

The unfamiliar and forbidden feel of his finger pushing relentlessly into her anus made Erin shiver. When she whimpered in her throat, Jared and Reese both caressed her, murmuring to her softly. Jared stroked her back. "It's okay, love. Just feel."

Reese stroked her hair back again. "Duncan is going to make you feel so good, honey. Just let him. Doesn't it feel good to have him in your tight little ass? We can't wait to take you there, honey. We're all going to love it."

Duncan twisted his finger inside her. "Her ass is unbelievably tight."

She couldn't stop trembling as he began stroking. A new and totally foreign sensation shot through her at this new invasion. She struggled to adapt to it, but with them touching her everywhere, she couldn't focus. Then her body just took over. Tightening on his finger made it feel even larger inside her, but she just couldn't stop. It felt as though he controlled her with his dual penetration. Moisture flowed from her pussy like never before as he moved in and out steadily in both openings.

Reese's hands tightened. "Fuck, her mouth is unbelievable. Erin, honey, I'm gonna come. Let go, baby. Let go. Shit. Damn it."

Erin doubled her efforts, holding onto his thighs tightly, needing his taste and wanting to give him the pleasure that they gave her.

"Fuck. Let go. Damn it. Come on, baby, oh, fuck!" Reese growled and she felt his cock throb against her tongue as he came. The salty, erotic taste of him did nothing to turn her off, instead she became greedy, wanting more and swallowed on him repeatedly, needing all of him.

She thrilled at his bit-off curses and groans and the way his hands tightened even more on her as his big body stiffened and shuddered under her hands. She continued to lick him clean, running her tongue over him until he slid from her mouth. His thighs trembled, making her feel both powerful and desired. Duncan slid his finger from her and she found herself trying to follow him, needing her now empty anus to be filled once again.

"Easy, baby. I'm going to use some more lube and give you two fingers this time." With Duncan's cock filling her pussy and his fingers working in and out of her anus, her lower body bloomed like never before. Inhibitions melted away. When Reese slid down until she lay on his chest, she gripped him, digging her nails in as she struggled with all the unfamiliar sensations.

Duncan's two fingers felt huge as he worked them into her, stretching the tight ring of muscle at her entrance and moving them around inside her.

She gasped at the darkly erotic fullness. "Oh, God. Oh, God." She knew her eyes had to be huge in her face as she looked at Jared, who had moved to lie beside her.

Jared stroked a hand down her back. "One day soon, we're going to fuck that sweet ass, love, and you're going to come like never before."

Erin held onto Reese as Duncan held his fingers deep, stroking her anus, the sensation so new and unfamiliar that she had no defense against it. At the same time she knew that Jared watched her face as though gauging her reaction as their brother invaded her most private opening.

Duncan's cock thrust into her over and over, driving deep inside her as his fingers worked her ass. She could never have imagined this feeling. The deep sense of vulnerability made her even hotter, surprising the hell out of her. His cock felt so hot and thick, this position allowing him to stroke deep. Relentlessly working that magical spot inside her, he had her body clenching repeatedly, making his dual invasion even more pronounced.

Jared smiled, his scar slashing deeply. "How does it feel to have Duncan's fingers fucking your ass while Reese and I watch?"

Oh, God. How could she tell him? His fingers tightened on her nipple warningly. "Tell us."

"Please." Her clit burned, throbbing painfully. "It feels so naughty. I feel so full. I've never...I can't...Ahhhh! Oh, God!" Sparks shot through her, and she fought frantically against the feeling as it threatened to overtake her. She absently heard Duncan's roar and deep groans as he swore, her own orgasm triggering his. "No. Make it stop."

Duncan cursed harshly and groaned. "Incredible."

Reese's arms tightened around her. "It's okay, honey. We've got you."

Jared's hands moved over her arms and back as he spoke softly to her, but she had no idea what he said. But his voice soothed her as she slowly began to fall back to earth.

Duncan's hands tightened on her hips as he held his cock deep inside her, stroking slowly.

She hadn't even noticed when his fingers had slid from her bottom, so lost in the riot of sensations. Everything sizzled, every nerve ending in her body screaming with pleasure. She'd never felt anything like what she'd just experienced. The repeated total loss of control terrified the hell out of her. Even more terrifying was the fact that on some level she had trusted them enough to allow herself to let go more than she ever had. She hardly knew them. How could that be possible?

She could think about it later. Right now she just struggled to recover, to pull that protective cloak back around her. Her heart still raced and her breathing sounded ragged. She smiled against Reese's chest when she realized they sounded just as bad. She couldn't prevent a groan as Duncan withdrew. She felt hands and lips everywhere, not knowing or caring whose as she closed her eyes and snuggled against Reese's heat.

She flinched at the touch of a washcloth between her legs. They'd apparently expected it as Reese halted her automatic jolt while someone ran the cloth softly over her. Barely awake, she felt someone lay her on the bed and tuck the covers around her. Then she knew nothing.

* * * *

Jared looked up from setting the table, smiling when Duncan walked into the kitchen carrying a big pot. "How are Mom and the dads?"

Duncan set the pot on the stove and turned the flame on low. "They're good, but upset. Mom is mad as hell and worried to death. I think Dads have their hands full trying to keep her away from here." He shook his head. "Hell, they're having a hard time staying away themselves."

Jared frowned worriedly. "But they will, right?"

Duncan nodded. "Yeah, I convinced them that the less people around, the better we would be able to protect her. I don't want anyone else in the line of fire." He rubbed a hand over the back of his neck and sighed. "I just wish we could figure out what the hell happened. I talked to Ace. No one can figure out why anyone would want to hurt Erin."

"Did he check out that Jacob that she dated?" Just the thought of Erin with another man, even if it had only been platonic left a bad taste in his mouth.

"Yeah, and it was just like Erin said. He wanted more and she didn't. Ace said the guy sounded intimidated by Erin and went along with her wishes without arguing. He talked to some people that she worked with in Houston. Nobody had a bad thing to say about her, but every one of them knew better than to piss her off." He chuckled. "It seems that everyone has always been afraid of Erin's temper. They say she strikes hard and fast and they never knew what hit them until it was over."

Jared grimaced. "She's made a lot of enemies?"

Duncan shook his head. "Not a one. They all seemed to respect her and Ace said that everyone he talked to agreed that she never lit into someone unless they deserved it. Afterward, she never harbored any bad feelings and the people she'd argued with had admitted that they deserved what they'd gotten. Most of her friends are people that she's fought with, but apparently she doesn't hold grudges and neither do they."

Jared chuckled. "Amazing. Wait until she lights into one of us. That should be a lot of fun."

Duncan laughed. "Our guts will probably be all over the floor before we even realize we've been sliced."

Reese walked into the room and moved toward the pot on the stove. "What's so funny? Is that Mom's chicken soup I smell?"

Duncan nodded. "Yeah, she thought it might be a good idea for Erin to eat light for a couple of days after being so sick. We'll have it for lunch."

Jared listened as Duncan told Reese what Ace had learned. Hearing a noise, he looked up to see Erin standing in the doorway, looking tousled and sleep soft, her eyes glazed and unfocused. And fell head over heels in love. Just like that it hit him with a force that nearly staggered him. Everything inside him jumbled. Want, need, and the overwhelming emotions of love, protectiveness, and possessiveness mixed together. Suddenly everything settled and a deep sense of peace and rightness washed over him as everything fell into place. Any lingering doubts disappeared in a heartbeat.

"Come here, love."

Still half asleep, and probably because of that, she obediently walked barefoot toward him, laying her head on his chest and leaning against him. She felt like a soft little kitten snuggled in his arms. He smiled inwardly knowing just how quickly she could become a spitting tiger.

Nothing in his life had ever felt so right. He tilted her face to his, searching her sleep softened expression before lowering his head. He pulled her against him even tighter, feeling her breasts with their little pointed nipples poking into him as he touched his lips to hers. He sank into her, her soft full lips warm as he pushed past them. His loins stirred as he feasted on the taste of her.

When he lifted his head he watched her blink several times, amused that her eyes looked unfocused. She glanced at Duncan and Reese and looked back up at him, biting her lip hesitantly. He smiled gently, realizing how new all this must feel to her. Remembering her words of the night before, that she couldn't go from one man to another, he realized she didn't want to hurt his feelings by going to one of his brothers. Guilt crossed her face and he could only imagine the thoughts going through her mind as she stood there, eyeing him uncertainly.

Kissing the top of her head, he turned her toward Duncan, who happened to be the closest. Watching her move into his brother's arms and seeing the emotion on his brother's face as he held her, he felt a deep sense of peace and purpose. This is what they'd been looking for. Moments such as this is what they'd always known they wanted.

His jaw clenched. They couldn't start a life with her until they figured out why some asshole wanted to hurt her.

"I'm going out. I need some air. I can't believe I slept so long."

Jared snapped back to the present. Erin stood in Reese's arms, smiling up at him. Reese looked happier than Jared had seen him look in a long time. Hell, they probably all did, except for the worry they all tried to hide from Erin.

When Reese looked up at him questioningly, Jared shrugged. "I guess we can go for a walk or a ride if you'd like. You haven't met Missy yet. Would you like to go after you eat breakfast?"

Erin shook her head. "I'll just get some coffee."

Reese got her a cup and poured it for her. "Go get dressed. We'll go as soon as you're ready."

Jared watched in fascination as dimples appeared on Erin's cheeks, making him want to grab her close and repeat the lovemaking they'd shared the night before. Erin had gone up in flames in his arms and had taken him with her. He'd never responded so fiercely to a woman before.

Her hair fell halfway down her back in beautiful waves that he couldn't wait to see fanned out on his pillow again. His hands itched to palm her full breasts and take those pebbled nipples into his mouth. He'd loved the feel of those long legs wrapped around him and he couldn't wait until he could have them around him again.

For the first time in years everything felt right. Not only had he and his brothers all fallen for Erin, but it appeared she affected each of them more than any woman ever had. He hadn't expected to get so lucky.

His fathers had found that in their mother, but after years of hoping and waiting, they'd just about given up on finding the same. They'd agreed that they might have to make do with a little less than all-out lust for a woman if they ever wanted to start a family.

Erin had been a hell of a surprise. He thought it adorable that everyone they spoke to talked about her no-nonsense and hard-as-nails attitude, but with him and his brothers, she seemed nervous and jittery. They had her off balance for now, but he knew it wouldn't last. They'd just have to make as much headway as they could before she got her balance back. Christ, she made him feel good.

He shuddered to think they had almost let her get away. When she'd stopped dating Reese and worked so hard to avoid him, they had pretty much given up on her. But the night they saw her at the club, the sparks between her and Duncan had settled their fate.

After they'd driven Erin home that night, they'd begun to make their plans.

Erin had done her best to avoid all three of them since then. She'd done a hell of a job of it, too. Frustrated, but admiring her skill in avoiding them in a town as small as Desire, they went behind her back and made arrangements with Boone and Chase to take her home from the Christmas party.

Then everything had blown up in their faces.

The phone rang and he glanced over as Reese went to answer it.

Duncan turned off the stove and went out to help Bud get the horses ready. Bud and Jim took care of the horses for them and their fathers and had for a couple of years now.

Sometimes they got so distracted while working on a piece of furniture that they forgot the time. Since their fathers had gotten older, they'd hired the men for both of them and it worked out well. The horses got fed when they got busy, and they didn't have to worry about their fathers getting hurt while trying to deal with them.

Reese hung up, smiling. "That was Jesse. She wanted to know how Erin felt and when I told her that we were going to take her for a ride, she said to ride over and they would ride with us. She wants to see Erin, and Clay and Rio want to make sure that Erin likes Missy."

Erin came out, smiling, wearing jeans and a thick sweater. "It'll feel good to get outside a little." Her stomach rumbled and she blushed adorably. "That soup smells delicious. I can't wait to get back to it."

Jared helped her into her jacket before going outside, not being able to resist nuzzling her neck in the process. The soft skin beneath his lips and her shiver had his cock jumping to attention.

They walked outside to find Bud waiting with the horses, his face lined and wrinkled from years spent in the sun. He almost never smiled but did now as he touched his hat when he saw Erin. "Ma'am."

"Hello, I'm Erin."

Jared saw Bud nod and turn red as Erin offered her hand. The older ranch hand had more common sense than most people Jared knew and had been informed of the situation. He trusted Bud to keep an eye out. Very little got past the older man.

Meanwhile, everyone had passed the word about Erin being in danger and he knew by now his friends would be on the alert. By now everyone in Desire would know what had happened. The men who lived here were furious that three women had been hurt on their watch in the past year. Jesse, Kelly and now Erin had all been injured in attacks. Meetings had been planned to discuss the fact that they had all become lax in protecting the women. They all felt guilty as hell, ashamed that they hadn't done their job.

The founding fathers of this town would be ashamed of them.

Jared took the reins for Missy from the older man. "Everything okay, Bud?"

The old hand nodded. "Yep."

When Erin blinked at the abrupt reply, Jared wanted to laugh. Bud never spoke more than absolutely necessary and a lot of people didn't consider him very bright, or observant. They quickly learned their mistake.

"If anything was wrong or if anyone came around, Bud would know about it." He smiled at her reassuringly. "It's hard as hell to pull the wool over Bud's eyes. He's ex-military and sees everything."

He turned to Bud. "Go on home, Bud. We'll take care of the horses when we get back from our ride."

"Might as well wait a spell." Bud turned and walked back into the stable.

Jared shook his head, smiling. Bud pretty much did what he thought best no matter what anyone else said. He winked at Erin, his smile widening when she blushed. "Come on, love. Let's go so we can get back and feed you."

Reese and Duncan came forward and introduced her to Missy. He smiled as he watched Reese help her onto the horse. They'd bought the filly for her but hadn't told her that yet.

They'd asked Clay and Rio about selling Missy because they knew how she'd been trained but also because she was almost exactly the same color as Erin's hair in the sun.

He eyed Erin's stirrups and saw that Duncan had judged correctly. After making sure she'd settled, he mounted his stallion, his brothers following suit. He could see her nervousness and shot a quick look at Duncan, who'd moved to Erin's other side so they flanked her. Duncan gave a quick nod and Jared knew his brother would also be ready to help if Erin had a problem.

After Duncan gave Erin a few quick instructions they started out. Reese moved to the other side of Jared and kept a conversation going with her as they rode. Duncan occasionally chimed in, but Jared just listened absently, keeping an eye on her. Missy behaved just as Clay had promised, although they'd already ridden their newest addition to be sure.

Clay and Rio really knew how to train horses and knowing that this one had been trained for Jesse made him feel even more secure. Jared knew Clay and Rio would do anything to keep Jesse safe.

Seeing that Erin seemed to be doing fine and with his brothers keeping the conversation going, Jared became lost in his own thoughts. Glancing at her again, he found himself taken in with her flushed cheeks as she tried to maintain the aloofness and seriousness that everyone talked about. It amused him that she had trouble keeping it around them.

She responded to every smile, every touch he and his brothers gave her, and it made him hard as a rock every time. No longer a kid, he'd been absolutely amazed at *his* response to *her*. He'd been totally unprepared for an erection while dancing with her and the swiftness of his arousal earlier. He couldn't believe a grown man in his forties could be as horny as a teenager over a kiss.

One thing that had bothered him had been the way she looked at him as though for understanding or approval before moving from him to his brothers. She looked like she'd felt guilty about wanting to kiss and cuddle with them, too.

Guilt had no place in a relationship like the one they wanted with her and he had to see what could be done about it. They'd be tiptoeing through what could turn out to be an emotional minefield. At least they could have some time with her. They would just have to take advantage of it and do their best to show her just how happy they could be. They could show her first hand just how well a ménage relationship could work.

It would take time and effort, both of which might be in short supply until they caught whoever wanted to hurt her. But by then she'd want to leave. It would be a juggling act but they had to make sure she accepted what they could have before she had the chance to leave them.

* * * *

Erin kept a close eye on a very quiet Jared. Not that he'd been much of a talker. But ever since they'd started riding, he'd been unusually quiet. It came as a shock to her to realize that she could already tell that something bothered him.

She'd learned that Duncan seemed to be the most intense of the three brothers, more intensely playful, quick tempered, and also more intense when it came to sex. All of them had proven to be more sexual than any men she'd ever known, but Duncan seemed to be the most daring, the one who pushed her the most.

She looked back at Jared through her lashes. He would have to be the most dangerous of the three. He acted the most possessive and was by far the most domineering. And when he got angry, his temper didn't flash like Duncan's. Jared's temper was ice cold. The look on his face whenever he talked about what had happened to her made her shudder.

Reese, on the other hand proved to be the most easygoing. She felt more comfortable talking to him than to the others but then again, she'd known him longer. The attraction she'd had for him when they dated continued to grow, but the way he looked at her sometimes made her think he hadn't shown all of his true colors yet.

Watching him unobtrusively as he spoke to Duncan, she thought about their lovemaking last night. Why hadn't he made love to her?

After all, he was the one she had a history with, but Jared had been the first to take her. Damn. Had that offended Reese? Did he feel that he should have been the first? The other two had had sex with her, but not Reese. She'd satisfied him with her mouth, of course, but still…

See? She knew she could never handle a relationship like this. How the hell did these women manage to do it? One man would be more than enough trouble, but three?

Forget it. She couldn't do this.

But she'd already fallen more than halfway in love with them.

Weren't men supposed to want sex with no strings? That's all she wanted, all she would be able to handle with these three. She'd just have to make it clear to them. Why couldn't she just go for the pleasure the way most men did? Christ, they made her feel giddy, like a teenager with a crush. She hadn't felt this way in so long she could barely remember. It was a lifetime ago, a different Erin.

"Ready to go a little faster?"

Erin spun to Duncan, startled. "Faster? Why do we have to go faster? How much faster?"

Duncan's evil grin had her clenching her thighs. His eyes, shadowed beneath his hat, glittered like gold as they roamed over her. Thankfully the jacket kept him from seeing just how her body had reacted to that mischievous glance.

"Just a little." He picked up the pace and Missy kept up.

She held on tighter. "What did I do?" Not knowing what she'd done to make the horse move faster made her realize she could accidentally do it again.

Duncan chuckled. "Nothing. Missy has been trained to keep up with the other horses riding beside her. The only thing you have to do is hold on and use the reins the way I showed you earlier to stop or turn."

Intrigued, Erin paid close attention as Duncan and the others sped up and slowed down, watching as Missy did the same. "Why has Missy been trained that way?"

Jared smiled as the others chuckled. "Missy was trained for Jesse. Clay and Rio wanted to teach her to ride but didn't want to take a chance that her horse could run off with her. Jesse liked to ride so much that they had to train Missy to remain still if she has a rider on her back and no other horses are around."

Jared moved closer. "Clay and Rio didn't want to take a chance that Jesse would ever try to ride alone so they made sure her horse wouldn't budge if she attempted to."

Erin nodded. "So this is Jesse's horse?"

Reese grinned. "Not anymore. We bought Missy last week."

Erin looked at each of them, confused. "Why would you buy a horse like Missy? Aren't all three of you good riders?"

Jared slowed his horse as they came to the Erickson's property. "Yes. We've been riding since we were kids. We bought Missy for you."

Erin's mouth fell open as Duncan and Reese came to a stop beside her, effectively bringing Missy to a stop also. "You bought a horse for me?"

Jared nodded and kept looking straight ahead toward the Erickson's back yard.

Stunned, Erin looked at the others. When they didn't say anything, she turned back to Jared. "You can't buy a horse for me!"

Jared kept his eyes forward and remained silent.

Erin turned to back Duncan, hoping he would understand. "You guys can't buy me a horse. I don't even ride!"

Duncan looked pointedly at her, then at Missy, and raised a brow.

"Today is an exception. I don't ride! You cannot buy me a horse."

Duncan grinned. "Apparently we can. Look, there they are. Let's go."

As they approached she saw Clay and Rio making adjustments to something before leading the horses toward them. Jesse came running out of the house. "Hi, everybody!"

Erin looked at the Erickson's horses. They all looked to be about the same size as the ones Jared, Duncan, and Reese rode. None looked as small as Missy. "I guess Jesse got a new horse."

Reese chuckled. "Oh, yeah."

As they got closer, Erin smiled at Jesse. "I understand Missy used to be yours."

Jesse grinned and Erin wondered how it could be possible that Jesse seemed to look more beautiful every day. She wore jeans and boots and a thick jacket and still managed to look trim. She'd braided her hair and wore a hat like the men's. "Yes. Missy's a good girl. Clay and Rio taught me to ride with her."

Everyone greeted each other and Erin couldn't help but notice how neither Clay nor Rio could manage to keep their eyes off their wife for very long. Jesse seemed to have the same dilemma, glowing at the attention from her husbands. What would it be like to love like that?

She turned to Duncan to find him watching her. She felt her face flush as she slid a glance at Jared and Reese only to find both of them eyeing her tenderly and smiling.

With her face burning, she turned away. How the hell did they fluster her so easily?

Jesse mounted her horse with one smooth move under the watchful eyes of her husbands. They'd waited until she'd settled before mounting their own. Jesse clicked her tongue and the horse moved forward.

Reese grinned at her. "You look like you've ridden your whole life."

Jesse laughed, earning indulgent smiles from her husbands. "Thanks. With these two I had to learn. They wouldn't take no for an answer."

Clay moved up beside her and leaned over to caress her thigh. "If we did, we wouldn't have gotten you."

Jesse beamed. "True. Thank God you didn't listen to me." She moved next to Erin. "We won't go far. It's your first time and you're going to be sore. I remember that feeling."

"I'll bet you do." Rio leered and Erin watched, fascinated as Jesse turned bright red.

"Shut up, Rio."

Jesse rode next to Erin as they started out. The women listened to the men mostly as they spoke about what Ace had learned so far. Jesse asked Erin how she felt and once Erin assured her that she felt fine, they let the men's conversation wash over them. Erin tried to forget everything and just relax and enjoy the scenery.

"It all seems so unreal." She'd spoken without thinking, grimacing as everyone became silent. "Sorry, I guess I was just thinking and it slipped out."

Jared moved closer, frowning worriedly. "Are you all right, love?"

Erin nodded and looked at each of them. "Yeah, I'm sorry. I was just listening to all of you talk and it just seems so unreal. How could this be happening? Why?"

"You have nothing to apologize for, baby." Duncan reached over to rub her thigh. "Are you sure you're okay?"

Erin nodded. "Yeah, let's talk about something else."

Rio looked over at her and smiled. "What do you think of Missy?"

Erin smiled. "I haven't fallen off yet, so I guess we're fine. I'm still nervous, though."

Jesse laughed softly. "If you fall off, she'll stop and wait for you to get back on. I know. It happened to me."

Erin gripped the reins tighter. "It did?"

Jesse nodded, smiling good naturedly. "Oh, yes. The first time I rode."

Clay reached over to tug Jesse's braid. "Scared the shit out of me."

Jared frowned and moved even closer to Erin, reaching out to stroke her thigh as Duncan had. "How'd you fall off, Jesse?"

Jesse giggled. "Rio made me laugh so hard, I let go and fell off."

Rio grinned. "I made up for it, didn't I?"

Jesse blushed again.

Erin caught the look Jessie shared with Rio. It made *her* face burn.

"Okay. Nobody say anything funny until I'm back on the ground again."

The men chuckled as Jared leaned closer and patted her thigh. "I'll catch you, love."

The place he and Duncan had touched tingled, the tingles shooting all the way to her center. Astounded that a touch from him, more like a little pat, could have that strong of an effect on her, had her shifting in the saddle and looking away. Looking at the scenery, she tried to listen to the others but she could focus on only Jared, Duncan, and Reese, feeling their gazes on her.

She had no experience at all with attentive men and didn't quite know how to handle it. She didn't care for being disconcerted by it. Damn it, she knew how to handle anything. Why couldn't she adopt that calm, cool demeanor she relied on so heavily?

She couldn't even blame it on the aftereffects of being drugged. This uneasiness with them had started long before. That's why she'd avoided them in the first place.

But she wouldn't be a coward about this. She wouldn't let the nervousness she felt around them push her away. Not having a long term relationship was one thing. She knew she could never put up with three men, but having a sexual relationship would be different. She saw nothing wrong with it. She didn't sleep around, but damn it, she sure as hell could have a relationship based on sex and enjoy it for as long as it lasted.

And they were incredible in bed.

Just remembering had her nipples tingling. Her panties had been wet since she'd cuddled with the men in the kitchen and it just kept getting worse. Even their glances felt like caresses on her overly stimulated body. Their deep voices washed over her, somehow both comforting and arousing her. Having no experience in dealing with feelings like these, she felt out of her element. She hated feeling so out of sorts. Not knowing how much more she could take, she struggled to concentrate on the scenery around her.

The next time she had sex with them things would be different. Now that she knew what to expect, she should be able to enjoy it without losing herself completely in it. As soon as she recovered her equilibrium, she'd be ready for them.

As they rode, Erin forced herself to pay attention to how Jesse and her men got along. She'd looked for any signs of jealousy and so far hadn't seen any. After the conversation she'd had with Jared, Duncan, and Reese she'd begun to see relationships like Jesse's and Rachel's in a new light. She hoped her sister and Jesse could be happy with their men. She just knew it would be something she could never be comfortable with.

They rode for a short while and Erin had to admit she really enjoyed it. They turned back and she knew that the others kept their horses at a slow pace in deference to her and she appreciated it.

She turned to Jared to thank him and jumped, startled when she heard a loud crack and fell off the horse. Lying on the ground, she heard the men's shouts and curses and covered her head when she heard the horse's hooves close, afraid of being trampled.

Erin felt a body land beside hers as another one, hard and heavy covered her. Her arm burned and lay heavily at her side as she fought for air. The breath had been knocked out of her when she fell and with the heavy body covering hers, she struggled to fill her lungs.

It seemed to be hours, but in reality had probably been only a few seconds before some of the weight lifted from her.

"Erin, talk to me. Are you okay?" Jared's voice sounded frantic above her. When she turned her head to look at him, the fear on his face took her by surprise.

She gulped in air and swallowed before speaking. "Yeah, I'm okay. I just got the wind knocked out of me when I fell off the horse. I think I fell on my arm. It hurts a little."

Beside her, Jesse's voice came out breathlessly. "You didn't look like you fell off the horse. You looked like you got knocked off of it."

Erin turned her head to see Jesse lying on the ground beside her, being checked over by a panic-stricken Rio, who covered her body completely with his.

Rio looked wild as his hands ran over Jesse. "Please darlin', tell me you're okay."

"I'm fine, Rio. I promise, honey. Why'd you pull me off my horse? Was that a gunshot?"

"Rifle," Duncan muttered from somewhere behind Jared. "Are either of them hurt?"

Rio turned to look over his shoulder. "Erin's arm but we don't know what else." He looked at Jared. "Any blood? Broken bones?"

Erin tried to sit up but Jared held her down as he continued to run his hands over her. "Let me up. What the hell happened?"

Jared shook his head, running his hands over her legs, irritating her that he'd refused. "In a minute—Clay, Duncan, and Reese are watching and waiting." He looked over at Rio. "Get Jesse the hell out of here."

Rio nodded. "We'll get both of them out of here. The five of us can protect them easier and better if we stick together."

Erin grabbed Jared's arm. "What the hell happened? You said it was a rifle. Did it scare Missy?"

Jared and Rio looked at each other. Jared grimaced. "I think somebody took a shot at you. Let me see where your arm hurts." He gently started to lift her arm out of her jacket.

Erin couldn't keep from crying out when he touched a really sore spot on the back of her right arm and tried to look down at it. She slapped at him. "Let go of me. I'll do it."

Again he ignored her. Jared's eyes widened in horror. "You're bleeding!"

Rio saw it immediately and started cursing.

"What?" The fear on their faces scared her enough to piss her off. She shoved at Jared, even angrier that he didn't budge. "Let go of me."

The men all gathered around her as Jared worked the jacket off of her, keeping Jesse close to her so that they surrounded both of them. The other men helped and she couldn't prevent a moan from escaping as pain shot through her arm.

"Did I break it?" Erin asked, trying to see, but with all the men's hands in the way she couldn't. Now that it had started hurting, it hurt like hell.

Jared cursed and looked up at the others. "She's been shot."

Erin could all but hear his composure snap.

Chapter Four

Very little conversation took place on the ride home from the hospital. The men only spoke to ask about her comfort. They'd worn the same grim expressions ever since they'd bundled her into their truck for the ride to the hospital.

The race to the ranch had been cloaked in unreality. Jared had held her tightly against his chest, flanked by Reese and Duncan, as they raced back to the stable. Clay and Rio had ridden behind them, Jesse tucked tightly in Clay's arms after Rio sent Jesse's horse back home.

Once they'd gotten there, they'd handed the horses over to Bud, quickly loaded Erin into their truck and sped for the hospital. The bullet had only grazed the back of her arm, making it not much more than a flesh wound. The fact that it had only been a flesh wound didn't appear to appease the men at all.

She knew Ace had been informed, but didn't hear all of the conversation. Duncan had called him and the doctor from the truck on the way to the hospital, but hadn't talked long. Jared's conversation with Ace at the hospital had lasted considerably longer and although she didn't hear all of it, it included some rather inventive cursing that had impressed even her.

Duncan had spoken to their parents, and she felt terrible that Isabel and her husbands couldn't even come near their children because of her. She'd asked for the phone and apologized profusely. Isabel had been more concerned for her and had told her that the apology hadn't been necessary and she couldn't wait until she could spend some time getting to know Erin better. That made Erin feel even worse. She had the feeling that Isabel thought she would be a permanent fixture in her sons' lives. When all of this finally ended, she'd have to sit down with her and set her straight.

Adding the events of this afternoon to what had already happened left Erin feeling slightly numb. None of it seemed real and she wondered how long it would be before she woke to find it had all been some kind of crazy dream. She wanted her damned life back. This vulnerability, this uncertainty had begun to seriously piss her off.

As they pulled into the driveway, Erin looked up at Duncan, who sat beside her. "I heard you talking to Chase."

Duncan nodded grimly. "Yes, he said he would talk to Boone. They've been passing the word not to let Rachel know. I think Chase said that he was going to the club and would start passing the word there."

Erin rubbed her forehead where a low level headache had started to form. "If anything happens to her or the baby, I'll never forgive myself. I thought I was doing the right thing in coming here for her, but I may have somehow put her in danger. I seem to be putting a lot of people in danger. Any one of you could have been shot by mistake. Can you imagine what Clay and Rio would have thought of me if the bullet had hit Jesse?"

Duncan's fingers bit into her chin as he turned her to face him fully. "None of this is your fault."

Erin leaned back, tired and frustrated. "Why is this happening?"

Jared stopped the car. "That's what we're going to find out. Duncan, stay here with her while Reese and I check out the house."

Lights shone in the truck as another truck pulled in the driveway behind them. Erin reached for the door handle, ready to confront this bitch, but Duncan pulled her back.

"It's okay. It's Lucas Hart, Devlin Monroe and Caleb Ward."

Jared and Reese got out of the truck and went to join them as Duncan pulled her against him.

She looked up at him, frowning. "Don't they have the security company?"

Duncan pushed her hair back from her face. "They do. Desire Security. They're also bodyguards."

She watched the men as they spoke quietly, unable to hear what they said. "Did you call them?"

"Yes, they're going to install a security system for us and check the place out."

Erin looked up at him, shocked. "You can't install a security system just because I'm staying here! That has to be expensive. I need to get back to my apartment. I can handle this on my own from now on." She searched the seat for her purse and remembered. "Damn, my cell phone's in the house." When she started to scramble out of the truck, Duncan gripped her arm to stop her again.

"You're not going anywhere." When she tried to pull away, he merely tightened his hold. "Listen to me, you little hellcat. We never installed a system because with just the three of us living here, we didn't need one. We always knew that we would get one some day, when we had someone to protect. Whether you want to listen or not, *you* are that someone."

Erin stared up at him in disbelief. "I told you I can't be what you want. This is all temporary. I appreciate all you and—" Her mouth closed with a snap when he grabbed her face in his hands and dropped a hard kiss on her lips.

He lifted his head and growled at her. "If you say that you're grateful again, I'm going to turn you over my knee and paddle your ass good."

Erin gripped the front of his shirt. "You just try it, buddy."

He scrubbed a hand over his face and sighed heavily. "Listen, my brothers and I care about you. A lot. We're not about to let anything happen to you and will protect you with or without your permission. We've claimed you and you live with us. That's the beginning and the end of this argument."

"If you think you're going to tell me what to do—"

"We are."

"Then you'd better think again!"

Duncan sat back and smiled so smugly she wanted to hit him. "You know, you really are beautiful. God, I love a woman with a temper."

"Arggghhh!"

Jared opened the truck door. "Well said, love. Lucas and Devlin have already checked out the house. Let's get you inside."

Erin turned to Jared. "Jared, listen, this is ridiculous. You can't install a security system. It's a big expense."

"Desire Securities gives us a discount. Come on, unless you need me to carry you."

"No, I don't need you to carry me. Jared, damn it, you're not listening to me."

"I listen to every word you say, love. Let's take this inside. You're too exposed out here."

Erin saw the way he and Caleb kept looking around as Duncan got out the other side and came around for her. She got out and the men surrounded her as she headed for the house. The idea that someone had a reason to hurt her seemed like a nightmare. None of this could be happening. "You know, I'm going to wake up and find that this has all been a dream."

Jared leaned close and whispered in her ear. "When you wake up, nudge me. I'll be sleeping right beside you."

Caleb's chuckle told her that he'd heard Jared's remark.

She turned to him. "Hi, Caleb. We've never formally met before, but I've heard good things about you. Do you have any idea how much business we do because of you and your partners?"

Caleb smiled mischievously and looked intrigued. "Really?"

Erin smiled back. "Yeah, women are always coming in trying to entice some of the men in Desire. You and your partners get your fair share along with several other men in this town. I understand all of you have a thing for pink."

Caleb looked startled at that and looked down at her but only smiled and continued his perusal of their surroundings, his gaze always moving. "That we do. You mean we have competition? Who's in first place?"

She grinned. "Now that would be telling."

His gaze slid to hers. "I can make you tell me." He looked up at Jared and Duncan and his smile fell. He cleared his throat. "Maybe not."

She looked up to see both Jared and Duncan frowning at Caleb, who appeared to be struggling to hide his grin. They walked in the front door to the living room where Lucas and Devlin stood talking to Reese. After greeting them, Erin moved to the kitchen. "I'm going to start some fresh coffee."

Lucas grinned. "A woman after my own heart."

Erin walked out of the room and into the kitchen, startled to find Caleb and Reese following her. "I'm not going anywhere."

Reese ordered her to sit as he made the coffee.

She plopped into the chair, wincing as it jarred her arm. "This is all ridiculous, you know. There has to be some kind of mistake."

Caleb sat at the table and opened his laptop. "Someone has tried to hurt or kill you three times already, Erin. If there's a mistake, whoever is doing this has made it, not you."

Caleb's overlong brown hair made him look more like a bad guy than a security expert. Pulled back into a ponytail, his hair looked as soft as mink and she knew for a fact that more than one woman had fallen in love with those deep blue eyes. She heard a lot of it in the lingerie store as woman shopped for things to tempt him and his partners.

When the coffee had finished, they all went into the living room as Lucas, Devlin, and Caleb installed a security system that also included the outbuildings. None of Erin's objections had any effect. Finally, in defeat, she gave up and curled up at the end of the sofa as the men worked.

Jared, Duncan, and Reese helped, but at least one of the men stayed with her at all times. It drove her crazy. How could she live like this? Some psycho had decided to do this and they all had to pay for it. She hoped she had a chance to get her hands on this woman.

Of course, Ace showed up, asking a lot of questions and nodding his satisfaction at the elaborate system being installed. The testosterone level in the house had become stifling as the seven very alpha males set about protecting her. Not that she didn't appreciate it, but she desperately needed some time alone.

When she stood, Jared and Devlin whipped their heads around, only reinforcing her decision. "I'm going to take a shower."

Jared frowned. "You'd better make it a bath. You're not allowed to get that bandage wet."

Devlin nodded and smiled at her. "We've already finished in the master bedroom and bath. We figured you might want to go to bed soon."

"Thank you." Her arm had starting hurting again. She was tired and smelled like horses and antiseptic. And some idiot wanted to kill her. She just wanted some time alone to soak.

Jared had to help her out of her shirt. Finally alone, she now sat in the biggest bathtub she had ever seen, even bigger than the one at Rachel's house. She knew the men installed it with the intention of sharing it with their woman one day.

A brief pang of regret went through her that she couldn't be that woman, but she knew her own limitations. It would be better to face facts now than to have to deal with heartache later on.

She leaned back and groaned, careful to keep her arm propped on the towels Jared had provided. The hot water felt heavenly on her sore muscles. She washed the smell of horse from her skin, happy that she had her bath supplies here. Like almost everyone else in town, she used products from Jesse's store. The bath oil she used smelled fresh like baby powder. Erin had almost fallen asleep when she heard a knock on the door.

She heard Reese's voice come from the other side. "Are you ready to eat or do you want to soak a little longer?"

"No. I'll be right out." Erin sat up and groaned.

"Are you all right?"

"I'm fine." She tried to get up and couldn't. "If I can get out of here."

"What did you say?"

Erin turned to face the rim of the tub and tried to lever herself, but she couldn't use her sore arm and the hot water had soaked out all of her strength. "Nothing."

She tried twice to come to her knees, holding onto the rim, but she slipped.

"Erin? I'm coming in."

Erin had no chance to protest as Reese came through the door. She yelped and tried to cover herself but the small washcloth offered no protection. "Get out! I can do it."

"That's why I heard you slip. You're going to kill yourself trying to get out of the tub before you'd ask anyone for help."

She groaned when she heard footstep approaching.

"What's going on? I heard Erin cry out." Duncan walked into the bathroom just as Reese bent to her and gripped her under her armpits, lifting her over the rim of the tub. No matter how often she saw it, she could never quite get over their effortless strength. She'd gotten too used to soft corporate men who couldn't lift more than their portfolios.

Erin gripped Reese's shoulders as Duncan reached for a bath sheet. Aware of the men's eyes on her, she blushed furiously as her body came to life.

Reese set her on the rug in front of him. "She couldn't get out of the tub but rather than call for help, she slipped."

Duncan wrapped the huge towel around her. "Christ, Erin. Did you think he was going to rape you?"

She tried to pull the towel from Duncan's grasp, but he ignored her and started to dry her off. "I was taking a bath. Baths are private." Her nipples had become diamond hard and she bit her lip as Duncan dried her breasts thoroughly, spending more time on them than was necessary.

Duncan chuckled. "We've already seen you naked, touched you naked and fucked you naked. Seeing you wet and naked isn't more intimate than that."

Reese reached for the shirt that Jared had left for her, tossing it onto his shoulder as Duncan continue to dry her. "You're so beautiful, Erin. Why would you want to hide your body from us? We'll all know it as intimately as our own before much longer."

Erin shook her head. "No. This is not going to happen. Sex is one thing but this…" She waved her good arm. "This is more intimate. I'm not doing this."

Duncan moved behind her and she felt him stroke the towel down her back and over her buttocks, making her tremble. Reese steadied her as Duncan carefully parted her thighs. "But the better I get to know your body, the better I can pleasure you." He knelt behind her, running the towel slowly up and down her legs, paying particular attention to the inside of her thighs.

Her toes curled into the plush bath mat as Reese touched a finger to one of her throbbing nipples. She groaned and reached out to grab his forearms for support, flinching as she used her injured arm.

Reese tucked it close to her and carefully avoided touching it. "Your nipples are very sensitive, aren't they, honey?"

Erin nodded, her head falling back when she felt Duncan's mouth on her bottom, his hands firm on her thighs. Reese focused on her breasts, cupping them and stroking her nipples. Her eyes snapped open when she heard Jared's voice.

"I wondered what was taking so long."

Erin jumped guiltily. She bit her lip, her face burning, but she couldn't seem to move away. "I…uh…they…hmm…ohhh! We—"

Jared moved closer and tilted her head back with a finger under her chin. "So I see."

Erin's knees buckled when he covered her mouth with his and he caught her against him, mindful of her arm. All three of them touched her, using their hands and mouths to draw her into their seductive web. She couldn't have stopped them if her life had depended on it. Jared's hot mouth devoured her. Her pussy clenched as moisture coated her thighs.

The hands on her breasts sent arrows of lust through her that settled directly between her legs. She felt Duncan part her bottom cheeks and moaned at the forbidden feel of his tongue darting between them. He licked and poked at her forbidden hole as they held her firmly. Before she could squirm away, Duncan moved.

Jared lifted his head and moved behind her as Reese took her mouth with his. Cupping her face, Reese tilted it to his as Jared's denim-clad thighs brushed against her bottom.

Duncan, now in front of her, parted her folds, licking at her slit.

Reese swallowed her gasp of pleasure as she tightened her hold on his forearms.

Jared went for the sensitive spot on her neck and her legs gave out. If his arm hadn't wrapped around her she knew she would have fallen.

When Reese lifted his head, she blinked her eyes open, dazed. The heat and tenderness shining in his had her holding onto him tighter as she leaned into him. What would it be like to stay here with them like this forever? She blinked rapidly, ruthlessly pushing that thought away. Damn it, she knew better than to allow herself to get emotionally involved with them. But just for a moment she could pretend.

With Jared holding her up, Reese cupped her breasts again. They looked small and pale in his hands. She looked down and saw Duncan kneeling in front of her. When the tongue on her slit slid through her folds again, she dropped her head back on Jared's shoulder and closed her eyes, crying out and moaning at the sheer eroticism of having all three men touching her like this.

Reese groaned and tugged her nipples. "Christ, she's beautiful. After what happened today, I need this with her."

She didn't hear Jared's response because Duncan chose that moment to capture her clit between his lips and begin to suck. Huge waves of pleasure washed over her, pleasure like she'd never felt with anyone else. Her hoarse cries sounded strangely primal to her own ears but she couldn't stop them. Slumping forward over Jared's arm, her body jerked as Duncan eased his touch, slowly bringing her down.

By the time he lifted his mouth from her slit, she felt like a limp dishrag. Duncan's mouth placed opened-mouthed kisses all over her mound and thighs and moved up to her stomach.

Reese moved back as Duncan stood before her. Jared released her, allowing her to slump against Duncan. "That's my girl," Duncan crooned, stroking her as she continued to tremble.

Jared's hand moved over her bottom. "Bring her out once she settles."

Held in Duncan's arms, she felt his arms tighten around her as his big hand cupped her head and held her against his chest. "You're so responsive, baby. You come so beautifully." He tilted her head back until she looked at him. "Your whole body is flushed and your eyes look so unfocused. It gets me every time."

His eyes darkened, the heat in them unmistakable. Although his erection pressed against her stomach, he just continued to hold her. Her eyes closed as he ran his thumb over her lips.

"Your lips are all red and swollen from my brothers' kisses. If I had my way I would keep you looking just like this all the time."

Erin smiled up at him tremulously, wishing it were possible. "I'd never survive it." She leaned in and kissed his chest, thrilling at his surprised hiss. He lifted her face and dropped a quick kiss on her lips. "Let's get you fed. You're going to have an adrenaline crash soon."

Reese held out the huge shirt Jared left for her. It went over her arm easier than one of her own shirts would have. They helped her dress in an old pair of her sweatpants and got her a pair of thick socks.

The conversation flowed over dinner, intriguing her as they talked about their childhood. "I can't imagine what it must have been like to grow up with three dads. Didn't you feel different from the other kids at school?"

Reese grinned. "They were all jealous. We played sports and our mother, and at least one of our dads came to everything. We always had somebody to ride horses with, somebody to help with our homework or just somebody to talk to."

Jared nodded and frowned at the soup remaining in her bowl. "If we went over there right now to talk and our fathers were busy doing something, at least one of them would be available to listen to us, offer advice."

Erin frowned back at him when he pointed at her bowl with his spoon. When he raised a brow, she sighed and took another small bite, knowing he'd hound her until she ate it. "But what if, say the three of you had children and Reese always left the two of you to do his chores so he could play with the kids?"

All three of them started shaking their heads before she'd even finished. Duncan offered her a piece of bread. When she refused, he just held it out until she accepted it. "We wouldn't do that. We already know that this is the kind of life we want to have and know what we have to do to make it work. It would depend on the circumstances. For example, Jared's better at math so if one of our kids needed help with math homework, Jared would probably be the one to help. For the most part, we'd take turns unless one of us was more suited to the task than the others."

Erin was silent as she digested that, and decided to play devil's advocate. "But what if it's sex? What if you're all working on something, say a piece of furniture that has to be done by tomorrow and your wife wants attention?"

Duncan and Reese grinned as Jared watched her soberly. "Then we all drop what we're doing and make our wife come so many times that she's exhausted enough to fall asleep and then stay up all night if we have to in order to finish the piece."

Erin narrowed her eyes at him. "Why do I get the feeling that you've thought about this a lot?"

Jared shrugged. "It's the way we were raised. We've known this is what we've wanted our whole lives. We've seen it work and seen how it works. We've also seen the results. It's worth it. Eat your damned soup."

Erin picked up her spoon again. "You're a pain in the ass."

Jared nodded. "Yep."

Resigned, Erin ate another spoonful. She had a feeling he would force feed her if she didn't eat it. She could argue with the best of them but had already learned that Jared didn't argue. Since he was a hell of a lot stronger, she knew he could make her eat it, which would only end up pissing her off.

They ate in companionable silence for several minutes. Erin closely watched the way they interacted with each other. Several times she'd observed a unique unity among them. They communicated often without words and a lot of times seemed to know what the others were thinking. Brothers, yes, but they seemed closer than the brothers she had known. Now that she thought about it, Clay and Rio seemed unusually close. So did Boone and Chase. Suddenly it hit her. They would be sharing all of their marriage problems and worries with each other more intimately than most brothers would.

They sat at the table talking amiably for quite a while. Lucas, Devlin, and Caleb each came in and had some of Isabel's soup, and went about their business. Jared, Duncan, and Reese came and went after that, helping them while at the same time making sure that she always had someone with her. Dinner had been cleared and she drank coffee with them as they roamed in and out. Lucas and his partners had the same ideas about sharing a woman and she asked them a lot of questions. They appeared to think a lot like Jared and his brothers and seeing her sincere interest, answered her questions patiently. They had all certainly given her a lot to think about.

Lucas, Devlin, and Caleb finished installing the system and explained it to them before smiling their goodbyes, promising to come back the next morning. Staying here with Jared, Duncan, and Reese, she knew everyone assumed that they had a more permanent relationship than they did, and treated her in a way that made her feel more a member of the community than she had before. Not that anyone had ever treated her with anything but the utmost kindness and respect, but their attitude toward her had changed subtly. She couldn't quite put her finger on it. But it had changed. Mentally shrugging, she decided that they would see for themselves soon that nothing had changed and would go back to the way they'd been before.

All of this had started to make Erin's head hurt. Her arm had been getting worse over the last few hours, but she wanted to put off taking a pain pill until she went to bed. She started to rise to get a glass of water to take it now and cried out as the muscles in her thighs protested. They'd tightened into knots and screamed when she'd tried to use them.

The men instantly moved to surround her. Duncan reached her first. "Oh, baby. You tightened up, didn't you? With all that happened today, I never gave another thought to the fact that you had your first horseback ride."

Jared knelt in front of her and his hands covered her thighs.

Erin tried to jerk away and hissed at the pain. "No. Don't touch me, damn it. It hurts." Erin swatted at his hands, breathing a sigh of relief when he removed them. She covered her thighs with her own hand and began to massage gently, wincing.

Duncan stood behind her and rubbed her shoulders. "Baby, we've got to rub you down. You can't even get out of the chair. Tomorrow you won't be able to move."

Reese stood behind her. "I'll get the liniment. We're going to have to carry her to bed."

Duncan chuckled and kissed her hair. "The first of many times."

Jared looked up at Duncan. "I'll carry her to bed. Reese, get the liniment."

Erin couldn't believe how sore she'd become. She hadn't really had a hard workout since she'd moved to Desire. She'd obviously gotten out of shape. "This isn't a good idea." She gratefully took the pain pill Duncan handed her and drank the water he offered. She groaned when Jared slid an arm under her thighs. "No. Don't move me. Just leave me here." Once the medicine kicked in she would be fine.

Jared chuckled. "All night? No, love. You need a rubdown." He slid an arm behind her back and straightened, lifting her from the chair.

Erin leaned against his shoulder. "I haven't been carried since I was a little girl."

Jared nuzzled her temple. "Get used to it."

Erin turned away, not knowing what to say to that and looked again at the large bedroom. When she'd first seen it, she had been overwhelmed by the sheer size of everything. It had the biggest bed Erin had ever seen. "Did you and your brothers make this bed?"

"We did. It's a double king. I used to sleep in it alone but we built it to share with our woman."

Erin thought it better not to comment on that. "The tub and the shower are huge, too."

Jared smiled. "They're meant to be shared also."

Erin looked up as Reese came into the bedroom carrying a bottle. Duncan threw back the bedcovers so Jared could lay her in the center on the crisp white sheets. She reached out a hand for the bottle. "Thank you. I can do it."

Jared shook his head. "No, love. We'll do it. You won't knead the muscles, and you can only use one hand. You need a good firm massage to loosen them up."

"No. You'll rub too hard. I'm not one of your damned horses."

Duncan left the room, smiling.

Jared and Reese both chuckled as Jared removed her sweatpants. He ran his hands from her feet to her slit, his eyes tender. "I'm very aware that you're a woman, love. Lay back."

Erin eyed him warily and lay back on the bed. "If you hurt me, I'll get even. And no funny stuff."

Reese laughed. Jared smiled faintly and leaned over her. "I have no doubt of your ability to get even. As for *funny stuff*, if you're referring to lovemaking, there isn't anything funny about it."

Erin gulped as his tone made her insides clench. The underlying steel in his voice did something unexpected to her. She'd always called the shots when it came to men, but these three hadn't been so easy to control.

Lying here with Jared positioned between her legs and Reese at her side, her body had already started to come alive. She knew they couldn't help but see that her nipples poked at the front of her borrowed shirt. Her clit throbbed and she could already feel her pussy prepare for them. She had to consciously keep her hips from tilting toward them in invitation.

She'd never been much for sex, never saw the big deal, but with these men it had become all she could think about. She had the uncomfortable feeling that when she left them she would miss it terribly. Between now and then maybe they could work out some sort of arrangement.

Resigned to the fact that she couldn't deny what her body screamed for, she closed her eyes and braced herself for their touch.

Erin moaned as Reese's hands covered her thigh. Her eyes flew open and she watched Jared as he started to work on the other. She bit her lip and closed her eyes against the need that shot through her. Their hands felt so hot and firm as they gently massaged her.

Her muscles protested, but the fire in her pussy caused her more torment. She hoped they thought her moans came from her soreness and not the pleasure they gave her. She wondered briefly if they could see the moisture dripping from her.

Their fingers firmed even more as they massaged the insides of her thighs. When they parted them, her eyes flew open. "What are you doing?"

Jared raised a brow. "We have to have some room to work, Erin. We've all seen you naked already, love. Relax."

Erin groaned when Jared's hands massaged more firmly. "That hurts, damn it."

Reese chuckled. "I can imagine the noise she's gonna make when we take her ass."

Jared shot his brother a look before turning back to her. "Erin, I have to get these muscles loosened. No. Don't tighten up. Relax."

Reese chuckled again. "That's the same thing we'll say to her when we open up her ass."

Erin glared at him. "Stop talking about taking my ass. I told you that I don't do that." She turned to Jared. "How the hell am I supposed to relax when the two of you have your hands between my thighs?" When they grinned she narrowed her eyes at them. "Let me do it." She sat up and tried to slap their hands away but they both kept going.

Reese's hands firmed even more and she cried out and tried pushing his hands away, but he didn't budge. "You won't do it hard enough to do any good. It's gonna get harder before we're through, but by then, you'll be putty in our hands."

Duncan came back into the room and got onto the bed, tumbling her onto her back again and lounging beside her. His hand slid back and forth over her stomach. "I talked to Boone. Rachel's going crazy to see you so we're going to have to do something about it and hide your injury so she doesn't worry."

Erin's hands somehow found their way to his hair as he leaned down and rubbed her lips with his. She opened enthusiastically and met his kiss with heat of her own. She loved the sensual feel of his lips on hers, soft but firm and so undeniably talented.

Feeling his hand on her bare breasts, she realized he must have unbuttoned her shirt without her even noticing. Her breasts felt hot and swollen as he traced his fingers over them, not touching her where she needed it most. She arched, trying to get him to touch her nipples, but he easily avoided her, chuckling into her mouth. Jerking her mouth from his, she shifted restlessly, growling her frustration. "You're a tease. Get away from me."

Duncan chuckled again and bit her bottom lip. "Demanding, aren't you?"

Erin cried out when he pinched her nipple.

"Your nipples are incredibly sensitive." He lowered his head to her other nipple at the same time she felt her legs being parted.

Her body had already experienced extreme pleasure at their hands and cried out for more. She tilted her hips, a sharp cry escaping when she felt a mouth at her slit. Reese came up beside her and Duncan released the nipple he'd been tugging. Reese's mouth captured it and began sucking it into his mouth.

Their hands and mouths touched her everywhere, all at once, and she couldn't keep up with all the sensations. Where one left off, the other began until she couldn't keep track. Touch after erotic touch threw her into a tailspin until they all blended together, keeping her mindless with need, her body trembling and clawing with lust.

Jared lifted her bottom and held her slit against his mouth, running his tongue through her folds. His shoulders pushed her legs even wider and she felt his tongue push into her pussy, gathering her moisture.

Her cries and moans sounded needy and desperate but she didn't care. Twisting and squirming restlessly, she found to her frustration that the grips the men had on her held her practically immobile. When Jared lifted his head, she whimpered.

His voice sounded low and harsh. "She's close to coming already. I could feel her clenching on my tongue."

"Oh, God." Erin couldn't believe how much his words aroused

her. She'd never had sex with a man who did a lot of talking in bed, but Jared, Duncan, and Reese spoke to her and each other frequently during sex and it made her hot as hell.

Duncan groaned. "Baby, you want us, don't you? No matter how much you try to deny it, you were made for us."

Erin's hips bucked when Jared started to push a finger into her pussy. "I can't give you more than this. Hurry."

Jared's finger stopped moving and both Duncan and Reese stopped touching her breasts, holding her still as she struggled to get them to touch her again.

"Why not, Erin?" The steel in Duncan's voice had to flood Jared's hand with her juices. She hoped he didn't notice.

Jared chuckled. "She liked that."

Damn.

Duncan turned her to face him, firming his grip when she tried to resist. "Nobody's moving until you tell us why."

She shuddered and knew they all felt it. "Damn you. It's none of your business. Either fuck me or leave me the hell alone."

Reese grabbed her wrist and raised it gently, but firmly over her head. Duncan gripped her chin while carefully holding her injured arm against her body so he didn't hurt it. "Everything about you is our business."

Erin bit back a whimper as he touched just the tip of her nipple with a rough finger.

Duncan pinched, then abruptly released the other. "Tell us or we'll torture it out of you."

"Because it's cheating!"

Jared stilled. "What?"

Erin couldn't move enough to get any relief as the three men held her. Duncan touched her nipple so lightly, it only made the throbbing worse.

Jared pushed his finger deeper but wouldn't move it, just held it there. He skimmed a calloused finger over her clit, making her jolt and cry out. "How is it cheating, Erin?"

"A relationship should only be between two people. Now let me go!"

"Never." Duncan covered her mouth with his again as she felt Jared move his finger inside her.

She bucked and arched as Duncan and Reese tugged at her nipples again. She felt Jared withdraw his finger from her and tried to arch her hips to follow.

Duncan lifted his head and looked down at his brother as Jared rolled on a condom and positioned himself between her thighs.

She felt Jared nudge the head of his cock at her entrance, holding her buttocks in his hands. Her pussy burned as he began to push into her, her inner muscles stretching to accommodate him. Needing this, needing his thick cock inside her, filling her, she tilted her hips to force him deeper.

"Easy, love." She heard the effort of holding back in his voice. "I don't want to hurt you, and your muscles and your arm are already sore. I'll give you what you want, Erin."

"Hurry up then, damn you."

Duncan and Reese continued to play with her breasts as they watched Jared's cock press into her. Knowing that they all watched such an intimate thing raised her arousal to a level she never dreamed of. She just couldn't understand how such a thing could excite her so much.

Duncan tugged a nipple. "Do you know how sexy it looks to watch my brother's cock go into you and know that I'm soon going to take his place? All three of us are going to fill that tight little pussy tonight." He pinched her nipple, sending a jolt of fire racing straight to her slit. Jared began to stroke into her, each stroke deeper and faster than the last.

She couldn't keep from clenching on him and flooding him with her juices. "Jared, more." When he lay over her, she wrapped her legs around him and winced.

Jared froze. "Am I hurting you, love?"

Erin shook her head and tilted her hips. "No. It's not you. It's from riding. I can hardly move. Please, Jared. Ohhh! God. I'm so close. I need—" It felt so erotic to be looking at all three of them at a moment like this.

Reese rubbed her thigh. "We'll give you what you need, love. Just lay still. Let us do all the work."

Erin grabbed Jared's shoulders, smiling up at him. "I like that. I'll just lie here and let the three of you pleasure me."

Duncan chuckled. "You do that."

Jared's mouth covered hers as his mind-numbing thrusts continued. The fullness had her toes curling as the pleasure washed over her. Burying her face in his throat, she licked at his skin, glorying in his taste and scent. As the first ripples began, she clenched on him. Just that fast she went over. She barely heard her own sobs. Jared swallowed them as she lost herself in her orgasm. Clutching Jared to her, she absently noted that Duncan and Reese both stroked her, touching her tenderly as Jared tightened around her, forcing his cock against her womb as he came, shuddering in her arms.

Jared lifted his head and stared down at her, brushing his lips back and forth over hers as he stared into her eyes.

The tension between them now scared her. It had grown even more with their lovemaking, something she hadn't expected. She wouldn't have been a bit surprised to see electric sparks shoot from her fingertips as she ran them over Jared's shoulders. It shouldn't happen like this. After the sex, all of that should have disappeared. Some of her fear and confusion must have shown on her face because he smiled at her reassuringly.

"It's all right, love. Slow and easy. We'll take it one step at a time."

He shifted and she dreaded his moving away and leaving her cold, but he only eased aside enough for his brother to move in. Duncan captured her lips with his, eating at her mouth while his hot hand covered her breast.

He lifted his mouth, staring down at her. "Reese, keep her arm still."

She grabbed his shoulder and realized he must have undressed while she'd had sex with Jared. When she reached for his cock, he grabbed her hand and placed it on the pillow next to her head.

"Not this time, baby. I'm too hot for you already."

Her hips continued to rock, her pussy already hungry to be filled again. She squirmed, trying to move closer as Duncan moved between her thighs.

"You stay right where you are, sweetheart." She felt Reese's hand slide under her and caress her bottom. "Once Duncan gets inside you we're going to work on stretching this ass a little more."

"Stretching it?" Erin squealed and tried to move away and felt a light slap on her left buttock.

"Hey! Ohh!" As Duncan spread her thighs with his, she tried to lift to him, but she groaned as her thighs protested the movement.

Duncan leaned over her. "Baby, stay still. We'll take care of you." His cock lay heavily on her abdomen and as she looked down, she saw it jump. Oh, God! It looked so long and thick, and she just couldn't wait until it plunged inside her.

Jared and Reese knelt on either side of her, each cupping a breast. Reese leaned down, turning her to face him and began to kiss her again as Duncan rolled on a condom and thrust into her. She groaned at the incredible fullness, feeling every bump of his cock as it slowly stroked into her.

Duncan held her hips tightly as Reese and Jared each caressed her. Jared's hand kept moving closer and closer to her bottom and she tightened in uncertainty. Duncan groaned when she tightened on him and gripped her hips even harder.

She squealed into Reese's mouth when she felt a coolness at her bottom hole. When Reese lifted his head and smiled at her, she turned to Jared, panting. "I don't know about this."

Jared's voice, laced with intent, sounded low and crooning. "We have to stretch your bottom to take us, love. That's the only way that you can take all three of us together."

When she felt Jared's finger begin to work into her, the way her body reacted to such a carnal sensation shocked the hell out of her. She wanted more. "Oh. Oh. Oh."

"I have to get these muscles to loosen. No. Don't tighten up. Relax, love."

Reese chuckled and nipped her shoulder. "I told you that you'd hear the same thing when we started to stretch your ass." He continued to pluck at her nipple, pinching it lightly and sending a jolt of lust straight to her clit.

Duncan had stopped thrusting when Jared had first applied the lube, but now he began again, stroking deeply, touching her womb with every thrust. He held her wide open, using his hands to pull her ass cheeks apart for his brother.

Erin groaned and cried out, pushing back to meet his thrusts and taking Jared's finger deeper into her bottom. The lube had made the entrance easier, but Erin shivered at the sensation that still felt unfamiliar and forbidden. She wondered if she'd ever get used to it. She felt her body open to Jared and Duncan's invasion as if having a mind of its own.

She felt Jared stroke her anus with his finger in a move so intimate it took her breath away. The combination of that and Duncan digging at a spot inside her that drove her wild had her turning to Reese and crying out against his chest. She felt their touch everywhere all at once and her body overloaded at all the sensations, tightening more with each stroke. The tingling began and in a blinding flash, her body became suffused with astounding pleasure. Her orgasm lasted so long she almost couldn't bear it, the waves relentless as they crashed over her.

Erin tightened on the finger and the thick cock inside her involuntarily, over and over again. She heard Duncan's growl and felt his cock pulse deep inside her as Jared bit off curses.

Jared kissed her knee. "Damn, she's got a tight grip."

Reese lifted his head and she could feel all of them watching her. "You're clamping down hard on Jared's finger, honey. I'm going to put a little plug in you now and fuck you with it inside you."

Duncan withdrew from her, running a hand over her thighs before disappearing into the bathroom. Jared kept working at her puckered opening. Feeling more of the cool lube, she winced as Reese moved away.

He undressed, and walked toward her completely naked. She couldn't take her eyes from his muscular form and the sight of his thick cock standing at attention. For her. Not until he'd almost reached her did she see the cone shaped object in his hand.

Jared's finger slid out of her at Reese's approach. "She's lubed good."

"What are you going to do?"

Reese chuckled. "I told you, honey. I'm going to put a plug in your bottom to stretch you a little more. Then I'm going to fuck you while it's in there."

Hearing the steely tone in his voice, Erin tried to scramble away from his hands. Large hands stopped her and she got two sharp slaps on her ass for her effort.

"Try again," Reese invited. "That would give me all the excuse I need. Jared and Duncan think you're too sore and want to be easy on you. If you can fight me, you must not be that sore."

"Easy, Reese," Jared warned. "If you hurt her, I'm going to have to hurt you."

Erin turned to Reese, smirking. "Yeah, you'd better not hurt me. Jared won't let you. Leave my bottom alone."

Another *really* sharp slap landed and Erin gasped in surprise because Jared had been the one to deliver it.

"Never think that you can threaten one of us with the other. You belong to all three of us. Now you can either lie still like a good girl and have a butt plug worked gently into your ass, or you can keep mouthing off and trying to escape and Reese will put you over his lap and we will *all* take turns spanking you before he fucks your ass. What's it going to be?"

Thinking fast, she gave him her best pout. "But I'm hurt." She never pouted but she thought this might be a good time to start. Something about pouting made her feel so *girly*. She never thought herself capable of pouting to get her way as she did now.

Jared's eyes narrowed. "And we're aware of that and won't hurt your arm or your sore muscles. I ought to spank your ass just for thinking that we would. Your pout could use some work."

Furious, Erin kicked out at him, only to have him grab her foot before it could connect. "Bastard." No one had ever talked to her that way. Why had it aroused the hell out of her? She was just about to jump up and tell them all off when fingers pinched her nipples, something hard pushed at her anus and a finger stroked her dripping slit while circling her clit all at the same time. Lightning shot through her everywhere.

Reese pushed the plug against her bottom hole. "You want this inside that tight little bottom, don't you, Erin?"

"Ohhh!" Erin felt it start to slide into her, widening her opening as it entered. She bucked, trying to get the fingers circling her clit to make contact.

Jared rubbed her stomach with one hand while running his fingers through her folds with the other. "That's it, sweetheart. Fuck the plug into you. That's a good girl."

Erin couldn't help it. She hated his superior tone, but suddenly her body craved the forbidden feel of something pushed inside her bottom. She got so aroused giving in to them this way. She didn't have to be on guard now. Damn, but they knew how to handle her. Sons of a bitch.

Lifting herself, she tilted her hips, taking more of the plug inside her, crying out at the fullness. Whimpering, she pushed up again, impatiently watching Reese roll on a condom. Finally he began to push his cock into her pussy.

Duncan licked a nipple. "Jesus. I'm already hard again."

Jared grinned. "Join the club."

Knowing that this aroused them, only made her hotter. They made her so hungry, so greedy, and she wanted it all.

"Reese?"

"Yes, sweetheart?"

"I want you to take me there."

Silence filled the room.

"What did you say?"

Erin continued to push back. "I need you. Just for tonight, pretend I'm your woman. Take me like you would take your woman."

Jared and Duncan leaned over her. Jared's eyes looked hard, his face tight. "You *are* our woman."

Erin shook her head, whimpering as Reese slowly withdrew from both openings. "No. I told you I can't. But just for tonight. Please."

Duncan lifted her and lay on the bed, donning a fresh condom and pulling her on top of him. "We'll show you tonight what it's like to be our woman, but don't for one minute think we're giving up on you. You're going to pay for pissing us off like this." He surged into her pussy with one smooth thrust, forcing a cry from her. Even now, Duncan held her forearm so her injured arm wouldn't be jostled.

Jared knelt beside her and she felt his cock touch her cheek. He gripped her hair and turned her face nudging her lips with it. "Open. I want to fuck my woman's mouth."

Erin opened her mouth and took him in. In her excitement, she took him too far and panicked.

Jared pulled back. "Nice and easy, sweetheart."

Jared remained motionless and Erin began running her tongue all around him and sucking him as deeply as she could. He caressed her hair and face as she worked to give him pleasure, loving the taste of him, the feel of every ridge of his thickness.

Duncan held himself still deep inside her, holding her steady. A whimper escaped when Reese began to push into her bottom. Duncan played with her nipples, murmuring softly to her. "Easy, baby. Relax your bottom. Let Reese in."

Reese pushed the head past the tight ring of muscle at her entrance and she panted, squeezing her eyes closed as she fought to relax.

It burned, and she questioned her decision as he continued to push into her. It made her pussy feel too tight to hold Duncan's cock, and her thigh muscles started screaming.

Jared slid his length from her mouth and leaned down to kiss her lightly. "Are you all right, love?"

Tears came to her eyes at the relief that he didn't seem to be angry at her anymore. "It burns!" She groaned loudly as Reese pushed more of his cock into her anus. She looked at Jared. "I don't think it will fit. Help me."

Jared caressed her face. "It will fit, love. Reese will take it nice and slow. Reese, slow shallow strokes. Don't go any further yet."

Erin felt Reese begin to stroke in and out of her bottom, the most forbidden and unfamiliar pleasure she could imagine. "I feel too full. Oh, God. It feels too…too… Ohhhh!"

"Intimate? Naughty? Submissive?" Duncan's growl sounded in her ear.

"Yes! Oh!"

Duncan's bit off curses filled her ears as she tried to concentrate on loosening her bottom. When Duncan reached down and touched her clit, she jolted and automatically tightened on Reese, making her anus burn even more.

Reese groaned. "Fuck. Don't do that again. She's too fucking tight." She felt him withdraw from her. "I have to use more lube."

Erin felt more of the cool lube being worked into her and when Reese withdrew his fingers, she once again braced for the feel of his cock.

"Relax, Erin." Reese began to push into her again.

The slippery lube made it easier, but she still had trouble accepting the large head through her sphincter. They both groaned when it passed through, and his momentum took him further into her ass than he'd gone before.

Wild with need, she couldn't keep her hips from grinding on Duncan and turning her head, took Jared's cock back into her mouth.

Jared stroked shallowly into her mouth, groaning. "Reese, go ahead, more on each stroke." He ran his hands through her hair. "Let's fuck our woman nice and slow."

Duncan and Reese set up a rhythm that had her groaning deep in her throat. Jared fucked her mouth with smooth short strokes. Having all three of them at the same time sent her senses reeling as lust all but consumed her.

She couldn't imagine being more aroused than she felt at that moment as she took them in every way. Her bottom burned as she clenched on Reese. The totally foreign sensation of having her ass filled with a thick cock had her shuddering. Goosebumps broke out all over her at the unbelievable fullness.

Reese panted as his strokes came faster. "She's too fucking tight. I can't last."

She didn't think it would have been possible to take something so deeply into her ass. She screamed in her throat when he plunged even deeper and gripped her hips tightly, forcing himself to the hilt inside her as he pulsed his release. It wasn't enough. She needed more. Oh, God. They'd taken her too far this time. She'd never find satisfaction from this raging hunger.

Rocking on Duncan, she whimpered as Reese slid from her. Jared pulled out of her mouth. "Oh, God. Oh, God."

"You need your ass full of cock to come now, don't you, love?"

Erin buried her face against Duncan, hiding what she knew must show on her face.

She heard the rip of foil and then Jared moved in behind her. He and Duncan held her hips still as Jared pushed the head of his cock against her puckered opening. He began to push in and groaned. "Fucking tight is right. Jesus, Erin."

Again she cried out as the large head entered her. They'd all become too aroused now to go slowly. She sure as hell didn't want slow. She needed more now. Jared quickly began to thrust deep into her bottom, both he and Duncan keeping her as still as they could to set up their rhythm.

Erin couldn't believe the wild lust going through her. She could die of such pleasure. The feeling of completely giving herself over to them made her respond with abandon, not caring about anything but the pleasure of having them this way.

She couldn't last and she felt the warning tingles start and groaned. "No! I don't want to come yet."

Duncan's grip tightened, his voice rough. "Come, damn it. You're going to fucking come right now!"

Duncan reached down, rubbing her clit and she flew. She couldn't hold it off any more. Pleasure flowed from her clit to her pussy and anus and up through her body. Even her toes tingled with sensation. She heard Jared's deep growl, followed closely by Duncan's as they drove their cocks deep, pulsing as they found their own release. She continued to rock on them, unable to keep still. Relief washed over her that the wild need inside her had been satisfied. She'd let go, given in to all her body's needs, and they'd fulfilled her.

It scared her to death.

She could still feel her body milking their cocks as she collapsed on top of Duncan. She couldn't seem to stop it. From the moans still coming from them, she knew that it felt just as good to them as it did to her.

Reese brushed her hair back from her face as she turned on Duncan's chest to face him, smiling faintly.

Erin buried her face in Duncan's chest again. "I'm tired."

Reese turned her back and kissed her lingeringly before nodding. "We'll talk tomorrow."

Erin moaned as Jared's cock withdrew from her. Reese picked her up. She moaned again as he pulled her off of Duncan's cock. "Come on. I have a bath ready. Your muscles are going to need another soak."

"No. Leave me alone." She just wanted to close them out for a while. They'd gotten far too close, taken more than she'd meant to give, and she just wanted to be alone.

He ignored her, carrying her into the large bathroom and stepped into the tub, lowering them both into the hot water.

Erin reached for the clip she had left on the side of the tub earlier and used it to put her hair up so it wouldn't get wet. Amused at the way Reese watched her, as though fascinated, she couldn't help but smile. "I just don't want to get my hair wet again."

"I love watching all the little things women do. *You*, I'm especially interested in. I couldn't figure out what that thing was."

Duncan climbed into the tub. "We have to bathe her and work on those muscles while they're warm, Reese."

Erin felt uncomfortable when Reese shot his brother a dirty look. "I'm just giving her time to relax and let them warm up."

Duncan chuckled, not appearing to be put off by Reese's answer, but she didn't want to start any trouble. She extricated herself from Reese's grip, sitting between them and reached for the soap. "That's okay. I can wash myself. I'm a big girl, you know."

Being naked in front of them during sex had been one thing but she didn't feel comfortable taking a bath with an audience. "I wish we were taking a bubble bath."

Jared had just started to step into the tub. "Bubble bath?"

Erin watched as got in. His cock looked impressive even now. Jesus, how could a woman take a bath with three to-die-for men and not be affected? "At least I would be covered."

Duncan grinned. "Yeah. We would have a lot of fun playing hide and seek. What kind of bubble bath do you use?"

"I use one of Indulgences'."

Jared frowned. "You don't smell like fruit or vanilla or like any of the others. What kind do you use?"

"She makes one that smells like baby powder. I like that one."

"That's what that is!" Reese shook his head. "I was going crazy trying to place that smell. I haven't smelled baby powder for a long time." He opened his mouth to say something else, but Duncan cut him off.

"Come here, Erin. Let's see what we can do about those sore muscles."

By the time they'd rubbed her down in the tub, she felt so loose that she thought she just might go down the drain when they let the water out. She'd ended up leaning against Duncan, afraid that he'd gotten jealous that Reese had carried her in.

Reese got out and dried off, reaching for her and Duncan handed her over to his brother without a word. She watched his face, but he didn't seem upset and for that she gave a sigh of relief. Right now she felt too tired to deal with jealousy. She could only imagine how many times it would come up and knew she had no stomach for it.

Reese carried her back into the bedroom and laid her on the bed.

"I can walk, you know."

He dropped a kiss on her lips before turning her over, careful of her arm. "I know. But it hurts you and we get pleasure out of carrying you. It's a win-win."

She tried to reach for the covers. "I'm cold." She looked over her shoulder when she heard Jared's voice.

"I know, love. Just give me one minute and I'll cover you up and we'll get you nice and warm."

Her eyes had fluttered closed, but snapped open when she felt him move between her thighs. "What are you doing?" She felt his hands on her bottom.

"Easy, love. We haven't done the back yet. Your bottom and the backs of your thighs have to be rubbed down, too."

She buried her face in the pillow and groaned.

"What's the matter, baby?"

She felt the shift of the mattress as Duncan moved to lie beside her. She kept her face in the pillow. "This is embarrassing. He's massaging my butt."

"Embarrassing? Both Jared and Reese fucked your *butt* and this embarrasses you?"

Erin raised her head, looking for jealousy that Duncan hadn't taken her there. "Are you upset because you didn't take me there?"

Jared tapped her ass. "Loosen up, Erin."

"I'm jealous as hell. I want that ass, too." Duncan leaned down to kiss her lightly. He grinned. "Next time I get it first."

She smelled the liniment as Jared began massaging her. She melted under his hands, her eyelids getting heavier by the minute. When he finally finished, she heard Reese grumble as Jared got into bed on the other side of her, leaving Reese to sleep either in his own bed or on the other side of Duncan.

Reese grunted. "We all sleep together. Right from the beginning. I'll sleep next to you tomorrow night."

Erin thought it prudent not to comment. How the hell could a person keep track? Two might be a little easier, but three? She'd have to remember whose turn it was for everything and didn't see how she could ever get it right. That's why she'd never allow herself to become permanently involved with them.

Duncan pulled her close, pillowing her head on his shoulder and she heard Jared grumble before moving closer to her back. It felt good to lie this way between them. But how long would it be before they slept in separate bedrooms? Fought constantly? Or worse, didn't speak at all? How long would it be before the cheating began? How long would it be before they found something in another woman's arms they didn't find with her?

Her life would be hell and so would theirs. After hearing the way they'd talked, she'd thought it might be easier, but she hadn't even realized the extent of the conflicts.

No, when this nightmare ended and she left, she wouldn't see them again this way. She just wasn't cut out for this kind of life. She knew it and accepted it. She'd just have to make sure they accepted it, too.

Chapter Five

Her own moans woke her. Erin buried her face in the pillow as strong hands firmly massaged her thighs and buttocks.

"Good morning, sweetheart."

Erin lifted her head and opened one eye, looking over her shoulder to a grinning Reese. "No more massages. That's how I got into trouble last night." Already aroused, her mind struggled to catch up. Lifted into his hands even as she fought not to, she dropped her head back onto the pillow again. "Go away."

He chuckled as he moved to sit beside her and brushed her hair back from her face. "You're not a morning person, are you?"

Hearing the amusement in his voice, she opened her eye again. He looked too damned good to deal with before she'd even had her coffee. Dressed in his usual worn jeans and chambray shirt, he looked rugged and sexy as hell. She had the added advantage of knowing just how good he looked naked and couldn't help remembering the look and feel of all that lean muscle. Groaning, she stuck her face in the pillow again.

She felt him reach under the covers and trace the side of her breast eliciting another moan from her. Already she needed his hands on her. Without opening her eyes, she rolled, arching to press her breasts into his waiting hands. "I'm not as sore."

Reese chuckled and leaned down to lick her nipple, making her gasp. "We rubbed you down in the tub last night and I've been working on you for a while already this morning. You sleep like the dead. We've all had our showers and gotten dressed, but you never moved."

Erin finally managed to open her eyes, only to close them again as Reese took a nipple into his mouth. "Hmm. You guys wore me out." It felt like an imaginary string connected her nipples to her clit and every time he tugged, she felt her clit pulse. Shifting restlessly, she clamped her thighs closed against the fluttering that had already started in her pussy.

Gripping Reese's forearms, she felt the tight muscle bunch, reminding her once again of his strength. Reaching for the buttons of his shirt, she fumbled to undo them, needing to feel his hot skin against hers. He leapt up from the bed, quickly shucking his clothes.

Her eyes popped open. She couldn't miss this. The sight of his large cock jutting out had her scrambling to her knees and reaching for him. She caressed him, watching in fascination as his eyes darkened to a brilliant green. She looked down and seeing a glistening drop on the tip, she caught it with her thumb and smeared it around the head.

Reese stroked her hair, grinning. "Now I know how to wake you up." He bent down to touch his lips to hers before straightening with a groan. "Every time I get near you, I get hard. Do you have any idea of the hell you put me through when you wouldn't see me anymore?"

Erin ran her hands over him. "I'm sorry, but when I realized you wanted me to have a relationship with all three of you, I thought it better to stop before someone got hurt." Stroking his cock, she reached beneath it with her other hand and cupped his sack. Her arm felt stiff but didn't hurt much anymore.

Reese raised a brow. "It looks like you were wrong."

Erin shook her head. "No. What's between us can never be more than this." She smiled seductively. "But we can have a lot of fun enjoying each other. This way we all get the pleasure and nobody gets hurt."

Reese cupped her breasts. "Erin, I want you to stay."

Erin leaned into him. "Let's not ruin this. Please, Reese. Take me."

He laid her back, covering her body with his as he pressed his thick length between her thighs. Grabbing her hair, he turned her face to the side and bit down on the sensitive spot on her neck.

She shuddered with need, wrapping her legs around him, needing to have him inside her. Moaning in distress when he denied her, she dug her nails into his shoulders.

Reese didn't even flinch. Instead, he cupped her face between his big hands and forced her to look up at him. "If you walk away from us without even trying to make this work, I'm going to turn you over my knee and spank your ass until it's so red you won't be able to sit down."

Erin knew her eyes had to be huge in her face as fresh moisture drenched her slit. Not used to being around men who intimidated her, Erin struggled not to show her trepidation and, yes, damn it, arousal at his words. When she felt the cock between her thighs jump, she knew that the image he'd created had excited him as much as it had her.

Erin swallowed and forced herself to sound firm. "Spank me? Spank me? Try it buddy and I'm going to kick your balls into your throat."

Reese grinned. "I love a challenge." He tugged her nipple and bit down again on her neck. "I think I can manage to get you over my knee no matter how hard you fight. And make no mistake, darlin', if you keep pushing, that's exactly where you're going."

Erin moaned and squirmed, trying to get his cock inside her. He kept playing with that spot on her neck and tugging at her nipples. Both drove her wild. "Never. I'm not as easy as the other women who live here, and I'll be damned if I'm going to let a man spank me."

Before she could prevent it, he'd turned her to her stomach and covered her body with his. When he pushed his cock against her bottom, she began to struggle.

Reese held her easily, alarming the hell out of her. "Nobody ever said you're easy, darlin'. In fact you're a hell of a lot of work. Have I mentioned how much I love your ass?"

She wanted him inside her so badly she shook with it, but it wouldn't do for her to let him see just how strongly his manhandling had turned her on. Jesus, what was it about a strong man that just made her melt. If any of them found out her weakness, they'd use it against her.

Reese lifted off of her and she heard the rip of foil before he brought her to her knees at the edge of the bed, spreading her legs wide.

As hard as she tried, she couldn't be still, rubbing her bottom against him as he positioned his cock at her dripping opening. Her nipples brushed against the blanket, arousing her even more.

Reese took his time, running his hands all over her bottom as he speared a thick finger into her pussy.

Mindless with need, she moved on his hand, moaning as the need for release continued to build.

He withdrew to trace her folds, his finger moving perilously closer to her clit.

She rocked her hips, struggling to get the contact she needed, but he deftly avoided her.

Reese removed his finger and held her steady. "You're so damned passionate. We knew you would be. You try to hide this part of yourself, don't you, sweetheart? You want everyone to think that nothing affects you, but we get to you, don't we?" He entered her with one forceful thrust, startling a delighted scream from her. "You don't think you're going to miss this if you leave? Your body knows us now. So does your heart. You're just too stubborn to admit it." His harsh groans told her just how little control he had left. The forcefulness of his strokes sent her senses spiraling and she struggled to match his rhythm to drive him deeper.

The bedroom door crashed back against the wall as Jared and Duncan rushed in. "Erin, oh, shit, Reese." Duncan chuckled. "Her scream scared the hell out of us. I'll go let the others know she's okay."

She absently heard the door close again, so caught up in her raging need, she didn't care who walked in at that point. "Harder, damn you. Fuck me harder." She felt the bed dip and realized that Jared had stayed in the room.

Reese's strokes had slowed. He tightened his hold, not allowing her to take him any faster. "You need this. You need what we do to you. Isn't that right, darlin'? Jesus, you're full of fire."

Erin shuddered, so close to coming she could almost taste it. "I'm going to hurt you. Oh, God. Faster."

The touch of his finger pressing against her puckered opening caused chills through her. Those irresistible tingles started slow, quickly building in strength as he pushed his thick finger into her. Knowing Jared was watching, she tried to tamp down her reaction but instead found her body opening to him. "Damn it, Reese, I, Ohhh!" Coming hard, she grabbed fistfuls of the bedding, burying her face in it as she cried out over and over as the waves of release continued to wash over her. Jared turned her to face him, covering her mouth with his and swallowing her cries.

She heard Reese's harsh growl as he came, grinding himself against her, into her. Unable to stop shuddering, she held on to the bedding as Reese continued to move his finger in her bottom.

Jared caressed her back, easing back, his face close as he watched her slowly come down. Unable to face him, she squeezed her eyes closed, gulping in air.

Reese slowly withdrew from both openings, caressing her hip and leaning over her to kiss her back.

She collapsed on her stomach, only to have Jared gather her close, his lips in her hair as he ran his hand up and down her back.

Jared smiled at her and kissed her once more before getting up and walking out of the room, closing the door behind him and leaving her alone with his brother.

When Reese lifted her into his arms, she stuck her face in his neck and giggled. "I've hardly walked since I got here."

He took her into the bathroom and lowered her to her feet, unwrapping the bandage from her arm, and studying the stitches. "You can have some time alone. Take a shower and come out into the kitchen for some breakfast. We have to put a new bandage on you." He kissed her again leisurely, his hands moving over, softly caressing before releasing her with a grin. "You're too passionate to deny what's happening between us. Stop playing games, Erin. We know what's inside you and we want it all, temper, passion, insecurities, all of it. I see that scares the hell out of you. There's no reason to be scared of what we feel for you. None of us would ever hurt you. But you're hurting all of us by pushing us away."

Speechless, Erin watched him go. She locked the door behind him, relieved to have a little time alone. She needed time to think and to shore up her defenses. She wondered why she bothered when all three of them tore them down at will. Eyeing the lock dubiously, she hurried toward the shower, not knowing how long her solitude would last.

With the hot water raining down on her, she looked around at the shower again, not believing its size. Tilting her face into the spray, she couldn't help but smile as the water washed over her still trembling body. She couldn't believe how easy it had been for them to get through her, up until now, impenetrable defenses. If they unnerved her so badly, why the hell was she smiling?

Jared, Duncan, and Reese sent her senses reeling every time they touched her. She had no experience with desire like that. Infrequent sex with men whom she'd never run into at work had been pleasurable, but she'd never allowed it to be any more than that. Sex had always been a quick release, nothing more.

She'd gotten a late start and had never really understood the big deal. She could get as much pleasure, sometimes more, from her vibrator and didn't have to make small talk afterwards. And she never had to fake it.

She'd been so young when she'd been thrust into the job of being

Rachel's guardian. Guilt had made her go overboard, she had finally admitted to herself years later. But she hadn't made any time for men back then. She'd been busy trying to pay the bills and keep Rachel on the straight and narrow. By the time Rachel had moved away, Erin had still been a virgin and a novice in the dating scene.

Her experience since then had left a lot to be desired, and she'd already made up her mind that sex was highly overrated.

Her need for Jared, Duncan, and Reese, shocked the hell out of her. But that shock was mild compared to what they'd taught her about her own desires. The sex with them was better than she'd thought it ever could be, but their connection with her and each other during sex had proved to be damned near irresistible. Somehow they'd touched something deep inside her, something that had never been touched before.

For the first time in her life, she felt out of her league. If she didn't get some barriers up soon, she was almost positive they would break her heart.

How had they managed to get so close?

She'd have to do what she could to put a little distance between them.

She reached for the shampoo and started lathering her hair. By the time she'd dried off, she realized that caring for them had made the jealousy issues even harder for her to tolerate and she knew that she would have to break away as soon as possible.

With only the towel wrapped around her, she reentered the bedroom with the intention of getting dressed. Instead, she found Jared sitting on the end of the bed, apparently waiting for her.

"Good morning, love. Reese looks happy. Why don't you?" He stood and moved toward her, his eyes full of concern. Remembering the promise she'd just made to herself, she started to back away.

Jared stopped. "Don't I get a good morning kiss?"

Jesus, he looked hot as hell, and that damned scar gave him a rakish appeal. When he looked at her the way he did now, unsmiling, he looked like a warrior, and it turned her on big time. Her pulse leapt and her stomach quivered as he looked down at her, and she couldn't help but smile at how damned sexy he looked. Amazed that he'd so easily seen right through her, she forced a playful grin. "Good morning. Didn't I give you several just a little while ago?"

Jared's eyes narrowed as he closed the distance between them. "Yes, but I want one while we're all alone."

Uneasiness stirred. Had he been jealous of her time with Reese? Leaning into him, she lifted her face for his kiss, wanting so badly to feel his arms come around her. Alarm bells sounded in her head when she realized how badly she needed to see him smile. "Good morning again."

He didn't disappoint her, gathering her in his arms and lowering his mouth to hers, his firm lips moving over hers lazily, his tongue tracing them erotically. Her toes curled into the carpet as his mouth worked its magic. His arms tightening around her, holding her close. Deepening his kiss, he ran his hands over her body, possession in every stroke. The force of his dominion over her senses staggered her. Everywhere he touched became his as flames of lust licked at her.

When he lifted his head she looked down to where his hand cupped a breast, dazed to see that her towel had fallen off.

He led her to the bed, reaching out for the tube of antibiotic ointment and the gauze he'd placed there. He pulled her onto his lap and applied a new dressing, his heated gaze sliding over her repeatedly. Shaken, she trembled, feeling both vulnerable and adored. It was a heady combination.

Between giving attention to her injury, he paused to stroke her nipples, smiling when she gasped. "You're such a responsive woman." He ran a hand down her back, his eyes flaring when she shivered. "A strong woman with strong passions. Irresistible."

Not knowing how to respond to that, she remained silent.

Jared finished bandaging her arm, set the gauze and antibiotic ointment aside and adjusted her on his lap, laying her back over his arm. "I love having you in my arms."

Erin gulped. How the hell could she resist him when he looked at her that way?

Disconcerted at the tug on her emotions, she nevertheless wrapped her arms around his neck as his own tightened around her. Held on his lap this way, completely naked while he remained fully dressed, made her feel small and feminine, something she'd never felt before being with them.

Then why did she feel safer, more desired, *cherished* more than she'd ever felt in her life?

Laying her head on his shoulder, she leaned into him as he began to stroke her from shoulder to thigh and back again. Unable to fight what he made her feel, she closed her eyes as he once again proved his mastery over her body. Feeling another set of hands, she opened her eyes to find Duncan kneeling beside her.

He met her gaze, smiling so wickedly it sent a fresh jolt of lust through her. The combination of Jared's attentiveness and caring, and the blazing hunger in Duncan's eyes shattered the last of her defenses.

Intoxicating her with their attention and touch, they stirred her up so quickly she found herself squeezing her thighs together to ease the ache that had already begun.

Jared lifted her, his mouth moving down her body, kissing, nibbling and making her skin ultra sensitive. His hand moved over her breasts as Duncan's moved down her body, his touch a little less gentle. When Duncan moved between her thighs and parted her folds, she writhed in anticipation, knowing just how devastating his mouth could be. He traced her inner folds with his hot tongue before pushing it inside her.

Jared put her injured arm behind his back, shifting her on his lap and holding her securely for his brother. Duncan's tongue continued to move over her folds, sliding over her clit, and making her cry out in pleasure. She shook in Jared's arms, the pleasure almost too much to bear.

She tried to close her legs against him, the pleasure almost painful in intensity. Of course Duncan would have none of that and gripped her thighs, holding her legs high and wide. Jared slid an arm under her knees, holding her in that position, and leaving Duncan's hands free.

"You're in big trouble now, love," Jared told her tightly, sliding his gaze to watch what Duncan did to her.

Duncan parted her folds, running his hot tongue over her slit from her clit to her bottom hole, never stopping in one place long enough. The chill from the air moving on her wet folds was a stark contrast to the heat of his tongue.

The combination of sensations drove her wild. "Oh, God! How the hell do you do this to me?" She fought to lower her legs against his demonic teasing, biting her lip to keep from crying out.

Jared chuckled. "You're only giving Duncan a challenge, Erin. Anything you try to fight will spur him on. Duncan, she's biting her lip to stay quiet. Do you really think we're going to let you keep all those sexy as hell sounds from us?"

Erin's only answer was a deep groan as she quivered in Jared's arms. She'd never felt so wanted, so needed as a woman. They somehow managed to draw every softness, every weakness from inside her, holding it up to the light and showing it to her.

Jared chuckled, gripping her tighter. "You're amazing, love. I love when you fall apart in my arms. Would you do that for me?"

Erin shuddered when Duncan nipped the cheek of her bottom. "I can't help it. I'm so close." She whimpered in her throat as fresh need clawed at her. "How can you make me want being with all of you? It's not right."

Jared raised a brow. "Anything is right as long as we all enjoy it, love. And we all plan to enjoy you in many ways. Do you want to feel Duncan's cock in your sweet pussy?"

"Oh, God, yes!" She looked up at him warily, fighting to keep the need at bay long enough to judge his reaction. "You're okay with this, right?"

She felt a chill go up her spine as Jared's eyes turned icy. Looking back and forth between them, she gulped nervously. Her thighs trembled under Duncan's hands. So aroused she knew she couldn't last much longer, she forced herself to meet Jared's eyes.

Duncan's hand landed hard on her vulnerable ass. "If you weren't hurt, I would turn you over my knee and give you the spanking you deserve for that question. You belong to all of us equally, and I know it's going to take time to get used to, but you're using up all my patience with this, Erin."

Erin kicked out at him only to have him grab her legs and spread them wide. "Damn it. I told you I can't do this. If you want to fuck me, then fuck me. I'm not playing by your fucking rules."

"You will." Jared stood and laid her gently on the bed and, gripping her jaw, turned her to face him. "I want to feel that hot mouth of yours on my cock." He slid his jeans down his legs and wrapped his hand around his throbbing erection as she watched. She'd never known men to be so open and free about sex before. Or so giving. It freed her, made her less inhibited and made it even harder for her to hide what burned inside her.

Smiling, she edged toward him, wild for his taste. Keeping her eyes on his, she used the flat of her tongue to lick the glistening drop from the tip, drawing a hiss from him. Opening her mouth wide she took him inside, moaning her pleasure at his taste as well as the way his hands moved over her breasts.

Duncan once again moved between her thighs, licking her slit, his hot mouth driving her crazy as he circled her clit without touching it.

How did they know exactly where and how to touch her to give her the most pleasure? How to tease her until she would do anything for release from their erotic torment?

She knew Duncan purposely avoided her clit. She knew he could make her come in a heartbeat and deliberately kept her on the edge. Knowing he could send her flying at any moment added yet another layer of anticipation to her excitement. The three of them challenged her on a level she'd never been challenged before. They never allowed her to hold anything back. They not only could handle her dark hungers but demanded all of them from her. She couldn't help but hold back. She'd been doing it for so long she didn't even know how to let go anymore.

When Duncan lifted his head she moaned, trying to close her legs to ease the throbbing of her clit. She heard the rip of foil and then he was back, forcing her legs apart again.

Knowing she would soon be out of her mind, she raced to give Jared pleasure. Sucking him further into her mouth, she heard his groan and felt his thigh muscles tremble. When Jared began to thrust more deliberately into her mouth, she doubled her efforts, using her tongue to try to make him lose his formidable control. She lost the ability to think as need drove her, her hunger for them giving them the reins.

Duncan poised the head at her slick opening and entered her with one smooth thrust, startling a desperate cry from her throat. His strokes began immediately, deep and smooth. With unerring precision, he dug at the place that drove her wild, a place it seemed only he and his brothers could find.

She moaned, shivering and groaning as Jared's length slid deeper until the head of his cock touched the back of her throat.

The sounds of their pleasure filled the room. The uninhibited and expressive sounds they made had the last of her inhibitions falling away and made their lovemaking even more intense. The feel of Duncan teasing her clit while he pumped his steely hot cock into her erased all thoughts from her mind. She gripped him tightly, making it all the more delicious. Not until she felt the strength of those incredible warning tingles did she begin to panic. Mentally struggling to tamp it down, she tried to move her hips to redirect his thrusts.

Duncan didn't allow that at all, Holding onto her hips tightly and never missing a stroke. "Baby, I'm gonna come, and you're coming with me. Don't you dare fucking fight it. I won't let you."

Erin couldn't let go. Her mind simply wouldn't let her. She felt almost primal in her need, wanting to go over so badly she could almost taste it. But her mind fought against the overwhelming loss of control they forced on her. She couldn't keep from clenching on Duncan as she took Jared as deeply as she could.

Jared's bit off curses as he urged her to go over grew increasingly desperate. With a harsh groan, he came, his cock pulsing on her tongue.

She loved Jared's deep groans of satisfaction and Duncan's hoarse growls of pleasure. Jared pulled from her mouth and lay beside her, his face a mask of fury. "You think you're going to get away with holding back, don't you? Well, you're not. Slow down, Duncan."

Duncan's thrusts slowed immediately as he partially withdrew, keeping his strokes deliberately slow and shallow.

Jared gripped her hair and forced her to face him. "You're such a fucking control freak, never wanting to let go. You think we don't know you? You always have to be in charge, don't you, Erin? Don't try to turn away from me, damn it."

Erin mewed in her throat when he nibbled at that sensitive spot on her neck. "I don't know." Oh, God. Her body burned everywhere.

Jared's eyes glittered darkly. "Your fight to be in control makes us crazy to strip it from you. You want us to come first and as much as you like the sex, we're getting to you and you don't want to give more than you have to. Well then, love, we're just going to take it. We're not going to give you any choice. We're not going to let you hold back. We're taking it all, love."

Erin fought to breath as Duncan's torturously slow thrusts took her closer and closer to release. "You have no right to ahh...try to take anything."

Duncan had already learned her body well and thrust just enough to keep her on edge without allowing her to go over. "That's what you think, baby. We're your men and have all the right in the world to demand everything you have to give." He groaned the words between thrusts.

Erin clenched her jaw. "You have no right to demand anything, you bastards. Let me go."

Jared reached under her to tug at a nipple while Duncan played with her folds. "Oh, God! Duncan, please. Jared!"

Duncan slapped her ass. "Scream for us, baby."

Erin clamped down on Duncan as he gripped the cheeks of her bottom. Jared's hand moved down her body until he touched her clit, rubbing it lightly. The pleasure undid her. She came, screaming, her whole body tightening and bowing. Duncan's low groan as he came excited her even more.

The incredible pleasure kept going, shock waves of it vibrating throughout her system. Collapsing on the bed with Duncan lying on top of her, she struggled to rebuild her defenses.

After several long minutes Duncan slid from her and shifted to her other side, joining his brother in caressing her and murmuring to her softly.

The feeling of being surrounded by them afterward, the heat of their bodies warming hers, the soft words and caresses added something to the closeness after lovemaking. It was a different kind of intimacy than she'd ever experienced. Their attentiveness and thoughtfulness, combined with their strength and conviction quietly and completely snuck through her defenses and became impossible to fight.

With a last soft kiss, Duncan rolled off of her and, still naked, went to his closet.

Erin couldn't keep her eyes off of his tight butt and watched him, smiling as he walked back with a fresh shirt for her. "I think I can wear my own clothes."

Jared turned her to face him and kissed her lingeringly, before raising his head and gripping her chin. "Our shirts won't be tight on your arm. And you're giving us a hell of a hard time. We're going to keep you as naked as we can. That way we can be sure you won't go outside so we can keep an eye on you and use every opportunity to get past those defenses you keep building. We're not going to stop until we have all of you, Erin."

Flabbergasted at his audacity, and terrified that they could actually do it, Erin poked him in the chest. "Listen buddy, I do what I want and come and go as I please. I'm going to get dressed and get the hell out of here."

Duncan slapped her ass, infuriating her even more. "Your clothes are hidden where you can't get to them. There's no place for you to go. Your apartment is off limits until new stairs are built. It's not happening right now. You can't go to Rachel's without worrying her and endangering her baby. No one will take you in because they'll know you're running from us. You can't even book a room at the hotel."

Erin punched him in the stomach, satisfied at his grunt but enraged that it didn't budge him. "You bastards!"

Jared gripped her chin. "I never thought of you as a coward, Erin. Stay here and fight it out. If you don't want us, surely you can resist and say no. Or is it yourself that you're afraid of?"

Erin slapped his hand away and grabbed the shirt Duncan held. "I'm not scared of anything. I said I wanted the sex. Couldn't you have just been happy with that?"

Not giving them a chance to answer, she stormed into the bathroom before they could see the truth.

They already had everything.

* * * *

Duncan watched her go, wincing as the door slammed shut behind her. "Damn it!"

Jared sighed and started to get dressed again. "She's going to bolt the first chance she gets. Christ, she's injured and sore and all we've done is fuck her brains out."

Seeing the self disgust on Jared's face, Duncan grimaced. "Yeah, but damn it, what the hell does she expect when she's holding back? Doesn't she realize that only makes us crazy and desperate to have it all? If we don't get through to her soon, she's going to leave and start avoiding us again. The only times we've been able to reach her is through sex and tenderness, and she still tries to hold back."

Jared buttoned his shirt, shrugging. "I have no fucking clue what's going on in that hard head, except that she's doing her best to avoid any emotional tangles. She wants what we can do for her sexually and that's it." He grinned. "But her temper snaps whenever we get too close. With the way she's been snapping at us lately, I'd say we're making progress."

Duncan frowned at the closed bathroom door. "I figured that out already. But why the hell is she fighting it so hard? She has to see how much we care about her. She responds like she was made for us, and I see the way she looks at you and Reese when you're not looking."

Jared nodded. "When you're not paying attention, she looks at you like she's starving for you."

Duncan grinned. "That's how she looks at you two." His smile fell. "Then what's the fucking problem?"

Jared sat down to pull on socks. "I don't know, but now we've pissed her off so she won't talk to us. Let's get out of here and leave her with Reese. We'll tell him what's going on and go work outside. She talks to him easier than she talks to either of us."

Duncan threw on his own clothes. "I don't like that either. She should be able to come to all of us."

Jared stood and started out the door. "I know. I know. But our main priority now is keeping her safe. Let's get Reese to calm her down. We'll get her to talk to us. One problem at a time. Jesus."

* * * *

Erin came out of the bathroom to find the bedroom empty, annoyed to discover it disappointed her. Dying for her first cup of coffee, she headed out to the kitchen, coming to an abrupt halt to find Reese sitting alone at the table drinking out of a thick mug.

He smiled when he saw her. "Coffee?"

When she nodded, he stood and got her a cup. "How about some breakfast?"

Erin shook her head. "No, just the coffee, thanks."

Jared walked into the kitchen. "Scrambled eggs and toast at least. She's going to take another pain pill, and I don't want it to upset her stomach." He looked at Erin and raised a brow when she opened her mouth to argue. "We were all pretty selfish this morning and took you while you're still sore. You're going to take it easy today."

Reese nodded and got up to fix her breakfast as Jared pulled on his boots.

Jared smiled apologetically. "We were all so hungry for you, especially after the scare we had yesterday, but that's no excuse for taking you that way while you're hurt. We'll have to start taking better care of you."

Duncan strolled into the kitchen, touching her hair as he went past her. "Speaking of that, I just talked to Ace and Bud. Bud is chomping at the bit to go up to the rocks behind the Erickson's and see if he can track whoever shot Erin. Rafe already had to stop Clay and Rio from going up there. Ace and the others are going up with Bud. He's the best tracker around."

Jared nodded. "If anyone could find anything, it would be Bud."

Reese had the bacon cooking and began scrambling the eggs.

Erin looked from one man to the other. "Aren't you guys going to eat something?"

"We ate hours ago, sweetheart." Reese smiled and refilled her coffee. "Devlin and Caleb have already been here and gone." He refilled his own cup and sat at the table, looking over at Jared. "We have another problem. Rachel knows."

"What?" Erin demanded. "How the hell did she find out?"

Reese shrugged. "How the hell do you women find out anything?"

Erin groaned. "I've got to get back to work. She should stay home."

Reese shook his head. "She already said no to that and right now Boone and Chase are doing whatever they have to in order to keep her calm. But she's worried and pissed."

Duncan moved to get his own cup of coffee. "You need to stay right here where we can keep an eye on you."

"No. I need to get back to work." When they all started to speak, she held up her hand. "I'm not suicidal. But I can't just sit here while Rachel's health is in danger. Would any of you sit hiding if you were in my shoes? Think of the baby."

Jared scrubbed a hand over his face, his jaw tightening. "Damn it, Erin."

Reese turned from the stove and winked at her. "She's right."

Clearly annoyed, Duncan narrowed his eyes. "Then she needs someone to stay with her."

When Jared just stared at her, scowling, Erin couldn't keep from grinning. "Don't tell me I won an argument with you. I don't think my heart could take the shock."

His scowl deepened. "Very funny. Don't get used to it. And you're going to have a bodyguard from the time you walk out the door until the time you get back home."

Erin chose to ignore the 'home' reference. "Bodyguard? Listen, I'm sure Lucas, Devlin, and Caleb are very good, but I just can't afford the expense. I used my savings to move here and buy half of the lingerie store." She accepted the plate Reese handed her.

Jared reached for his coat. "You're not paying for them. We are. And I already told you that they give the residents of Desire a discount." He lifted a hand when she opened her mouth to object. "We can easily afford it, and it's already done. Someone will be with you whether you like it or not. Eat your breakfast."

Erin glared at him. "You really don't argue worth a damn."

Jared raised a brow. "Remember it. I can see I'm going to have to put my foot down where you're concerned. You'd argue with the devil." He turned to Reese. "Did you or Caleb find anything when you checked outside?"

"No. Jim didn't either. We went over the barn and the stables. Lucas and Caleb went over the yard again this morning."

Erin paused with the fork halfway to her mouth. "So can I go to work today?"

Jared shook his head. "No. You have to wait until tomorrow. We have to talk to Lucas and the others and we want you to take a day to recover. We shouldn't have made love to you the way we did. It's just that we were all so worried and it got out of hand. If you relax today, you can go to work tomorrow."

"But—"

Jared cut her off. "Don't push me on this, Erin. You'll lose. Be happy with what you got. If I had my way, you wouldn't leave the house until we catch this bitch."

Erin bit her lip and nodded, deciding not to push the issue. She'd become very adept at picking her battles and Jared's face had hardened into a look that she'd come to learn meant he couldn't be pushed any further. She decided to spend the rest of the day doing laundry, not wanting them to ruin her delicate lingerie. She'd bet her clothes from yesterday were still in the hamper. They wouldn't have thought of hiding them. Once she washed her jeans and sweater from the previous day, she could get dressed.

* * * *

Jared and Duncan went out soon afterward, leaving Reese alone with Erin. He leaned against the counter, sipping his coffee and watching her straighten the kitchen, finding it difficult to keep his eyes off her long legs. She looked sexy as hell only wearing one of

Duncan's shirts. "Would you tell me what's bothering you?"

Erin finished wiping the table and went back to the sink, her graceful movements becoming jerky.

He scowled at the way she kept her head down, hiding her face from him. He let it go for now.

Erin squirted soap into the sink. "Not a thing. I just want to go back to work. I hate not being there for Rachel."

Furious at the lie, he kept his tone cool. "That's not what I meant, Erin, and you know it. I don't care much for lying." He knew damned well that she didn't either.

Erin sighed and finally turned to face him. "You and your brothers won't accept the fact that I know my own limitations. You want more than I'm capable of giving. If you keep on this way, somebody's going to get hurt."

"What if you're wrong?'

"I'm not."

Reese closed in on her, setting his coffee on the counter and reaching for her. Cupping her jaw, he ran his thumb over her bottom lip, delighted that it trembled. "You are wrong. You've denied part of yourself for so long, you'd forgotten it was there. It won't be held back forever, sweetheart. Jared, Duncan, and I want *all* of you, Erin. You don't have to hide anything from us. Good or bad, we want it all."

Erin took a shuddering breath. "I can't."

The panic in her eyes alarmed him. "You won't. Tell me who hurt you."

Erin pulled away. "No one."

"Another lie."

Her eyes flashed with temper. "It has nothing to do with you."

Reese watched her race out of the room before picking up his coffee. Staring at the empty doorway, he fought the need to go after her. "That's where you're wrong, sweetheart. It has everything to do with all of us."

* * * *

Hours later Erin walked into the kitchen as Jared, Duncan, and Reese came through the back door. They each looked pointedly at the clothes she'd washed and put on. Winning that small victory cheered her immensely.

Lucas, Devlin, and Caleb came by after lunch and agreed with the idea of her going back to work. They seemed angry and anxious to flush out whoever kept trying to hurt her. Sitting at the table, they'd grimly informed Jared, Duncan, and Reese that since they couldn't find anyone new in town, they believed that whoever had hurt her had to be local.

Lucas sighed, going through his notebook. "Hell, we don't even know if it's a woman. Michael and John both suspected the same thing but figured Ethan and Brandon would have told them. For the sake of argument, we'll say she. She has to be someone from around here. How else would she be able to target Erin so specifically? She had to know where Erin lived and had to know where *you* live and that Erin would be staying here. It had to be someone who knew you'd be riding that day."

Jared frowned. "*We* didn't even know we'd be riding until just a few minutes before we left."

Duncan leaned forward. "But if it was someone local, how come no one at the Christmas party recognized them?"

That sent off a flurry of cursing, especially when Ace came and joined them. "Whoever it is wore some kind of disguise. The blonde hairs we found behind the bar belonged to a wig."

The men sat around the kitchen table discussing possibilities and motives until Erin couldn't take any more.

"Can I use your office?"

Silence settled over the room as the men looked up at her. Jared got up and moved toward her, gripping her elbow and escorting her from the room. When they got to the living room, he lifted her face to his, his features drawn. "I thought you were going to make yourself at home here. You don't have to ask permission to go anywhere here, damn it."

"Okay. Okay. You don't have to get so bent out of shape. I just didn't feel comfortable going into your office—"

"Enough! I have my hands full with everything that's going on. When this is over, love, you and I are going to put an end to this bullshit once and for all."

He swooped down to capture her mouth with his. His hands on her bottom pulled her close. His mouth took control of hers, filling her with the taste and heat of his. His firm lips moved on hers and she automatically leaned against him.

It felt like coming home.

When he lifted her, she wrapped her legs around his waist and squirmed closer. The feel of his chest against her breasts and his tight stomach against her mound had her rubbing against him.

When he lifted his head, his eyes glowed with golden sparks. His lips twitched before he leaned down to nip her bottom lip. "You really are like a cat. I love the way you rub against me when you're aroused. I don't think I could ever get enough of you, love." He dropped a hard kiss on her mouth and lowered her to her feet. "We'll deal with all your objections after we find this bitch. Until then, treat this as your home." He lifted her chin. "This is your last warning, Erin."

Watching him walk away, she stuck out her tongue at his back, surprising herself at the immature gesture. She recognized his serious tone, but she still didn't know him well enough to know what he would do. He'd threatened to spank her before, but she didn't think he'd actually do it. Reese, maybe. Duncan, in a heartbeat. But she didn't know about Jared, and right now she didn't want to think about the fact that the thought of being out over his knee made her hotter.

Shaking her head she went into their office. She had to call Rachel and calm her down and let her know that she would be in to work tomorrow. Maybe getting away from the men for a little while would help put all this into perspective.

After her call to Rachel, she went into the living room and sat in the oversized chair, staring out the window. The pain pill she'd taken earlier had started to wear off, but she didn't want another just yet. She'd have to go into the kitchen to get it and she could still hear the men in there talking.

She just wanted to think. Rachel had asked her several times on the phone if something was wrong and Erin did her best to reassure her. Realizing that she did sound different, *felt* different, she tried to blame it on the pain medicine. But she'd lied. She hated lies. She'd lied more since meeting Jared, Duncan, and Reese than she had in her entire life. Lied to them. Lied to Rachel. Lied to herself.

She hadn't been acting like herself at all. This entire situation had rattled her and she just wanted to get back to normal.

Before that could happen, however, they had to figure this out. They'd missed something. Why the hell would anyone have any reason to hurt her? Why now? She'd been here for a few months with no problems. Why all of a sudden did someone feel the need to hurt her? She went over it in her mind over and over and had come no closer to finding an answer. Suddenly it hit her.

She raced into the kitchen where all of them sat, laptops and papers strewn all over the table. They all looked up at her entrance. "It's not about me. It's about you."

* * * *

The men all began talking at once until Ace stood and whistled. When the room got silent, he looked at Erin. "What are you talking about? Why do you think it's about your men?"

"They're not—" She normally would have met their icy glares with a smart comment, but the hurt in their eyes had her swallowing it before it could spew. "I've been racking my brain trying to figure out what I could have done to piss somebody off enough to come after me. The only thing I've done new since I came here is seeing them."

Lucas rubbed his chin. "Yeah, you have been seeing Reese for awhile."

Erin blinked. "You knew about that?"

Devlin's brows went up. "Of course we knew. You'll find there aren't many secrets in Desire, even less when it concerns the women. We all watch out for the women here and make it our business to know what they're up to. Now that you've been claimed, everyone will back off but we'll all still watch out for you."

Erin stared at each of them aghast. They all stared back as if *she* was the one who was crazy. "Damn it! I don't need a babysitter. I'm a big girl and can take care of myself."

Lucas looked pointedly at the notes and readouts covering the table and opened his mouth, only to shut it again when Jared spoke.

Jared stared at her coolly. "You know the rules of Desire. I know damned well Boone and Chase spelled it all out for you. Once you moved here, you became subject to those rules. They're neither flexible nor negotiable."

So angry she couldn't speak, Erin stamped her foot. "Arhhh!" She kicked Jared in the shin on her way out, angrier when it hurt her toes, but he didn't even wince.

* * * *

Jared watched her storm from the room, not grinning until she disappeared through the doorway.

Caleb watched her go and turned to Jared. "Your woman's got quite a temper."

Ace grinned and slapped Jared on the shoulder. "All the good ones do."

Reese leaned forward. "Speaking of tempers, Mom said that when she and the dads went to town the other day, she saw Hope Sanderson light into you."

Ace's smile fell. "Damned fool girl. Have you seen her drive? I swear she can't keep it under eighty on the road into town. We give her a ticket every time, but do you think that stops her? No, not Hope. She knows damned well where we set up radar, and she just flies right by."

Lucas frowned. "She could get herself killed doing that. She needs to be turned over one of her daddy's knees."

Ace snorted. "Garrett, Drew, and Finn can't do it. They tried. She bats her eyes at them and her daddies just melt. Gracie's getting worried, though. One of them is going to have to take her in hand."

Caleb shot a conspiratorial grin at Jared. "Maybe I should go talk to them. Since nobody's claimed her, I can volunteer to spank her bottom for endangering herself that way."

Ace whipped his head up from where he'd been looking at his notes. "Stay the hell away from her. She's just a kid."

Duncan, Reese, and Devlin laughed outright. Devlin wagged his brows. "Hope hasn't been a kid for a long time. She's looking real good since she graduated from college. Hell, she looked good before she left, but now..."

Ace stood to his full height, all six and a half feet of muscle and leaned over the table, getting directly in Devlin's face. "You stay the hell away from her. You are *not* spanking Hope. Do I make myself clear?"

Devlin leaned back in his chair, totally unperturbed. "You said it yourself. She needs to be disciplined for putting herself at risk that way. Since her daddies can't spank her, it's up to one of us to get their permission and do it ourselves. You heard what Lucas just said to Erin. You know the rules. We all watch out for all the women. Somebody's gotta do it."

Ace's face turned to stone. "I'll take care of it. Just stay the hell away from her."

Not at all surprised at Ace's reaction, Jared touched his arm.

"You'd better claim her before she ends up hurting herself. You know damned well she only speeds to get your attention."

Ace shook him off. "She's just a little thing. And she's too young. You know damned well how I am. She'd never be able to handle it."

Having problems with his own woman, Jared could sympathize. "I think Hope's a lot tougher than you give her credit for. She knows all about your need to be dominant in bed."

Ace paled and spun around to make sure Erin couldn't hear them, lowering his voice. "How the hell does she know about that?"

When they all just stared at him, Ace wiped a hand over his face. "Damn it. That's the problem with living in a small town."

Lucas went back to his laptop. "I'm eliminating people who live here one by one but it *is* a small town where everyone knows everyone else's business. So how come no one knows who the hell would have a grudge against Erin?"

Ace looked back over his notes. "Okay. She dated Reese but broke up with him. So it wasn't until the Christmas party that you decided to see her again?"

Duncan chuckled. "No. We had already decided to go after her after the night she and Rachel snuck into the club. But she avoided us. We had already set it up with Boone and Chase to be the ones to take her home after the party."

Lucas looked up from his laptop. "Who knew that you would be making your move at the party?"

Duncan frowned and looked at his brothers. "No one. The three of us talked about it from time to time, but we were always alone when we did. Of course Boone and Chase knew."

Lucas frowned. "Where did these conversations take place?"

Jared shrugged. "Here, mostly. Why?"

Devlin started tapping his keyboard. "Have you stopped seeing anyone lately?"

Reese looked toward the doorway before answering. "We weren't really seeing anyone. We'd been messing around with a woman named Debbie but none of us was serious about her. She tried to play us off of each other to make the others jealous." He shrugged, looking at Lucas. "You know that kind of shit can't work. We broke it off with her but there were no hard feelings. She just liked the sex, I think."

"Are you sure?" Ace scribbled furiously. "What's her last name?"

Reese gave them the information they wanted as Devlin typed it into his laptop.

"I'll check it out." Lucas stood and stretched, looking over Devlin's shoulder as he typed.

Jared stood to refill everyone's coffee. "I really doubt that it was her. I think you're wasting your time."

Ace scribbled in his notebook. "A lot of what we do is nothing but dead ends but we have to—"

Jared almost dropped the coffee pot when he heard the loud crash of glass shattering coming from the living room. Slamming the pot down, he raced out of the kitchen, the others right behind him, dreading what he'd find.

Chapter Six

Flipping through the channels, Erin finally settled on a nature show. Before she realized how it happened, she found herself totally engrossed in the life of hippos. When one of the males approached the mother and the baby to check out the newest addition, Erin held her breath. If the male decided the baby posed a threat, he would kill it in a heartbeat. Rooting for the mother as she put herself between the male and her baby, Erin was on the edge of her seat, urging the baby to move faster.

Just as the male hippo got around the mother and moved close to sniff the baby a loud crash and flying glass startled her so badly she fell of the sofa. "What the hell…?" With a hand over her heart, Erin stood to see that the living room window had been shattered.

Jared came rushing into the room, wrapped a hard arm around her and took her back down to the floor before she could blink.

The other men had rushed into the room with him, cursing inventively. The front door opened and the sound of running feet surrounded her as the men scrambled everyone at once. Ace barked out orders, demanding the others to stay back, but Lucas and his men ran out right behind him.

Jared brushed the hair back from her face. "Are you okay? Are you hurt?"

Erin shook her head. "Just my arm when I hit the floor. What the hell happened?"

Duncan knelt beside her. "It was a rock. Are you okay, baby?"

Erin's arm burned and she struggled to sit up. "Let me up. My arm is killing me."

Jared moved off of her and helped her to sit up. "Don't stand. Stay out of sight until we find out what's going on."

Erin looked down at her arm, pissed off that it had started bleeding again. "Damn it. This is going to stain. I need my clothes."

She didn't even have the chance to object before Duncan gathered her against his chest. Lifting her, he kept himself between her and the window as he raced for the kitchen. Putting her in a chair, he started to pull off her sweater. "Let me see it."

Erin slapped his hand. "I'm not undressing in the kitchen. In case you've forgotten, we have company. I must have ripped the stitches."

Reese rushed into the room carrying one of his t-shirts and the first aid kit. "Get that sweater off. You can put this on so we can take care of your arm." He reached for the hem, helping her out of it.

Erin managed to get into the t-shirt right before Lucas and Caleb came back inside. She reached for a napkin to wipe the blood but Jared beat her to it. Since it was on the back of her arm, she gave up and let him.

Lucas leaned over to see for himself. "Does she need more stitches?"

Erin shook her head. "No. She does not. Just slap a bandage on it. Did you find whoever threw the rock?"

Lucas shook his head, his lips thinning. "No. Bud and Jim were outside and neither one of them saw anything either. They came running when they heard the glass shatter."

Ace walked into the kitchen just as Jared finished taping the gauze in place. Holding up a bag where everyone could see it was the rock with a piece of paper tied to it with a string. The writing, in thick black letters was plainly visible.

Bitch Go Home

* * * *

Erin walked up the steps to the lingerie store the next day with

Lucas and Jared on either side of her. "I really don't think this is necessary. Whoever it is won't have the guts to come at me here." Silently, she hoped she would. She would just love to get a shot at this bitch one-on-one. So far she'd drugged her, shot at her, and threw a rock. All attacks from a distance. Erin would love to go hand-to-hand with her and put an end to this nonsense.

Both men ignored her, as she'd expected. When she unlocked the door, Lucas pushed past her to check out the store while Jared stayed with her as she opened for the day. Rachel came in soon afterwards.

"Damn it, Rachel." Erin stood with her hands on her hips and glared at her sister. "I came in so you didn't have to. I don't want you anywhere around me right now."

"Too bad."

Frustration mixed with pride that Rachel didn't back down. But she was more of a hard ass than Rachel could ever be. She turned to Boone. "Take her home. She doesn't need to be here."

Boone shook his head. "She's going crazy not being able to see you. You're both protected here. If I thought there could be any danger to her I would have her out of here so fast her head would spin." Ignoring Rachel's outraged gasp, he continued. "Chase and I will be in and out all day. So will your men and either Lucas, Devlin, or Caleb will be here at all times. Several men in this town will also be on the lookout."

"Damn it! I hate this." Erin spun to glare at Rachel again. "If you get upset, I'm kicking your ass out of here."

"You can try."

Erin smiled in a way that made hotshot corporate assholes back down. "I can do it and you know it."

Glaring at her, Rachel opened and closed her mouth several times before nodding in defeat.

Satisfied with her victory, Erin turned to the men. "Don't bother the customers."

Lucas grinned and saluted. "Yes, ma'am."

The number of people that stopped by the store that day amazed her, the locals voicing their anger at what had happened. By the afternoon it seemed to calm down and Erin starting restocking merchandise. She smiled as Hope came into the store. "Hi! I hear Boone and Chase and the others finished the remodeling in the building you and Charity bought."

Caleb poked his head out and smiled when he saw who it was before going back to the kitchen.

Hope grinned. "They did. That's why I'm here. Where's Rachel? I want to talk to both of you."

Rachel came out with several nighties on hangers. "Hi, Hope. Did my husbands really do a good job on your place or are they just bragging?"

Hope laughed, making Erin smile. She really liked the young woman who looked cute as a button but could be tough as nails when necessary.

"The place looks fabulous, but I'm afraid that once the men of Desire find out what I'm using it for they're going to be a little upset."

Erin leaned forward, loving it already. "Okay, give. What are you going to use it for?"

Hope looked around to make sure that no one could hear and leaned close, making Erin even more curious. "Charity and I are starting a women's club."

Erin gaped at her, shooting a glance toward the back. "Are you serious?"

Hope nodded. "Dead serious. The women in Desire will get huge discounts on their memberships, just like the men's club. I've already advertised online for other members. They don't know it yet, but I'm going to have Desire Securities check everyone out. I trust Lucas, Devlin, and Caleb to weed out all the women who wouldn't be right for us."

Careful to keep her voice down, Erin leaned closer. "Why not the sheriff?" To her amazement, Hope blushed furiously.

"No. I'd rather get Desire Securities. Anyway, it's going to be great."

Erin couldn't help but be caught up in the young woman's excitement. "So what do we do at the club?" Having been at the men's club she had some idea of what went on in there and wondered if Hope had underestimated what the men's response to this club would be. She had a feeling that the men would be beside themselves. Oh, God, this was going to be a hell of a lot of fun.

Hope grinned again, showing her dimples. "We're having a party there Saturday night, seven o'clock. We'll explain everything then. It's a party for women only, of course. We're not letting the men know that it's going to be a women's club until after the party."

Erin grinned. "I'll be there." Her smile fell. The last thing she wanted to do was endanger someone else. "Oh, wait. I don't know."

Hope touched her arm. "I know what's been happening to you and I'm glad you're okay. It's an exclusive party and only the women of Desire are invited. No one should be in any danger. Ace already knows about the party and that I was going to invite you. He and his deputies will be around anyway."

"In that case, I'd love to come."

Rachel shot a glance toward the back and smiled. "Count me in. Oh, the possibilities."

"Good." Hope nodded happily. "Like I said, Saturday's party is only for the local women. They'll be some business opportunities for you within the club. Same with Jesse and Kelly. Just like Club Desire promotes Jake's jewelry store, Logan's leathers, and Beau's adult store, I want to make the out-of-town members aware of the businesses here."

Erin shared a look with Rachel. The lingerie store did well but any chance to increase business would be great. She looked back as Hope continued.

"You'll be able to host lingerie parties at the club which all of the members would be invited to. The same with Indulgences."

Erin looked at Rachel again, her head already spinning with ideas. "That would be wonderful! Thank you so much."

Rachel nodded, looking thoughtful. "Yes, thank you, Hope. We'll definitely be there Saturday night. I've already got some ideas. And I can't wait to see the men's reactions to the club. Boone and Chase are going to freak and then put their foot down. You're certainly going to start a stir in Desire. I can't wait."

Hope shrugged. "I know the men aren't going to like it. But Ace better keep them from doing anything. Our good sheriff better not even think about stopping us, no matter what he thinks of our idea."

Erin frowned and raised a brow at Rachel, who just shrugged. Something seemed to be going on between Hope and the sheriff. *That should be interesting.*

The bell on the door sounded and Erin looked up, surprised to see Ace Tyler, the town sheriff walk in as if on cue. Every time she saw him, she was taken aback at his size, made even more noticeable as he stood next to Hope, making the young woman look even more petite. The only man in town as big as Clay and Rio, Ace stood six-and-a-half feet tall, every inch of him thickly muscled. Sexy as hell, he had a grin that would stop traffic and make women drool.

Or as in Hope's case, struck speechless. Erin could practically see the sparks flying between them and shot another glance at her sister. Rachel winked at her and smiled a greeting.

Ace smiled faintly, his eyes darting around. "Hello, ladies. Where are your men?"

Erin sighed at the reminder. "Caleb and Reese are in the back." Before she finished speaking, both men appeared in the doorway from the kitchen.

When the men moved away to talk under their breath, Erin, Rachel and Hope changed the subject.

When they finished, Ace nodded and moved to stand in front of Hope. Folding his massive arms across his chest, he scowled down at her. "You said you wanted to talk to me. What is it?"

Even from this distance, Erin saw Hope's shiver. Appearing to gather herself, she put her hands on her hips and lifted her chin defiantly. "You could have called my cell phone."

Erin hid a smile at the tiny young woman going toe to toe with the much larger sheriff.

Ace raised a brow at her tone. "I did. It's off. What did you want me for?"

"I want you to do your job Saturday night. Charity and I are having a private party and we don't want any men trying to get in."

"Why the hell would men want to come to one of your women's parties?"

To Erin's immense delight, Hope sneered at Ace. "I don't know. Some men just seem to like trouble."

"And some little girls like playing games." The menace in his voice made even Erin shudder. "Are you afraid that I can't handle the men who throw a fit when they find out you've opened a women's club in Desire?"

Hope gasped. "How did you find out?"

Ace leaned down until he stood practically nose to nose with Hope. "I know what goes on in my town, and I know everything that you do, little girl."

Erin watched in fascination as Hope's skin took on a rosy hue.

Hope turned to them. "Erin, Rachel, I'll see you Saturday." She shot one last glare at Ace before storming out.

Ace turned to them, grinning wickedly, and Erin wondered if Hope realized just what she would be getting into. "That went well." Looking at Erin, he gestured toward the men still standing in the doorway. "Listen to your men and stay safe." Turning to Rachel he smiled tenderly. "And you, soon-to-be momma, be good and let your husbands take care of you."

The bell over the door sounded and they all turned to see Duncan walk in. Erin sighed. "Here comes the next shift. Damn, I wish this bitch would just come at me."

* * * *

Erin forced another smile and almost gave in to the urge to leave Hope and Charity's party. She knew that this would be a good business opportunity, but she really didn't feel like being here. She couldn't focus and wished she could just have some time alone to think. Jared, Duncan, and Reese dominated her thoughts.

New Years had come and gone. She'd been staying with them for several days now and every day she lived there she fell deeper under their spell. Somehow they'd gotten through her defenses and made her fall in love with them.

Each one of them.

She'd never been so scared in her life. She'd never imagined she could fall in love with one man and she'd fallen in love with three. She had actually become involved in a ménage relationship and she still didn't understand how in the hell they worked. Somehow, together and separately, Jared, Duncan, and Reese had chipped away her defenses.

Each had different qualities, but had the same values and strengths that proved irresistible to her. They'd proven to be men unlike any she'd ever encountered and, if she was honest with herself, she had to admit they'd started making cracks in her defenses from the first time she'd met them.

In one way or another, they all got to her.

Jared was the bossiest. He took things seriously, sometimes too seriously. He didn't argue worth a damn, though. He stated his opinion and when someone disagreed, he seldom changed it. She would have better luck arguing with a brick wall. He had more patience in bed than she thought any man would be capable of. A very dominate man, he wouldn't allow her to hide anything from him. He wanted it all and wouldn't stop until he got it. He just kept breaking her resistance more and more each day. Slowly. Methodically.

Thoroughly.

Duncan's heat and intensity made her crazy for many reasons. During sex, he was always the most vocal, urging her to do and feel things she never had before. He pushed the envelope, especially with her and did it with a focus that she still hadn't gotten used to. She hoped she never got used to it. He made sex always fresh, always new, always moving to another level. He also loved to argue. She could see the amusement in his eyes sometimes, loving the challenge of it.

Reese had been the easiest for her to talk to. He listened and would argue, if necessary but knew how to admit a mistake and would sometimes change his mind. Or get her to change hers. He charmed her out of her bad moods and got her to say things she'd had no intention of revealing. He never seemed to get enough of her and that kind of attention was hard to resist. He also had a dominant streak, and a hot temper. Like Duncan, he liked to play and she had a lot of fun with him. She found herself opening to him more and more without realizing she'd done it until afterward. He finessed her like no one else ever had.

Used to taking care of herself, she didn't like how they appeared to be taking over. None of them seemed reluctant to go toe to toe with her, earning her respect. Used to men backing down, she sometimes felt out of her element when Jared, Duncan, and Reese wouldn't give an inch. They all stood up to her with no reservations.

Why did she find that sexy as hell?

She sighed and looked around, determined to think of something else. The place really did look nice. Boone and Chase and the other men who helped them out had really done a good job with the space.

Most of the women from Desire had shown up and now they all took their seats to hear Hope speak.

"Ladies, first let me thank all of you for coming. As many of you know, the purpose of this party is to tell you all about the women's club, Lady Desire that Charity and I are opening. This club will be similar to the men's club. The women of Desire can join at a substantial discount. You may be asking yourselves what we would do here." She grinned. "Pretty much what the men do at their club but with a woman's touch. We will have a place to go to talk to each other about how to make relationships such as the ones we enjoy in Desire work from a woman's point of view. We will have special guests to answer questions and show us techniques for pleasuring our men, making them putty in our hands."

She stopped, smiling as women applauded and laughed.

Erin sipped her water, wondering how she would be able to listen to how happy all these women were in their marriages and smile. She kept her eyes on Hope until the applause ended.

"We will have things such as belly dancing classes, parties for lingerie and body lotions." She looked at Jesse, Kelly, Erin, and Rachel in turn. "We will also have some of the more erotic guests." She paused for effect. "Several dominatrixes with their male submissives will be our guests on a regular basis. They will teach us things that we can do to pleasure our own men."

She paused again as the women in the room went wild. "They will show us exactly what drives men crazy, how to keep them from climaxing, and a host of other things. The same rules apply here that apply at the men's club. All women who are married or claimed can look but not touch." She paused until the applause and laughter died down. "Those of us who are single can do whatever we want with them. Either in private, or in front of everyone, your choice."

Charity went to stand next to her sister. "You can also come here just to talk, have a drink, whatever. We asked all of you to keep the purpose of this party secret until tonight because we didn't want the men of Desire to rush through the door before we could talk to you."

Everyone laughed again while Erin got herself another bottle of water. Great. Once Jared, Duncan, and Reese went out of her life, she could get her jollies from a male sub. She listened with half an ear as Hope and Charity talked about their plans for the club. She knew if she missed anything good, Rachel would tell her later.

"Erin, are you okay?"

Erin looked up to see Jesse's sister, Nat Langley standing beside her. "I'm fine, Nat. How are you?"

"Fine. Listen, I've heard about what's been happening with you and I can't believe it. Women are always well protected in this town."

Erin nodded. "I know. Lately, though, the ones that have recently come to town aren't having much luck with that."

Nat nodded. "And the men are furious. Jake told me that they've been having a lot of meetings at the club trying to come up with new safeguards. The men here think they've gotten soft. They're deciding on new ways to protect 'their women'. God help us."

Erin started laughing and found she couldn't stop. "You're kidding, right?"

Nat smiled. "I know what you mean. They could get even worse than they are now. I mean, have you ever seen such a group of men in your life?"

Erin sighed. "No." Thinking about the way Jared, Duncan, and Reese had made love to her that morning and the way they'd taken care of her when she'd been injured made her wish she could have the happily ever after she'd thought an illusion.

"No, I've never known men could be this way." She'd kept her fears and feelings bottled up for so long and the sympathy in Nat's eyes had her blurting, "Nat, I think I may have to leave Desire. I may have to leave Rachel."

* * * *

Jared stood with most of the men in the town, taking turns staring out the windows of Club Desire. They all watched the building across the street and had been struck speechless for a full minute when the sign 'Lady Desire' had lit up.

"I thought it was a party." Rio moved away, once again getting out his phone to call his wife.

Chase came back from his pacing and looked out one of the other windows. "We should have known it would be something like this when we did the bar. Damn it."

Jared looked across the room to where Hunter and Remington Ross fucked one woman while Dillon Tanner and Ryder Hayes took turns spanking another. The screams of pleasure from both women had him grinding his teeth. He wanted Erin. "What the hell are they doing over there? It's nothing like this club, is it?"

Chase looked over at what went on across the room and blanched. "No. Not a chance. Rachel's pregnant, for God's sake." He pulled out his cell phone and starting punching in numbers.

Rio came back over, followed by Clay. "I just talked to Jesse." He grinned. "She's pissed because we keep calling her. She said that they're going to have submissive men, just like the subs here. But, she said that the rules are the same as they are here. Once you're married or claimed, you can't participate."

Jared could feel all the blood drain from his own face. Suddenly he felt sick to his stomach. "Damn."

Rio frowned. "Erin lives with you. She's already claimed."

Jared shook his head. "She says she can't have a relationship with three men. We've been trying to convince her but with all that's been going on—"

Rio patted his shoulder. "Hell, man, I'm sorry."

Clay stared out the window. "Jesse would never participate. She would never cheat on us."

Rio grinned again. "No, she wouldn't." His smile fell as he glanced across the room and back again. "But can she watch?"

"Oh, hell no." Clay's face hardened as he grabbed the phone from his brother.

"Look!"

Jared looked at where Chase pointed to see the women pour out of the club, laughing and smiling.

Jared headed for the door and out into the street. He heard footsteps behind him and briefly wondered if any men except the ones currently fucking the subs had stayed behind.

Even Blade came out and headed for his wife. His face tightened dangerously. "What went on in there?"

Kelly grinned. "Probably just the same stuff that happens in your club."

Blade's jaw clenched. "Come on. We're going to discuss this."

Erin hid a smile when Kelly winked at her as she allowed her husband to lead her away. Erin grinned, knowing Kelly would have a good time alone with her husband tonight.

Jared, Duncan, and Reese surrounded her. Jared stood directly in front of her with his hands on his hips, scowling down at her. "What *did* happen in there, Erin?"

Erin couldn't keep a giggle from escaping. "You were in the men's club and you're worried about what I was doing?" She crossed her arms over her chest and raised her brows. "What went on in there?"

Reese didn't look any happier. "Not a damned thing. We were all staring out the window all night."

Erin laughed until her sides hurt. When the men just frowned at her, looking back and forth in concern, she laughed even harder. "I'm fine, I promise. I only drank bottled water. But you have to admit, it's funny as hell that you guys spent all night worried about what the women did."

"Yeah." Duncan grabbed her arm and started toward the truck. "Funny as hell. Let's go."

* * * *

Everything played out in slow motion. It always did. The same angry faces she'd seen hundreds of times never changed. Harsh words she knew but couldn't hear continued to spew from both of them as they moved through the house.

Knowing what would happen, she tried to scream at both of them, but to her horror, no sound came out. As the argument moved outside, she followed, screaming frantically at both of them. But still no sounds came out.

The silence was complete and scared her the most. She couldn't make them hear her.

No matter how many times this happened, no one ever heard her.

Knowing what would happen, she raced toward them as they jumped into the car, tears blurring her vision as they sped away. Horrified that she'd failed once again, she squeezed her eyes closed as the tears continued to fall.

The sounds she'd never heard came next, so loud they hurt her eardrums. Covering her ears against the sounds of the crash and the screams, she sobbed her horror and guilt. It was all her fault. She'd killed them again.

"No! Come back!"

* * * *

Duncan came awake when Erin started whimpering. By the time she screamed, he'd already pulled her into his arms. "It's okay, baby. It was just a nightmare."

Holding her face against his chest, Duncan saw Jared reach for her, surrounding her from the other side. Reese got out of bed, turned on the lamp and came around to sit beside them.

Shocked that the strong woman they all knew and loved, shook with sobs in his arms, Duncan rocked her as he would a child.

Erin grabbed onto him tighter. "I killed them again. It's all my fault. I killed them again."

Duncan shot a glance at his brothers. "Who did you kill, sweetheart?"

"My parents. I couldn't stop them. I killed them again."

Jared rubbed her back, his lips in her hair. "You couldn't kill anyone, love. Reese, get her some water."

Duncan, feeling completely out of his element, felt a momentary surge of panic at Erin's deep sobs. Pulling her more tightly against him, he did his best to calm her. "It's okay, baby. We're all here with you. It was only a bad dream."

* * * *

Now that the horror of the nightmare had started to fade away, Erin hid her face against Duncan's naked chest, mortified. Both Duncan and Jared held onto her as she pushed at them, desperate to get away. She hated the feeling of vulnerability at being seen this way, intensified by her nudity. "Let go of me." Relieved that they released her, Erin scrambled from the bed, pulling on her robe before accepting the glass of water Reese held out for her. She started out of the bedroom. "Thanks. I'm sorry I disturbed you. I'm fine. Go back to sleep."

Walking out to the living room, she curled in a chair. Sipping the water, she stared out the window. It had been months since she'd had the nightmare, and she'd hoped she'd never have it again. Hearing the men come out, she hurriedly wiped her damp cheeks. She continued to stare out the window they'd replaced, hoping they'd leave her alone.

She should have known better.

As Reece approached, she braced herself, slapping and kicking at him when he started to lift her. Despite her struggles, he held her against his chest as he sat back down in the chair, holding her on his lap.

"Are you okay, honey?"

Feeling far too fragile, Erin tried to get up. Reese simply tightened his grip, holding her in place. She flicked a glance at the sofa where Jared and Duncan sat there watching her. "I'm fine. I'd like to be alone. Can't you leave me alone for one fucking minute?"

Reese pulled her against his chest, holding her there when she resisted. "Not when you're hurting. Can you tell us what the dream was about?"

Erin sighed. "It was just a bad dream. No big deal." Erin swallowed the lump in her throat as she tried again to push out of Reese's arms. Every time she had the nightmare, she relived their deaths.

Reese grunted when she managed to elbow him in the stomach, but still held on. "This wasn't just a bad dream, Erin. You said you killed your parents again. That you couldn't stop them. You were screaming for them to stop when Duncan woke you up."

Duncan leaned forward. "I thought your parents were killed by a drunk driver."

Erin held herself stiffly, avoiding their gazes. "They were. Can you let me up now? I want some more water."

Jared stood and took the glass from her and headed for the kitchen.

When Reese tried to turn her face to his, she slapped at him, not wanting to face any of them until she could pull herself together. He firmed his grip and in desperation, she fought him. Sitting on his lap she didn't have a lot of leverage but did her best to pull away. "Let go of me, damn you."

He blocked her attempt to elbow him in the stomach. When she swung her other fist, clipping him in the jaw, he grabbed her hand. Not until then did she realize just how much he'd been holding back.

"Enough, Erin." Reese took her to the floor, despite her struggles.

Duncan stood. "Jesus."

Erin couldn't believe how quickly Reese had overpowered her. She'd never seen this side of him before. She'd seriously underestimated him. "Leave me the hell alone. Damn you! Let go of me."

Reese easily pinned her, using his weight to hold her down.

Gripping both of her wrists in one of his hands, he raised them over her head. Not until he had her secure did he lift some of his weight off of her. "Always the hard way with you, huh, Erin?"

"You bastard! Get the hell off of me."

Duncan knelt next to her, his face lined with worry. "Baby, what's this all about?"

Her robe had come loose during her struggles and she was uncomfortably aware that her breasts were bared. "Get this asshole off of me."

Jared came rushing back into the room, setting the glass of water on the coffee table. "What the hell's going on?"

Duncan shook his head. "I don't know. Reese was just trying to talk to her and she went nuts. I've had about enough of this."

Erin swallowed her panic. She wanted it to be over, didn't she? "Good. Then get Reese off of me so I can get the hell out of here."

With his free hand Reese gripped her jaw until she faced him. "That's not what Duncan meant. We've had enough of walking on eggshells around you. We've been careful with you too often. You've been hurt and have someone stalking you, and something in the past is keeping you from allowing yourself to commit to anyone. You've made taking care of Rachel your life's work and you feel guilty about your parents' deaths."

Duncan leaned close, getting right in her face. "No more. If you're going to be our woman, you're going to understand what's expected of you. For this to work, we all have to be open and honest. Spill it, Erin. Why do you feel guilty about your parents' deaths?"

"I don't. Leave me alone. I don't want to be your woman."

Reese narrowed his eyes. "Liar. You're crazy about us. And I know you feel you killed your parents. You told us you did."

"Damn it! This is none of your business!"

Jared leaned close, his eyes flashing. "That's your first mistake, love. You made it our business. You're fighting your own demons, demons that keep you from allowing yourself to have a relationship with us. We want you, Erin, and we're not letting go without a fight. For whatever reason, you've decided that being with the three of us is somehow cheating. You're wrong, damn it."

Erin jolted when he slammed a hand down on the table hard enough to make the water glass jump. She looked at him in amazement. Jared *never* lost his temper like this.

Jared closed his eyes, taking several deep breaths before speaking again. "You've got some sort of misguided guilt when it comes to your parents' deaths and you've spent seventeen years, half of your life, damn it, trying to make it up to Rachel."

"You don't know anything about it!"

"No, because you won't tell us! I can't fight what I can't see, Erin. Neither the person who wants to hurt you or this. I'm sick and fucking tired of fighting shadows. The person that wants to hurt you will be dealt with but this, *this* is something only you can tell us. We intend to have you. Rachel has two husbands to take care of her. It's time for you to get on with your life. With us."

"Damn you! Who are you to try to tell me what to do?"

"Your future husbands, damn it!"

Erin stared at him in shock and looked over at Duncan and Reese. Marriage?

Duncan cleared his throat. "Not exactly how I would have proposed, Jared." He looked at her. "We all want you to be our wife, baby. We all love you very much."

Erin looked up at Reese, who nodded.

"I've been in love with you for quite a while."

Erin gulped and looked up at Jared.

Jared smoothed her hair back from her face. "I love you and want nothing more than to spend the rest of my life with you. But we can't even begin to build a future with you until you get rid of this guilt and get ready to get on with your life. Now, either tell us or we'll go talk to Rachel."

Erin glared at Jared. "Marriage? Three husbands? Look, I've been honest about the way I feel since the beginning. I know I can't live with three men. Why can't you just accept that and leave me the hell alone?"

Jared drew a finger down her cheek. "Because we're all crazy about you and know damned well you feel the same way. You're lying to us and to yourself. You care for all three of us but you won't allow yourself to let go. And in case you hadn't noticed, you *are* living with three men. You have three lovers, Erin, who absolutely adore you."

Being backed into a corner brought out the worst in her and she snapped. "Don't you dare try to tell me how I feel. I'm not going to let you pressure me into anything I don't want."

Reese tightened his grip when she struggled again. "You usually don't avoid things, Erin. You face them head on. Why don't you do the same with this? You're hurting all of us, including yourself by not facing this."

Erin closed her eyes, shutting them out. Why couldn't they give her some space?

Reese was right. She hated feeling like a coward. Maybe if she told them, they would understand why she couldn't do this. Perhaps talking about it would put it in perspective. "I feel like I'm being unfaithful to each of you."

Reese eased his grip. "Was your father unfaithful?"

Erin opened her eyes, prepared to see pity on their faces. "Yes."

"Did your mother find out?"

The compassion in their eyes had her own stinging. "Yes."

Reese tightened his hold when she struggled again. "The night they died?"

Jared touched her shoulder. "What happened that night, love?"

Erin gave up and blew out a breath, "They had a fight. Dad got in the car to leave. Mom jumped in and tried to stop him, but he took off with her in the car." Even now she could remember her mother's screams as her father sped away.

Duncan urged her on. "Then they got hit by a drunk driver?"

Erin closed her eyes again, remembering that night. "The house smelled like popcorn. Rachel wanted popcorn, so I made her some. I haven't been able to eat popcorn since. Isn't that silly?" She swallowed the sob that came out of nowhere.

Jared caressed her cheek. "The police came to tell you that your parents had been killed by a drunk driver?"

Erin opened her eyes again, uncomfortable at the tenderness on their faces. "No." She didn't want to do this. She didn't know if she could do this. Already she felt her throat closing.

"What happened, love?"

"Let me up." They met her glare coolly. "Damn you. You won't *ever* tell *anyone* any of this?"

Jared ran a finger over her cheek, his eyes full of emotion as he looked at her. "We would never repeat anything that our woman told us in confidence."

When they just waited silently for her answer, she sighed. "My dad was the drunk driver. They hit a tree. No other cars were involved."

Reese released her chin and her arms, frowning. "I can understand why you wouldn't want Rachel to know that. But why do you feel guilty about it? If your mother couldn't stop him, I doubt if you could."

Erin pushed him, grateful that he let her go. Rising, she picked up the glass of water and moved to the window. She'd never told anyone before, never wanted to. Suddenly the weight of it felt too heavy and she wanted to unload it. With her throat clogged, her words barely sounded, but Jared, Duncan, and Reese listened quietly.

"I was leaving a friend's house and I saw my dad come out of a motel room with another woman. I stood there for several minutes, stunned. I couldn't believe it. He drove right past me. He was smiling. I hadn't seen my dad smile in a long time, unless he was with Rachel. God, he loved her." She took a shuddering breath. "All of a sudden it hit me. What he had done. Nothing would ever be the same again."

She took a sip of water, trying to get rid of the lump in her throat before continuing. "I hated him then. My mother had always been there for all of us, and at that moment I saw our family would never be the same. I ran home crying. Rachel was up in her room. Mom was in the kitchen fixing dinner."

Jared and Duncan sat back down on the sofa, their eyes steady on hers. Reese came to his feet but didn't come any closer. The concern on their faces nearly undid her. "Mom asked what was wrong and I was so angry and upset that I blurted everything. She was devastated." She drank more of the water as her throat clogged again.

They didn't speak as she composed herself. Grateful for their patience, she struggled to get herself together. "Dad came home about an hour later. We sat and ate dinner together. Only dad and Rachel talked. Mom just sat there looking stunned. I couldn't eat, just sat there watching Mom. After dinner, Rachel went to her friend's house next door. I started helping mom clean up the kitchen while Dad went out to the living room to have a drink. Mom followed him."

She went back to curl in the chair, staring down at the glass. "I went around the other way. I stood in the dining room and watched them fight in the living room mirror. I watched him pour another drink as they fought, and then another. He threw his glass against the wall. Then he said he was leaving. He didn't want to hear Mom's nagging any more about another woman. He was the man of the house, and he could do whatever he wanted. He went out and got in his car. Mom tried to stop him and jumped into the passenger seat. I ran outside behind them. The door was still open when he took off. I was afraid that Mom would fall out. I ran toward them screaming, but he sped off and as he did, the door slammed closed with Mom inside."

She got up again, unable to sit still. "I cleaned up the broken glass and put the liquor away. Then I went to get Rachel and brought her back home. When she asked where Mom and Dad went, I told her that they had gone out to a movie. She asked for popcorn and wanted to watch a movie on television." She wiped her eyes when her vision blurred.

She accepted the tissue that Jared offered her. "When the sheriff came, I knew. I told Rachel that they had been hit by a drunk driver on the way to the movies. She never knew that the reason they fought, or that the reason Dad got drunk was because I had told Mom about his affair."

A sob broke through and then another. She couldn't seem to stop. Strong arms held her as she cried brokenly against Reese's chest. "All these years Rachel hasn't had a mom or dad because of me. She was only thirteen years old, a baby."

* * * *

Reese sat and held the woman he loved as she cried. If he hadn't loved her before, he certainly would have after hearing her. He rocked her, offering comfort as Duncan and Jared surrounded her, stroking her tenderly. He wanted to make up for the love she'd been denied. Listening to her, it had been clear that her father had loved Rachel but not Erin. The shallowness of her father made him want to hit something. Instead Reese buried his face in her hair. "So you did what you could to make it up to her."

Erin nodded against his chest. "Please don't ever tell her the truth. She'd hate me."

Jared kissed her hair. "If you believe that, you're not as smart as I thought you were. Rachel loves you very much. But none of us will ever tell her. That's your secret, love. Telling her would only make her hate her father, and she'd feel guilty as hell that you gave up your life for her."

Reese lifted her face to his and kissed her, loving the feel of her soft lips beneath his. "I want you to think about something, Erin. None of this is your fault. It's your father's. He's the one that got himself and your mother killed. He's the one who had the affair. Do you really want to give him the power to take away your life, too?"

"No." Her voice sounded so small and pain filled, he wanted to wrap her in cotton and protect her from everything.

Duncan took her from Reese's arms and sat with her. "Then don't. Come on, baby. Give us a chance to prove to you how good we can be together. Stay here with us."

Erin looked at each of them and Reese could almost hear her mind working.

"I can leave whenever I want to?"

Jared smiled at her tenderly. "Don't expect us to make it easy for you to leave, love. No leaving in the middle of a fight because you're mad. We work it out. If you're mad and don't want to sleep with us, fine. We'll sleep in other rooms, but you sleep in the master bedroom here."

Erin stared down into her glass. "I don't know. I can't deal with jealousy. I can't keep track of whose turn it is to sleep next to me and stuff like that. I'd just get it all messed up."

Reese knew they were winning and struggled not to grin. "That's our problem. We just want you to be comfortable. No more secrets. If something's bothering you, tell us. Okay?"

"I'm not agreeing to marry you, just to living here for a little while to see if we can make it work."

"Understood." Reese nodded, relieved and hopeful.

Duncan set her back on her feet and kissed her tenderly. "Thank you, honey. You won't be sorry."

Chapter Seven

Erin waved goodbye to Rachel and Boone as they pulled away. Walking toward the house, she looked over at her dust covered sports car and grimaced. She'd bought it shortly after moving here but because of everything that had happened, she hadn't been able to drive it since the Christmas party.

She missed her car.

Turning to Reese, who stood on the porch waiting for her, she smiled. "My poor car's filthy. I'm going to have to wash it before I can drive it again."

Reese opened his arms and she walked into them. "We'll take care of it. You can't drive it alone until we find out who's after you. Did Lucas finish?"

She snuggled into his warmth. She couldn't wait to get home from work every day, missing all three of them every minute she was gone. It had been a long time since she'd felt that way. Probably not since Rachel left home. "Yes, he and Devlin left when we did."

Lucas and Devlin had been at the shop for several hours. They'd been turning the room that they'd finished for Sammy, the little boy of the lingerie's shop new employee, Marissa, and Rachel's unborn child into a safe room. They'd installed special locks and had a new cell phone brought over that they wanted to remain in that room at all times.

It had been a sobering experience but Lucas had smiled reassuringly. "You're probably never going to use this, sweetheart. But it would be nice to know that you have a safe place to go if you have to, and with the children inside, the men feel much safer this way."

"Yes, but it feels terrible to need this. Is this one of those plans that came out of all the meetings you guys have had?"

Instead of Lucas smiling as she'd expected, he had nodded grimly. "Yes. We're all disgusted with ourselves at how soft we've gotten with protecting our women. We're doing rooms like this all over town."

Erin knew better than to argue that. She'd already seen firsthand just how the men in Desire treated their women. They wouldn't change no matter what she said. "I really appreciate this, especially for Rachel and Marissa. It's good to know that with the children there, there's a safe room."

Lucas smiled tenderly. "It's to protect you, too."

Erin sighed and nodded. "I know. I just wish they wouldn't go to so much trouble for me, especially Jared, Duncan, and Reese. They just don't listen. They're really not my men, you see. I mean, I know everyone thinks they are. Even you and your partners think that but..." She waved her hand, wondering how she could make him understand. "I mean, it's just that they're…one day we might be but..." She shrugged, uncomfortable that she'd given so much away and frustrated that it hadn't come out at all like she'd hoped.

His lips twitched. "Sure they are, honey. You just haven't figured it out yet."

"You don't understand—"

Lucas grinned and she wondered how many hearts he'd broken with that smile. "No, Erin, *you* don't understand. Those men want you and it's making them crazy that they can't claim you the way they want to with this threat hanging over your head."

Unable to stand still, she moved around the room straightening things as Devlin walked in. He looked back and forth between them but when Lucas shook his head, he remained silent.

Erin sighed. "I can't believe how all of you think. I don't need to be claimed. What's wrong with just having some fun?"

Lucas chuckled. "Not a thing. But it goes beyond that for all of you and you know it. You're not a stupid woman, Erin, so I can't figure out why you pretend there's nothing between you and the Prestons when it's plain that there is."

She plopped on the small sofa. "Look, I'm living in their house. That's all I can do for now."

Lucas nodded. "Yes, and they're protecting you as their woman, but those of us who know them can see that they're handling you with kid gloves. They're distracted and can't give you the attention you need until this is over."

Erin didn't know how they could give her any more attention. Thinking about just how much attention they'd been giving her made her body tingle with remembered pleasure.

She hadn't been able to wipe the grin off her face since she got up this morning. Last night and again this morning, Jared, Duncan, and Reese had all done their best to show their appreciation for her giving them a chance. She felt *very* appreciated.

She'd been very careful not to make the first move on anyone, not wanting to stir any jealousy, but she knew that she couldn't remain that way forever. It had been hard as hell to keep her hands off of them. She knew she wouldn't be able to handle it if she caused any problems between them.

Now held in Reese's arms, she lifted her face for his kiss.

Reese obliged her, sending her pulse racing. He patted her bottom. "I've got to run into town and check on some things at the store. Stay out of trouble. Jared and Duncan are in the workshop."

Feeling carefree despite the circumstances, Erin smiled as she went into the house. Going straight to the bedroom, she put the bag she'd brought home with her away. She couldn't wait to see the men's faces when they saw her new lingerie.

She quickly changed into jeans and a sweater, disconcerted with the way the warmth from Reese's pat on her bottom lasted. The warm feeling added to the slickness between her legs. Thinking of their lovemaking all day, she couldn't wait to be with the men again. Reese's kiss had only whetted her appetite. She left the room and moved through the house with the intention of heading out to find Jared and Duncan. A heavenly aroma in the kitchen made her stomach rumble. Opening the oven, she saw that someone had already put in a roast. Good. She didn't have to worry about dinner. She liked the fact that they could take care of themselves, not expecting her to do it. It was just one more point in their favor.

Grabbing her jacket, she walked out to their workshop. Breathing deeply, she filled her lungs with the brisk evening air. The closer she got to the barn, the louder she could hear some kind of machine. Not wanting to startle anyone into losing fingers, she waited until it stopped before she went inside.

Jared and Duncan knelt next to a table, apparently checking something with the legs. They wore jeans and soft looking t-shirts, pulled tight over rippling muscle. Their jeans had lightened from repeated washings and hugged their butts and thickly muscled thighs lovingly.

She leaned against the doorway, taking in the view. "Now that's what a woman wants to see when she gets home from work."

Her pulse leapt when they straightened, turning to her with wicked grins. She looked down, raising a brow at the impressive bulges in their jeans. "I see you missed me, too." Walking into their workshop, she closed the door behind her and started toward them. They had a large heater in the room, and with the door closed, the warmth surrounded her. Since Duncan was the closest, she moved to him, reaching out to cup him through his jeans. "Another nice view."

Duncan's grin widened as his arms came around her. "Hi, baby. We missed you like hell today." His mouth covered hers before she could answer, strong fingers on her jaw holding her in place. Her pebbled nipples brushed against his chest, drawing a moan from her and dampening her panties with a speed that stunned her. The bulge in his jeans grew beneath her hand and her body responded by preparing for it, her pussy clenching, already anticipating the pleasure he would give her. She gave him a last squeeze as he lifted his head and she turned to find Jared waiting for her.

His smile had disappeared to be replaced by a look of hunger. She'd never been much of a flirt, but discovered that now she wanted to play. It felt good. Walking toward him, she reached out to place her hand over the bulge pressing against his zipper. "Is this for me?"

Jared raised a brow, his lips curving, clearly delighted with her playfulness. "Exclusively. Come here and I'll show you." He yanked her against his chest, his warm, firm lips covering hers and sweeping her into the storm that had begun the moment she'd walked in. The feeling of power it gave her to know she could inspire such a response called out to everything soft and feminine inside her.

These feelings were strangers to her and she still hadn't gotten used to them. She reveled in them, though, as Jared took her mouth, his hands hot at her waist, possession in every sweep of his tongue. From behind, Duncan removed her jacket, unerringly finding that sensitive spot on her neck with his lips.

Jared raised his head, his eyes dark with need. "Let's see what kind of view Duncan and I can get." He pulled her sweater over her head and froze when he saw the teddy she wore underneath. Red and sheer, the teddy left nothing to the imagination.

"Jesus." Jared moaned and reached for her breasts. "I love having a woman with a lingerie shop."

Duncan wrapped his arms around her and reached for the fastening of her jeans. "I want to see more." He undid her jeans and started to pull them down. When he got them down to her knees, he knelt behind her and nibbled her thighs, sending waves of hot lust through her. "We're going to have to put you on the table so that we can take off your shoes. I don't want you to step on anything in here. Once you're on the table, you have to stay there."

Erin eyed the table dubiously. "Will it hold me?"

Jared stroked a nipple. "Of course, love. We built it. Now I want to see you all spread out on it."

Duncan lifted her onto the table, removing her jeans and shoes and laying them on a nearby work table. "Now we've got you right where we want you. Trapped, aroused and losing clothing fast." Running his hands over her, his gaze heated as it slid over her where she lay sprawled on the table. Placing a hot hand over her mound, he moved to stand between her legs as Jared moved above her head.

Her whole body already quivered with need and seeing the looks of lust on her lovers' faces drove her even higher. "Now that you've got me like this, what are you going to do with me?"

From behind her, Jared helped her to sit up and lowered the straps of her teddy pulling the material down until it bunched around her waist. "Explore. Touch. Taste." His firm touch trailed a path over her exposed breasts, leaving a trail of heat in its wake. Cupping her, he massaged gently while lowered his lips to her neck. "Look how much Duncan wants you. Look at how he's looking at your breasts and these pointed little nipples." Using his thumbs, he flicked her nipples, making her moan as more moisture ran from her slit. "Put your arms around my neck."

She obeyed him eagerly, the movement lifting her breasts higher. Leaning back against him, she tried to squirm enough to get him to touch her nipples, but he just held her breasts cupped in his hands. Duncan leaned forward, his face inches from her breasts as he looked up at her smiling. With his thighs between her legs, she couldn't close them and she waited breathlessly for what he would do next.

"What pretty little nipples." He reached out to stoke one, making her gasp. "We already know how sensitive they are. I could just play with them forever." Leaning forward, he licked each of them in turn and blew on them, making her writhe in Jared's arms.

"Oh, please. Do something. I can't stand it."

"How about this?" Duncan asked, lightly stroking her nipples as Jared kept them cupped in his hands, as though offering them to his brother.

"Yes!" The soft pressure on her nipples only made her hungry for more. Her pulse raced as they touched her, always surprising her with their eroticism. They were always so *physical*! She'd feel more in control if it wasn't only their touch that affected her. The sounds they made never failed to thrill her as they voiced their pleasure, encouraged her, praised her.

Duncan pinched her nipples lightly and she arched, crying out at the pull that went straight to her slit.

She felt a sharp tug between her thighs as the snaps gave way. Duncan lifted her bottom slightly to slide the teddy out of the way, leaving it bunched at her waist.

Duncan lifted her legs, bending her knees and pushing them wide. Between them, they laid her back on the table. Jared clasped her wrists in one of his hands, raising them over her head, while his other hand traced lightly over her breasts, barely skimming her nipples. She arched into his touch, moaning even louder now as lust took over.

Duncan touched his fingers to her folds, parting them and kneeling down between her thighs.

Jared ran a hand down her body. "Get her nice and wet. We don't have lube out here and I want to watch you take her ass. Would you like that, love? Duncan's going to fuck that tight ass while I watch and then he's going to watch me take that hot pussy."

Jesus, the way they talked aroused her so much. She started thrashing and cried out in surprise and pleasure when a large finger thrust into her.

Duncan chuckled. "She's already nice and wet." He straightened and withdrew from her, reaching for the fastening of his jeans.

She heard Duncan's zipper being lowered and shook in excitement. Hearing the rip of foil, she looked down to watch him roll on a condom.

Jared's hands on her breasts drove her crazy as he plucked and pulled on her nipples. He grabbed her hands and put them on his belt. "Keep your hands right where they are. If you move them, do you know what will happen to you?"

"I won't move them. Please hurry." She arched her hips in invitation.

"Does my baby need a cock inside her ass? Let me get my cock nice and wet first." With that Duncan surged into her pussy. Her cries got even louder as his thrusts deepened. She held onto Jared's belt as he pinched her nipples and slowly pulled upwards. "Ahhh, oh, what are—? Ohh!"

When Duncan withdrew, she whimpered in frustration. "Hang on, baby. Now it's going in your ass." Using her flowing juices, he lubed her bottom and pressed the head of his cock at her puckered opening.

Erin held her breath, shaking with need as he began to push into her.

Duncan supported her thighs on his arms as he leaned forward, lifting her bottom off of the table and pushing his cock slowly, steadily into her. The level of intimacy startled her as Jared just held her as he watched his brother take her ass.

Jared tugged her nipples. "Duncan looks like he's being tortured."

Duncan groaned as he finally worked his cock all the way into her. "It feels like I'm being tortured. Delicious torture."

Erin cried out as he filled her again and again, robbing her of every bit of the control she struggled to hang on to. "Yes. Ohh!" She couldn't believe how completely her body surrendered to him when he took her this way.

Duncan spoke through clenched teeth. "I can't last. She's too fucking tight. Milking me too hard."

Her anus stretched around his thickness as his cock forged deep into her tight passage. His slow deliberate thrusts controlled her, robbing her of all reason. Her complete surrender to being taken this way never failed to alarm her. At this moment they truly dominated her, a sensation she'd never experienced until meeting them.

Jared leaned over her, cupping her breasts and running his thumbs back and forth over her nipples. His rough, calloused hands provided a mind-blowing friction on her sensitive flesh. He kept his face close to hers, his lips brushing her jaw, mesmerizing her with his rapt attention. "You see what you do to us?"

Erin gulped in air, her stomach quivering as his hand slid over it and down to her clit. The combination of Duncan holding himself still deep inside her and the touch of Jared's rough finger on the throbbing bundle of nerves did her in. She screamed, writhing on the table within their tight hold.

Duncan's curses filled the room as he groaned, tightening his hold on her as she bucked. "Jesus!"

Jared eased his finger from her clit. "She clenches hard, doesn't she? Look at her."

Duncan leaned over her, his hands braced on either side of her waist, still holding her legs high and wide. "Beautiful." Leaning in, he kissed her, his mouth brushing over hers repeatedly. "If you think we're ever letting you go, you're crazy." Straightening, he ran his hands down her thighs, watching her closely as he slowly withdrew.

Erin couldn't hold back a whimper as the head passed her tight opening.

Jared wrapped his arms around her as Duncan moved away. With sudden insight she realized that at least one of them held her firmly every time she came.

Duncan approached, fully dressed again and took her wrists in one big hand and held them over her head. "Now I get to play while I watch Jared take you."

"Oh, God."

Jared spread her thighs, moving between them. Pushing two fingers into her pussy, he began stroking. "You're nice and wet, love, just the way I like you."

She arched, her eyes closing as Duncan used his free hand to pinch her nipples while Jared ran his fingers through her slit. Hearing the sounds of Jared preparing to take her, she shuddered, clenching her hands into fists.

Duncan released her hands, leaning over her from above to take a nipple into his mouth. One hand covered her belly as the other teased her other breast, circling but not touching her nipple.

Already her clit throbbed again and she reached down to ease the ache.

Jared slapped her hand away. "Oh, no, you don't. You leave that clit alone."

Duncan lifted his head. "Every time we let go of your hands you go for that clit. You're too used to pleasuring yourself. No more, baby. That's our job now. I guess we'll just have to hold onto you." The fight she put up proved worthless as Duncan easily captured her hands again, laughing softly at her curses.

She gasped as Jared plunged deep, her body tightening. His cock felt like hot steel inside her.

Jared's quick thrusts gave her no chance of holding back. He took her hot, fast and hard, just what she needed.

How did they always know?

The insistent friction on the spot inside her made her clench on his steely cock. His hoarse moans blended with hers. "You feel so fucking good, love. Hot. Tight. Wet. Hungry."

With Duncan's attention to her breasts and Jared's thick hardness fucking her deeply, she couldn't hold on any longer. Her body milked him, her pussy clenching on him demandingly, drawing every drop of his release from him. She felt him tremble, felt his thick cock pulse inside her, heard his groan. He took her with him, forcing her over. "Damn, woman, you take all my control."

Duncan ran a hand down her side as Jared leaned over her, laying his head on her breast. When Duncan released her hands, she fisted them in Jared's hair, holding him to her.

Duncan bent and teasingly licked the seam of her mouth before entering and she whimpered in her throat as she tried to lift to him. His kiss tasted like sin, hot and wild.

Jared wrapped his arms around her, crooning to her softly until her trembling stopped. He lifted his head, his lips moving over her jaw as he withdrew.

Duncan stroked her hair. "Easy baby. You go so high it's hard to come down, isn't it? I love you this way." Duncan rubbed his lips over hers.

Erin smiled faintly, not ready to give him what he wanted. "I think my bones melted."

Duncan chuckled as he and Jared helped her up. While Jared held her, nuzzling her lips and neck, Duncan gathered her clothes and both men helped her dress as she stood, still trembling. She moved sluggishly as though drunk.

After they'd helped her dress, neither seemed to be in a hurry to get back to work. They each held her, stroking her back and making small talk, asking her about her day. Jared lifted her face to his, dropping a lingering kiss on her mouth. "Go on up to the house and get warm. We'll just put this stuff away and be up in a few minutes."

Erin kissed them each in turn and went to the door. Opening it, she stood on the threshold and turned, grinning. "Oh, by the way, I like the table. It's sturdy. Is the kitchen table this strong?"

Duncan leered. "We'll just have to check it out."

She closed the door on their laughter and crossed the yard to the house, waving to Bud and Jim where they stood by the fence. Bud smiled but Jim just lowered his head, probably embarrassed. Erin's face burned when she realized they'd probably heard her.

Mentally shrugging, she walked inside. They were all adults and something told her it wouldn't be the last time.

* * * *

After dinner had been eaten and cleared away, Erin got her things together to take a bubble bath. Her injury had healed enough and she'd looked forward to this all day. She knew the men would love her bubble bath ritual and couldn't wait to see their reaction. They'd been fascinated by her bottles, lotions, and perfumes, opening them and smelling each one of them. More than once she'd caught them fingering her lingerie hanging to dry.

Although she'd tried hard to keep her clutter to a minimum, they seemed to find pleasure that her belongings joined theirs around the house. It touched her immensely. She couldn't deny that she enjoyed being surrounded by their things and that little things, like watching them shave, gave her a warm fuzzy. Reclining on her bath pillow, she soaked in the hot, scented water, relaxing more by the minute.

Hearing a knock at the door, she opened one eye. That hadn't taken long at all. "Come in."

Reese stuck his head in the door. "Do you mind if I—Hey! You're taking a bubble bath."

Erin bit the inside of her mouth to keep from smiling, in the mood to tease. It got harder to hold back as he came into the bathroom, looking at the huge tub of bubbles as though in awe. "Yes, I know. Did you want something?"

Watching the way he eyed the bubbles as he moved closer, Erin did her best to keep a straight face. She almost lost it when he reached out and scooped up a handful of bubbles, looking at them as though he'd never seen bubbles before and eyeing the tub longingly. "Reese, did you want something?"

"Uh, yeah, I, uh wanted to know if it was okay if I took a shower while you were in here but—"

"Sure, go right ahead. But could you shut the door, please? I'd like for it to stay warm in here."

"Oh, sure, okay. No problem."

Closing her eyes, she listened to the sounds of him undressing and the water running. She heard him showering and within a few minutes, heard the water go off. Feeling his presence, she opened her eyes to find him kneeling beside the tub.

"Do you need me to wash your back?"

The hopeful look did her in and she couldn't suppress the laugh that bubbled out. "Would you like to take a bubble bath with me?"

Reese grinned. "Hell yeah!" He scrambled into the tub so fast she wondered if he'd been afraid that she would change her mind.

Pointing to the opposite side of the huge tub, she smiled. "You'll find another bath pillow over there if you'd like one." She tried *really* hard to keep her eyes from wandering to his thick erection and failed miserably.

His smile fell. "Bath pillow?"

Erin firmed her lips, again struggling not to laugh. How long had it been since she'd had so much fun? And how could he look so adorable and so damned sexy at the same time? "That way you can lay back and relax like I am. That's the whole purpose of a bubble bath." She almost gave in. Already her stomach had tightened with need. The sight of his steely length, muscular physique, and roguish grin was so enticing and she knew she wouldn't be able to resist for long.

"But I thought—"

"Oh, I thought you wanted to relax with me. If you don't want to then the towels are right there."

"No! I'll get the pillow."

Reese sloshed water as he moved to get one of the bath pillows, and she heard him chuckle when he saw that she'd gotten enough for all four of them.

With her eyes narrowed to slits, she watched as he leaned over to see how she'd positioned hers and carefully fixed his the same way. He sat directly across from her, tangling his legs with hers. "This *is* nice."

Trying to appear relaxed as he caressed her, Erin closed her eyes. "Mmm, hmm." They popped open again when she heard another knock on the door.

The door opened and Jared stepped inside. "Reese are you— Hey!"

Erin watched Jared approach and saw Reese's smug grin as he

looked up at his brother.

"You guys are taking a bubble bath!" Jared accused.

Erin blinked up at him. "Is that a problem?"

Jared smiled indulgently at her. "Of course not, love. This is your home and you can do whatever you want." He turned to glare at his brother. "I thought you were going to take a shower."

Reese grinned. "I did. Then Erin invited me in." He frowned as Jared started undressing. "You can't get in Erin's bubble bath if you're dirty."

It took tremendous effort not to laugh when Jared took off for the shower, hastily throwing off the rest of his clothes and showering with amazing speed. She kept her eyes closed when she heard the shower turn off and the door open and close.

Feeling Jared's hands on her shoulders, she smiled faintly without opening her eyes. "Finished with your shower already?"

His hands slid down to cover her breasts beneath the surface of the water and massaged them gently. "It gets lonely in there without you." His warm breath on her ear made her shiver. "I like showering with you, washing you, running my hands over your slippery soft skin."

Erin moaned at the pleasure his touch and his words gave her. His hands felt wonderfully firm as they continued to slide over her breasts.

He toyed with her sensitized nipples as he cupped her breasts and lifted them until her nipples rose above the surface of the water. Using his thumbs to wipe her nipples free of bubbles, he continued to caress them. "Would you like me to wash you, love?"

Erin turned her head to smile up at him. "In a little while. Right now I'm just soaking. Would you like to take a bubble bath with me?"

"Then can I wash you?"

"Maybe." She giggled, surprising herself. Until she'd come to live with these men, she *never* giggled. Her heart was filled with such joy. She couldn't remember ever being as happy as she felt right now. The implication of that sobered her.

The water sloshed as Jared got into the tub. Reese, sounding superior, told Jared about the bath pillows and she kept her eyes closed and had to bite the inside of her mouth to keep from laughing.

Jared settled next to her, pulling her legs toward him and running his hands over her calves.

"Hey! I was rubbing her feet." Reese complained and her eyes shot open.

"Too bad. It's my turn," Jared told his brother laconically, leaning back on the pillow and closing his eyes as he ran his hands up and down her legs.

Erin eyed Reese nervously, not relaxing until he grinned at her and lay back. Anticipating it, she didn't even open her eyes when she heard the knock. "Come in, Duncan."

"What the hell's taking so—That's a bubble bath!" Duncan moved to kneel behind her, leaning down to kiss her shoulder. "Baby, you look so sexy sitting there in a tub full of bubbles. It makes me feel like playing hide and seek." He swiped away a mound of bubbles that covered her breasts, exposing them to his gaze. "Look what I found." He nuzzled her neck as he smoothed his hands back and forth over her breasts.

Erin gasped when he found the sensitive spot on her neck, shuddered when he traced his fingers over her breasts, circling closer and closer to her nipples.

Jared's hands crept slowly up her leg and she could feel the water slosh and Reese's legs brush against hers as he moved to her other side. Streaks of pleasure raced through her body from all directions.

Duncan slid his arms under hers and resumed his caresses on her breasts while his mouth continued to wreak havoc on her senses as he nuzzled her neck and shoulder. When Jared and Reese bent her knees and parted her thighs, she would have fallen if not for Duncan's hold on her.

"I love when you're slippery and wet, baby." Duncan's deep

growl in her ear made her shudder. His deep chuckle told her that he'd felt it.

Reese's hand moved up her thigh and to her center and she moaned when a finger slid into her. "She's slippery and wet everywhere."

Erin gripped Duncan's biceps, thrilling at the feel of the rock hard muscles bunching under her hand.

Reese moved between her spread thighs. "Damn it, let me get my jeans."

Erin watched him lean over the side of the tub for his jeans and dig a condom out of his pocket. She closed her eyes as Duncan and Jared continued their ministrations. Reese quickly returned. His big hands gripped her bottom, lifting her and sliding his cock into her with one smooth thrust. Wrapping her legs around him, she dug her heels into his taut butt silently urging him to move.

Water splashed over the sides of the tub as his thrusts deepened. His features tightened while his eyes remained on hers as though transfixed. His thickness stretched her wonderfully as he thrust deep, his strokes coming faster and faster.

Their touch and the way they all spoke to her and each other during sex added incredibly to the erotic atmosphere.

Duncan growled in her ear. "That's it, baby. Damn, you're beautiful."

Jared ran his hand over her thigh. "I love the sounds you make, love. I'm already hard as a rock and can't wait to have you again."

Reese lifted her bottom higher. "Damn, Erin. You feel too damned good, honey. Fuck."

Duncan and Jared tormented her breasts delightfully while they watched their brother take her.

Duncan pinched a nipple and Erin involuntarily clamped down on Reese's thickness. Reese cursed through clenched teeth. "Damn you, Duncan. Erin, you're going first. I mean it."

Erin believed him. The stroke of his cock on her inner walls made them quiver around him on each thrust. When his thrusts shortened and he dug at that sensitive spot inside her, the hoarse sounds that came from deep in her throat startled her. She'd never heard such desperation in her voice before. What they did to her never ceased to amaze her.

Panting and writhing as Reese took her hard, Erin struggled to catch her breath. The sounds of Jared and Duncan's encouragement sent her higher and higher. A sharp pull on her nipples sent her over. Digging her hands into Duncan's arms, she cried out as her body tightened in ecstasy. Sparks of pleasure radiated out from her center and touched every part of her.

Reese sat back in the tub, pulling her out of Duncan's arms and down on top of him, so she straddled his hips, burying his cock deep inside her as he groaned his release. Laying her head on his shoulder, she wrapped her arms around him. His hands and Jared's moved over her until her trembles lessened. The attention they gave her afterward touched her deeply each and every time. It lessened some of her insecurities at such a loss of control.

She had no warning at all before a thick finger slid into her bottom.

Erin jolted and sat up. "Ohhh! Oh, God!"

Jared's voice sounded erotic in her ear. "Look at this ass spread wide, just inviting trouble."

Nerve endings came alive and she couldn't keep from gripping him tightly. Hearing the rustle of clothing, she glanced over to see a naked Duncan, stroking his steely length and holding a tube in his hand. It was probably one of the most erotic things she'd ever seen. His look of primal lust had her bottom clenching in anticipation, tightening on the finger buried inside her.

Duncan's huge erection pointed toward his stomach, the head purple and dark. As he approached, she stared mesmerized as he slowly stroked his length, his eyes never leaving hers. A drop of pre-cum appeared at the tip and she involuntarily licked her lips.

"Come here."

Erin blinked at the steely command. Bristling at his tone, Erin opened her mouth to deliver a snappy comeback only to swallow her words. Instead a moan came out brought on by the way Duncan cocked an arrogant brow at her while Jared moved his thick finger inside her and Reese tugged her nipples simultaneously.

Before she could move, Jared wrapped an arm around her waist from behind and with his finger still imbedded in her ass, helped her lift off of Reese and placed her on her knees in the tub in front of Duncan.

"Open." Duncan's soft command sent a thrill racing through her that she struggled to hide. Unable to stop clenching on Jared's finger and the desolate emptiness in her weeping pussy, she obeyed eagerly.

More than a little disconcerted in her response and the extent of their command over her body, she fought to hide it. Somehow they'd reached inside her and pulled the dark hunger she'd denied and kept hidden to the surface. It was too late to deny it now, but that didn't mean she wasn't determined to make them just as helpless to the pleasure as they made her.

Gripping Duncan's hips, she leaned forward and licked the plum-sized tip, gathering the glistening drop of moisture on her tongue. Humming in approval of his erotic taste, she opened her mouth wide to take the head of his cock inside. When she used her tongue to caress the sensitive underside, his hands tightened in her hair as he attempted to pull back. She gripped his hips tighter, to prevent it, moaning.

Jared slid his finger from her, leaving her empty. She shuddered when it quickly returned, this time coated with the cool lube. It felt even colder than before on her over-heated skin.

"Easy, love. I know it feels cold, but I've got to lube you good so Duncan can take this luscious ass again." Jared withdrew, only to return with more of the lube to push two fingers into her.

Moaning around Duncan's cock again, she drew a hiss from him as his thighs trembled. Jared's fingers stroked deep and she trembled at such a forbidden sensation, wondering briefly just how much her response gave away. The sharp pinch and erotic burn seemed the same every time as an entirely different group of nerve endings came alive, but somehow still forbidden and new. The way they controlled her unleashed a torrent of needs, wild and powerful, yet submissive and feminine. They seemed to contrast but complemented each other in a way that staggered her.

Wild now, she stroked Duncan's cock with her mouth, taking him deeper with each stroke, conscious of the fact that both Jared and Reese watched everything.

Reese cupped her breasts, his thumbs stroking lightly over her nipples. "You look so sexy, taking Duncan like that. He won't last with that hot little mouth sucking him in that way."

"He loves it. We all do." Jared growled. "All Duncan can think about now is how good that mouth of yours feels and how tight your ass is gonna be when he works his cock into it. And all I can think about is getting back in that pussy again, having you hot and wet and tight all around me."

Wrapping her hand around what wouldn't fit into her mouth, she stroked the base of Duncan's cock. He felt so hot, so hard, velvety against her tongue. She just couldn't get enough of him. Moaning at Jared's strokes in her bottom, she trembled in anticipation of the hot steel in her mouth replacing them. Duncan's tortured moans sounded harsh and she could tell that the rein on his control had slipped. It thrilled her that she could have such an effect on him.

"Enough! Jesus, that mouth is incredible."

Jared withdrew his fingers from her bottom, and she couldn't prevent a moan from escaping as her anus clenched at the emptiness. Leaning over her, he nuzzled at her neck as he spoke to Reese. "Give me a towel."

Duncan withdrew from her mouth, rolled on a condom, and climbed into the tub, turning her to face Jared.

She wanted to laugh when she saw Jared's cock almost completely covered with bubbles. When he rinsed and dried himself, his eyes on hers, all thoughts of laughter fled and her mouth watered. The large head rose gloriously from his thick shaft as his cock thickened and lengthened before her eyes.

Duncan bent her at the waist from behind until Jared's cock touched her cheek. All playfulness vanished as hunger took over. She wanted all of them and no longer cared if they knew how much. Her body shook, her lust blooming until she demanded satisfaction from her lovers.

Jared grasped her head in his hands and she opened her mouth, hungry to take him inside as Duncan's hands tightened on her hips. She became even more demanding, craving the pleasure she knew only they could give her. Jared groaned as she began to suck him. "That mouth is so hot, Erin. It feels like I'm fucking hot, wet velvet, almost as good as your tight little pussy. Take me deeper inside, as far as you can. I want to feel that hot little tongue. Swallow on me, Erin. Let me feel your throat work on my cock."

She did as he demanded, his harsh groans urging her even more. She did it again. And again.

Duncan's touch became even firmer as it did when she'd shaken his control. "Christ, her ass is tight. Loosen up, baby. Damn. Even with all this lube, ah, fuck."

Erin whimpered in her throat when the head of his cock passed through her tight entrance. It burned as it penetrated her and if not for their hands holding her up, she would have fallen.

Duncan's hands on her hips tightened even more. "Come on, baby. Relax those muscles for me. As much as you like that bite of pain, I don't want to hurt you." More of her defenses crumbled. How had he known that? She felt hands caress her back. It had to be Reese. Duncan groaned and bit off curses. "Come on, baby. I want to fuck this tight ass nice and deep."

Without meaning to, she clenched on him, his words adding fuel to the hunger already raging inside her. Her whimpers and moans blended with her lovers' harsh groans and praise. Making more of her own demands, she moved on both of them greedily, sending off another round of curses.

Bent over at the waist with a cock invading her at each end, Erin's body quivered uncontrollably as the pleasure just kept increasing. Moaning when hands covered her breasts and began to tug at her nipples, she felt even more of her juices flow from her, causing her to move faster on both Jared and Duncan and they cursed soundly.

With a hiss and a groan, Jared pulled his length from between her lips and began to caress her back

Duncan's thrusts kept getting faster and deeper and she cried out, moaning as the burn in her bottom got worse.

"Ohh. Ahhh! It burns. More." They caught her as she fell forward.

With a last forceful thrust, Duncan slid deep until she felt his sack against her bottom. Moaning at the incredible fullness, she jolted when he wrapped an arm around her waist and pulled her tightly back against him. With the help of his brothers, he sat in the tub with her on his lap, his cock planted firmly deep inside her ass.

Sitting on him this way pushed his cock even deeper, the sensation of fullness and being so completely taken overwhelming her and she shuddered, screaming as she came. She absently heard a litany of curses as the muscles in her ass contracted on Duncan repeatedly. Her orgasm went on and on and she twisted and jolted at the strength of it.

Duncan's hold on her tightened. "Easy, baby. Fucking incredible. I've got you, baby."

Jared caressed her stomach. "That's it, love. Let it have you. Let us have all that passion you try to keep bottled up."

When after an eternity, the waves began to diminish, she opened her eyes to find both Jared and Reese watching her, their eyes glittering. Duncan reclined on the bath pillow, holding her against his chest, one hand low on her abdomen, the other on her breasts.

Duncan used his own legs to spread hers wide, his cock shifting in her bottom at the movement. Her inner muscles caressed him, burning her. Even being on top, she felt dominated, invaded, and kept in position in the most intimate way she could possibly imagine.

Jared's eyes stayed on hers as he moved between her spread thighs, leaning down to touch her lips with his softly, then with more heat. He lifted his head and eyed her hungrily. "How does it feel having that tight, little ass full of cock?"

Erin moaned as Duncan's cock jumped inside her. "Full. Deep."

Jared ran his hands over her breasts. "You're about to get even fuller." He reached out and picked up the last remaining condom from the rim of the tub and rolled it on. Bracing an arm on the side of the tub, he positioned his cock at her slick opening and began to push into her.

"Oh, God! Ohhh! Ahhh!" Erin's cries and Duncan's bit-off curses accompanied Jared's slow, deliberate invasion. She could feel every ridge of both of their cocks as they stretched her impossibly.

Jared groaned as he began moving, his slow, deliberate strokes taking him deeper and deeper until finally he buried himself to the hilt inside her. The fluttering of her inner muscles made her feel even fuller and drew hisses and deep groans from both of them.

Gripping Jared's shoulders, she held on for dear life, as they inundated her with overwhelming pleasure. Bucking and writhing, her movements restricted by Duncan's firm grip on her, she gave herself over to the pleasure. Sandwiched between them, their heat surrounding her, she could do nothing but let herself go. She no longer had any control over her body or responses. Reese caressed her legs and her breasts, pinching and rubbing her nipples, his hands always moving so she couldn't anticipate where the next touch would be. It was too much. Filled completely, held almost immobile, the pleasure became almost unbearable.

She screamed as she flew, clamping down on both of them helplessly. Jolts of pleasure came with the engulfing waves of it until it became more than she thought she could stand. Screaming their names over and over, she begged and whimpered, feeling completely lost.

Duncan's hands tightened on her and even Reese leaned in to help hold her. Water sloshed everywhere as her body bucked against the enormous power of it.

It lasted forever and when she finally began to recover, she became dimly aware that they had both found their release. So lost in her own pleasure, she'd been unaware that she'd taken them with her. Leaning heavily against Duncan, she frowned thoughtfully as she realized how much she had come to trust all of them. She let go with them in a way she never had with anyone else.

They led her to go further and further during sex, and even doing something like what they just did, she trusted them completely. The way they stroked her soothingly after sex, the way they watched her closely, told her they knew what they did to her, knew how vulnerable and overwhelmed she became. The fact that they already knew her so well and controlled her so easily sent up warning flags that she was just too worn out to deal with.

Jared caged her in as he kissed her, and she opened to him without hesitation. When he lifted his head, his eyes darkened with emotion as he smiled tenderly and withdrew from her.

Reese leaned down sliding his lips over hers and nuzzling her jaw before he and Jared lifted her off of Duncan's cock. Reese lifted her in his arms and carried her to the shower.

She leaned against him, giggling. "So much for my bubble bath."

Reese chuckled, nuzzling her jaw. "I love your bubble baths, sweetheart."

Jared stepped in and started the shower. "Yeah, they're very nice. I'm already looking forward to the next one."

When Reese lowered her to her feet and Duncan joined them, she looked at each of them sternly. "My bubble baths are sacred and you can't come in unless you're invited. That's not negotiable."

Jared raised a brow but said nothing as he reached for the shampoo. With jets everywhere no one had been left out in the cold and the steam rose all around them.

Duncan took her loofah from her and began to soap her body as Jared lathered her hair. "So we're not allowed to get into your bubble bath unless you invite us?"

"That's right. A woman's bubble baths are very important to her. It's a way to relax."

Reese grinned as he soaped his own body, looking pointedly at the way she leaned against Duncan. "You look pretty relaxed to me."

"Not at all negotiable, no matter how good the three of you are at sex." She firmed her lips, trying not to laugh at their expressions. She knew damned well they would try to get into her tub at every opportunity and she would have no chance of keeping them away, especially when they gave her pleasure like they just had.

They made her laugh, tickling her as they washed her. Afterward they dressed in jeans and t-shirts while she donned a cotton nightgown and they spent the evening watching a comedy on television. Not until she lay between Duncan and Reese in the dark bedroom much later did it hit her that she hadn't thought about the person trying to hurt her all night.

Chapter Eight

Several days went by with no further incidents and Erin really started to believe it had ended. Furious that she may never know who'd done those things to her, she lamented the fact that she would probably never know why or get the opportunity to get even. She started to relax her guard, but the men just became more worried and diligent.

"I don't like this." Duncan muttered under his breath one night as he paced back and forth. Erin looked up from where she sorted through drawings the designer had given them of some of the new nightgowns. She had to choose a few for the shop and had spread them out on the bed in what used to be Reese's bedroom.

Distracted, Erin barely glanced up. "What don't you like?" She really liked one of the designs and wanted one of them for herself. Jared, Duncan, and Reese liked all the racy lingerie she'd recently developed a fondness for and she loved to surprise them.

The sex just got better and better, but she couldn't help but remember what Lucas had told her about them holding back. Wondering if it had to do with jealousy kept her constantly on guard. Sometimes it exhausted her.

"I don't like how this bitch has just disappeared."

She flicked another glance at him before looking back at the patterns. "You said that they checked out that woman you'd been seeing and it wasn't her, right?"

He stopped pacing. "Right. It wasn't the guy you were seeing either."

She pulled one of the patterns aside that she definitely wanted for the store. Several women in town had purchased a similar gown and she knew they would love it. "I just dated him when I needed a date for a function, Duncan. I don't date."

"You bet your ass you don't date! Not unless you go out with us."

Erin looked up at his tone, frowning before his words registered. Laughing softly, she shook her head. "I meant before." She sobered quickly. "Please Duncan, don't push this. Let's just take it day by day the way we have been."

She looked down again and decided on a longer gown. In the process of putting aside the patterns, she jumped when Duncan gripped her chin and lowered his face until it came level with hers. "We want children with you, Erin. A family. This isn't fun and games for us. We want *you,* baby. We're not going to let you go without a fight."

Erin froze at the mention of children. She'd always dreamed of having a family of her own but hadn't really held out much hope for it. How ironic that she could have it but in a relationship she didn't think she could handle.

She sighed wearily. "Duncan, we've talked about this before. I care very much for you and Jared and Reese, but I'm just not sure if we can make it work. You're wonderful men, but I have a difficult time not feeling like I'm cheating on all of you. I'm nervous about jealousy and I still can't get comfortable. I'm too nervous about doing something with one of you that would make the others jealous or hurt their feelings."

Duncan frowned. "Erin, baby, we can't live like that."

Erin stood and started out of the room, looking at him over her shoulder. "That's what I've been telling you."

* * * *

Later that night, Erin walked into the living room. The men looked up from their action movie and smiled. Jared patted his thigh.

"Do you want to watch something, love?"

Erin shook her head, looking distracted. "No. Some of my things have been cut up. Sliced. Ruined."

"What?" Jared jumped up from his chair and moved to her, gripping her shoulders. The monotone she'd spoken in alarmed him.

Reese turned off the movie. "What things?"

Erin rubbed her arms as though chilled. "Some of my lingerie. Two pair of high heels. A couple of my dresses."

Pale and visibly shaken, she went willingly with Jared as he moved back to the chair and pulled her down onto his lap. He clenched his jaw when she shivered and pulled her against his chest, rubbing her arms.

Duncan moved to kneel beside her. "Where are these things? I want to see them."

Jared felt the shiver that went through Erin's body and tightened his arms around her as he looked at his brother. Even though Duncan spoke softly, Jared could see the rage in his eyes, the rage he also felt when the implication set in.

"I left them on the bed. My powder is missing. I don't know what else. But some of my things have been moved. I'm usually very careful of my things, more so since I came to live here. I've tried really hard to keep my things out of the way. Somehow, she got in and went through my things. I didn't see anything of yours damaged, but I stopped looking."

Jared wanted to throw something against the wall. Someone had been in their *bedroom*. Someone had actually trespassed and violated the place that their woman slept. The place where Erin should feel the safest, where they made love to her and where she lay trustingly in their arms had been breached. Erin looked shaken, more so than at any other time since this fiasco had started, and he vowed to put an end to this shit and do whatever he could to make her feel safe again. Enough was enough.

He ignored the comment about her being careful not to get in their way for now, filing it away for a future time. "Reese, why don't you take Erin to the kitchen and fix her some hot tea."

Reese wiped the frustration and anger off his face as she turned to him. "Come on, honey. Let's get something warm to drink and then I'll make a fire for you. We can curl up on the sofa."

Jared dropped a kiss on her hair, watching as Duncan did the same before they turned her over to Reese. After watching her walk away, he dropped his guard and turned to Duncan. "I've had enough of this. She's been in Erin's *fucking bedroom!*"

Duncan's hands clenched into fists. "I don't know about you, but I'm tired of being Mr. Nice-Guy. We've walked on eggshells and let everyone else handle it. This has shaken her badly. She feels violated." His face looked tight, almost as though carved in stone. "I'm not going to sit back anymore. This bitch has been in our fucking house. I say we stop this bullshit and do what we have to do to end this."

Jared nodded and started toward his office. "Call Lucas and Ace and tell them what's happened. Maybe they can get some fingerprints. One of us stays awake and with Erin at all times. This woman's got a knife and a rifle."

Duncan's jaw clenched. "So do we."

* * * *

Erin sat on the sofa in front of the fire Reese had made for her. He had covered her with the afghan as the shivering continued and held her as they watched the flames.

Lucas, Devlin, and Caleb had shown up, looking mad as hell, followed quickly by Ace. The sheriff's face had looked hard and cold, harder than she'd ever imagined he could look. He must have seen how all this had shaken her because his face softened and he smiled at her, but she could see it didn't reach his eyes.

She felt so cold inside. She would rather someone come after her head-on than do this. This made her feel so vulnerable and helpless. To know that someone had actually been in the bedroom where she slept with Jared, Duncan, and Reese made her feel more violated than anything ever had.

She'd taken away Erin's false sense of security and made it impossible for her to relax at all. She knew she'd never get to sleep in that room tonight. Hating herself for relying on Reese's presence, she sent him to help the others. He hadn't wanted to go, but she'd insisted she wanted some time alone. It infuriated her that she'd taken this so badly.

The men went in and out of the house for what seemed like hours, always checking on her. Each time they did, it added fuel to her temper. How dare this woman think she could scare her? Who the hell did she think she was that she could march into their bedroom and ruin her things?

Thinking clearly for the first time since she'd found her things sliced to ribbons, Erin got up and started to pace. She'd let herself fall right into this woman's trap. Whoever had done this would be laughing right now if she could see how much she'd upset her. No one, *no one,* would make her feel helpless and vulnerable like this ever again.

She started a fresh pot of coffee, knowing how fast all the men went through it and stood looking out the window as it dripped. Bud and Jim walked toward the stables. The poor horses hadn't been ridden since the day that she'd been nicked with a bullet.

Suddenly needing some fresh air, she started for the door, spinning when she heard her name called.

"Erin, where are you?" Jared sounded slightly panicked.

"I'm in the kitchen." She started toward the living room but he had already made it to the doorway. "I'm making a fresh pot of coffee."

Jared nodded, his face hard, the way it had been for several hours now. "Just stay close."

"I need some air. The house is starting to close in on me."

"No. You stay inside."

"But Jared, it's still light out and I won't leave the yard. You guys are all over the place. I'll be fine."

Erin's eyes widened as Jared very deliberately moved toward her, not stopping until the heat of his body pressed against hers. He gripped her arms and lifted her to her toes, leaning down until his nose almost touched hers. She gulped at the expression on his face. The composed and unflappable Jared she'd come to know had disappeared and been replaced by someone she almost didn't recognize.

"Disobey me on this, Erin and you'll find your bare ass over my knees. You won't be able to sit down for a fucking month. We haven't done such a good job protecting you. That mistake won't be repeated. You're going to have to be tough in order to deal with us so you might as well learn the rules. You fucking obey us or you're going to pay the consequences. We've gotten too soft with protecting our women. The founding fathers of this town would be turning over in their graves if they saw this." He dropped a hard kiss on her lips before he released her and turned away, walking back into their office.

Speechless, Erin stood there like an idiot for several long seconds, staring after him. "Rules? Obey?" She repeated in disbelief. Who the hell did he think he was? She didn't answer to anybody! If he thought that she would sit calmly by while he and all the other studs took care of her, he had another think coming.

She wouldn't be a victim, damn it. She kept telling them that she could take care of herself, but did any of them listen? Staring out the window, she watched as Duncan went into the workshop. Good. Duncan could be counted on for a good argument. Not like macho man who just gave orders and walked away. Grabbing her jacket, she looked defiantly over her shoulder and headed out the door.

Crossing the yard, she pulled on her jacket. The temperature had dropped several degrees and being confined to the damned house all day had made it feel even colder. Striding determinedly toward the outbuilding, she forgot about the cold and looked forward to her upcoming argument with Duncan. *That* would heat her blood. Especially the make-up-afterward part.

Pulling open the door against the stiff breeze that had suddenly picked up, she barely had time to get inside before it slammed shut behind her. Duncan spun at the noise and once he moved, she could see Jim standing behind him with a smile on his face that fell as soon as he saw her.

Duncan started toward her anxiously. "Baby, what are you doing out here?"

Erin watched in stunned disbelief as Jim picked up something from their work bench and struck Duncan from behind. "Duncan!"

Erin raced over to where he'd fallen, her hands fisted as she threw herself at Jim. "You son of a bitch! You hit Duncan! Why did you hit him?"

"Stop it, you bitch! This is all your fault!"

Distracted by Duncan's groan, one of Jim's fists got through her defenses. Seeing stars she staggered back to shake it off. "What the hell are you doing?"

"You think you can just waltz into town and take Jared, Duncan, and Reese from me?"

Stunned, Erin just gaped at him. "*You're* the one behind all this? You dressed as a woman and drugged me? Shot me? Cut my stairs? Stole my things?" Her anger turned to rage and she welcomed the chance to take it out on the person who deserved it the most.

Jim looked down at Duncan, smiling tenderly. "They're mine. I started working here just to be close to them. They like me. I knew someday I could make it more. But then you came along and ruined everything! Damn it, look what you made me do to Duncan."

Erin stared at him, incredulous. "What *I* made you do? How the hell did I make you hit Duncan?" She started toward Duncan only to come up short when Jim pulled out a huge knife.

"Stay away from him. It's your fault. I didn't mean to hit him, but you walked in and I panicked. I have to get rid of you. They've been talking about marrying you and I won't let you take them."

Glancing at Duncan, she saw he was still unconscious. The piece of wood Jim had hit him with had really knocked him out. She could only pray he was still breathing. Carefully loosening her stance, she moved closer to Jim. This is what she'd been waiting for, a chance to go toe-to-toe with the person after her. She pushed down the rage that threatened to overwhelm her at the attack to Duncan. She needed to stay cool. She figured Jim to be only a few inches taller than her. Although he outweighed her and was probably stronger, she could tell by the way he held himself he didn't know much about fighting. She did. And she was definitely meaner. "I'm going to kick your ass, you know that, right?"

* * * *

Jared slid the clip into the nine millimeter, looking over to see his brother preparing his own weapon. He listened absently as Ace objected, cursed and barked out orders to his deputies. Jared clipped the hunting knife onto his belt. He'd be glad when all this was over and they could start their lives with Erin.

He and his brothers would stand guard each and every night until they caught whomever had come into their bedroom. They were going out now to set a few traps. Furious that someone had been able to shake Erin, he vowed that she would never have to worry about her safety again. Damn it, they were supposed to protect her. Ace had been right at the meetings they'd had. The men in Desire had become far too soft.

Ace swore again. "I want all of you to stay here. My deputies and I will—"

Reese slid his own knife into his boot. "You do whatever you have to do. And we'll do the same. That's our woman. You would do exactly what we're doing if it had happened to your woman. I'm going to go get Erin and have Duncan come in and stay with her while we set up the traps. He went to get some things from the workshop." He strode out of the room.

Ace swore again and nodded, resigned. "Damn it! All right. But if you see or hear anything, don't do anything stupid."

Jared glared at him. "I'm not going to hurt a woman. But I'll be damned if I let someone get away with doing this to Erin. Don't worry, I want to see her arrested, not dead." He turned when Reese came running back into the room. "What's wrong?"

"I can't find Erin. She's gone."

Fear like he'd never known slammed into him, almost paralyzing him. "Fuck. Damn it. Where the hell could she be? She's got to be around here somewhere. She was in the kitchen. Who the hell could have taken her without us knowing? Why didn't she scream for help?"

Reese went white as a sheet. "Maybe she couldn't."

Jared started out toward the back, through the kitchen where he'd last seen her and out the back door. He turned to Reese and Ace who'd followed him, but before he could say anything he heard a man's scream.

Reese took off at the same time Jared did. "It came from the workshop."

They ran to catch up with Ace who had already reached the workshop door.

"You bitch!"

Ace opened the door and ran into their workshop. Jared and Reese nearly ran into him as he came to an abrupt halt inside. Moving around Ace, Jared stepped forward and couldn't believe his eyes.

Erin knelt next to Duncan on the floor. Duncan looked dazed as she helped him sit up.

Jim sat on the floor several feet away, holding his arm. "Look what she did to me!"

Jared flicked a glance at him and moved to help Erin and Duncan. "What the hell's going on?"

Duncan groaned and held his head. "What the fuck?"

Erin smoothed back his hair and looked over at Ace who had knelt next to Jim. "He's the one behind all this. He did it because he's in love with the three of you and thought I was in his way. I came out here to see Duncan, and Jim panicked and hit him, knocking him out. He came at me with a knife. He was trying to get rid of me while Duncan was out. He was going to convince all of you he ran out to help."

With Ace's help, Jim got to his feet. "She's lying. She hit Duncan. I was only trying to help him. She came at me with the knife. Then she broke my arm. I would never hurt Duncan. I'm from Desire. She's an outsider. Who're you going to believe?"

Jared and Reese helped Duncan to his feet. Jared couldn't believe that they'd never even thought of Jim. They'd trusted him all along. Once Duncan was steady, he approached Jim. "Why? Why would you hurt our woman?"

"I didn't. I was trying to protect Duncan. She's the one who hit him."

Ace raised a brow at that. "Stay put. I need to find the knife."

Erin pointed to the ceiling. "It's up there. I know I'm an outsider, but I'm not a liar."

They all looked up. Jared stared open mouthed at the knife sticking into the ceiling. "How the hell did it get up there?"

Erin started for the door. "I kicked it out of his hand. Broke his arm at the same time." She paused at the door, looking over her shoulder. "You'll find his fingerprints on it, Sheriff. Not mine."

"Erin!" Jared watched her go as he and Reese held Duncan up when he swayed. He turned back to Jim. "I can't believe you did this."

Jim looked up at him, his eyes huge. "But I love you."

Disgusted at himself that he'd never even seen it, Jared turned back to look at the empty doorway. Although she'd struggled to hide it, he'd seen the hurt in Erin's eyes. How could she think they considered her an outsider? Apparently they hadn't made themselves clear. They'd take care of that as soon as possible.

Chapter Nine

Hearing voices, Duncan forced his eyes open. Where the hell was he? It all came back in a rush. "Erin!"

"Shh. I'm right here."

Duncan looked around. Seeing that he lay in a hospital bed and that his parents stood with his brothers, he groaned. "What the hell am I doing in the hospital? I told you not to bring me here."

Erin leaned over him to kiss his forehead. "You passed out again on the way to the truck. They had to x-ray your head. Thank God it's hard enough to withstand a two by four."

His mother leaned over him from the other side, gripping his hand. "Thank God you're all right. When we heard what happened, we couldn't believe it."

"Mom? What are you doing here?"

Isabella blinked. "Where else would we be?"

His father, Ben came forward. "Of course we're here, son. Why wouldn't we be?"

"Who's watching the store?"

Another of his fathers, Wade, shook his head. "Caleb and Beau are handling it. Nothing for you to worry about. With those two running the store, every single woman within ten miles will shop today. Everybody's been calling to see how you are."

Duncan dropped his head back onto the pillows and winced. "Why the hell does my head…he hit me. Jim hit me from behind when Erin walked in. Baby, did he hurt you?" He pulled her closer, frantically looking for injuries.

Jared and Reese both chuckled. Reese came close, putting his arm around Erin. "Erin had disarmed him, broken his arm and was trying to help you when we ran through the door."

"What? How—"

Jared sat at the foot of the bed. "It seems our woman took martial arts classes when she lived in the city."

Duncan smiled, grateful that she hadn't been harmed. "You're full of surprises, aren't you, baby?" He grimaced. "She would have been totally defenseless. He knocked me out cold. What would have happened if—?"

Erin covered his mouth with her finger, making his lips tingle. "Nothing else happened. I keep telling you I'm a big girl and can take care of myself. I was happy to get the chance at him. He kept coming at me from a distance, and I couldn't do anything about it. Face-to-face I can handle."

"You sure can."

They all turned to see Ace and his deputy, Rafe come through the door. Ace winked at her. "It's nice to see a woman who can handle herself that way. You might want to talk to Hope. It would be great if you could teach some of that self-defense to the women here. I'll work with you."

Rafe nodded, smiling. "So will Linc and I. It would be great if we can get as many women as possible to take the classes. Now that you're one of us, we'll have to put you to work."

Erin looked around the room at the others. Jared looked anxious. Their fathers, Ben, Wade, and Cord nodded, smiling encouragingly.

Isabella nodded and patted her hand. "You *are* one of us now, sweetheart. You belong here."

Duncan held his breath as he saw how moved Erin was by all this. Her nonchalant shrug didn't fool him for a minute. As close as he was to her, he could see the tears shimmering in her beautiful eyes.

Erin turned back to Ace and Rafe and nodded. "I'll do that. Where's Jim?"

Rafe's lips twitched. "He's getting his arm set. Linc's with him.

We just came up to see how you are and to ask some questions."

Reese put his arm around Erin's waist. "I have some questions of my own."

Ace nodded. "I'm sure you do. Let me tell you what we found and then you can ask your questions."

Rafe began. "I went to Jim's house and found the stuff we think he used to drug Erin. It's at the lab being analyzed to make sure. We found his rifle. He had the hunting knife we believe he used on your things. I uh, understand you kicked it out of his hand and it stuck in the ceiling."

Reese leaned down and kissed her hair, chuckling. "Boy that story's going to be circulating for years."

Rafe shook his head. "I'm sorry I missed it. Anyway, we found some lingerie and think he might have taken it when he ruined the other things. We need you to identify it." He flipped through his notes. "I didn't know anything was taken."

Erin shrugged. "I stopped looking after I found some of the things. I haven't looked again. I'll identify it, but I don't want it back."

Rafe grinned. "Understood. But all this is just icing because he's confessed to everything."

Duncan didn't care for the appreciation in Rafe's eyes as he looked at Erin. Glaring at the deputy, he growled harshly. "Get your own damned woman."

To his utter amazement, Rafe sobered, looking pained. "Linc and I have one. As soon as she's free to come here, we're dragging her here, by the hair if necessary."

Ace shook his head, resigned. "Just don't do something I'll have to arrest you for. I don't want to have to hire more deputies."

Erin slapped Duncan's leg. "Leave Rafe alone."

Duncan twisted his fingers in her hair until she was forced to lean close. "When I get rid of this headache, you and I are going to have a little talk."

Ace stepped forward, looking at Erin. "For the record, I never doubted you or thought you were lying. It was a little odd to run in to rescue you and your assailant was the one in need of medical assistance. I can't tell you how proud I am that you took care of yourself."

Erin untangled her hair from Duncan's fingers and straightened. "Okay. Thanks." She turned to Duncan. "You don't scare me."

Duncan couldn't resist pinching her fine ass. "I will." He looked back at Ace. "So he admitted to everything?"

Ace nodded. "Everything."

"Why the hell did he drug her?"

Ace looked pointedly at the women.

Duncan exchanged a glance with his fathers, but before he could say anything Erin broke free from Reese's arms and rushed over to Ace, poking him in the chest with her finger. "He drugged *me*. We're all adults here, Sheriff. I want to know why, and I'm not leaving the room so you can talk behind my back."

Ace's lips twitched as he looked over at him, enraging Erin even more. "It's up to the men if you can hear this."

Duncan opened his mouth to have his fathers take them out of the room when he met both Erin and his mother's stony glares. "To hell with it. Somehow they'll hear it anyway."

Ace nodded. "Jim knows about the woman the three of you have been seeing and that it was… casual. He figured if Erin acted like her, you would be done with her after one night. He didn't want to hurt her, just make her very, uh, needy. He gave her a little and when that didn't seem to work he gave her a little more. He didn't drug anyone else. Since he knew the names of everybody, no one gave it another thought when he lied about who sent him."

Rafe leaned against the wall. "He cut her stairs while she was at the hospital. He knew they would find the drug in her system so he cut the stairs to make it look like someone wanted to kill her. He figured when she came home, she would fall and no one would have any reason to suspect him. He wasn't really thinking clearly at that point. He was really upset that Reese and Jared were the ones who'd gotten hurt."

Duncan's stomach churned when he thought about what might have happened. "But he shot her!"

Ace nodded. "Yeah, well he blamed Erin for Jared and Reese getting hurt when it was supposed to be her. He convinced himself that she was no good for you and wanted her out of the way. Like Rafe said, other than planning the thing at the Christmas party, nothing else was planned. He'd really hoped that it would work and when it didn't, he panicked."

Jared sighed heavily. "And that's why we couldn't find anybody when the rock came through the window. Bud and Jim both told us they ran out front. Turns out they weren't together when the rock hit. Bud was in the stable and Jim said he was by the fence. When Bud came out, he saw Jim around the side of the house and Jim told him to hurry because he'd heard a loud crash out front. Bud's furious that he managed to fool him all along. He said Jim's been acting strangely, but Jim told him that a girl he was seeing broke up with him so he attributed it to that."

Reese nodded. "He fooled all of us. Anyway, when Jim threw the rock through the window he ran to the back and when he saw Bud he just stopped and changed directions."

Rafe answered his walkie-talkie. "Jim's ready. I'm going down so Linc and I can take him in."

Ace nodded and watched his deputy leave before turning to Erin. "Lucas, Devlin and Caleb are kicking themselves right now for not listening to you before. You said the bartender reminded you of a man and that the attacks had to be because of your men, not you. Lucas especially is not happy that he didn't pursue that more actively."

Duncan struggled to sit up, grateful when Erin pushed the right button. Christ his head hurt. "How could he have known about Jim? Jim worked for us for years and we never even suspected he felt that way."

Ace shook his head. "You know Lucas, a control freak if I ever saw one. He doesn't like mistakes and is mad as hell that somebody got past his radar. Hope and Charity asked him to do background checks to approve memberships to the club they opened. I'll be going over them, too."

Duncan grinned as Erin grumbled under her breath. "They'll be lucky if anyone gets approved."

Isabella paced at the foot of the bed. "I don't understand something. How did Jim know that my sons were still interested in Erin? It looked like she and Reese were through. How did he know they would be attempting to get Erin to see them again at the Christmas party?"

When Erin came close, Duncan reached for her hand, needing the contact. "Good question."

Ace shrugged. "He said he was standing outside the workshop and heard you talking about it. He said that he knew by the way you were talking about her that it was serious. He flipped, frantic to do something but not quite sure what. He came up with drugging her. We found out where he got it and informed the state police. His supplier will be arrested."

Reese used a finger to lift Erin's chin. "Why the hell did you go outside anyway? We told you to stay in the house."

Duncan squeezed Erin's hand. "Another good question."

Erin sighed and tried to pull her hand away but Duncan held firm. "If you must know, Jared made me mad and I was on my way out to the workshop to pick a fight with you."

Duncan's eyes narrowed. "Pick a fight with me?"

Erin shrugged. "I wanted somebody to fight with. You're always willing to argue and Jared won't."

"It sounds as though you're beginning to know your men, baby." He ran his thumb back and forth over her hand, loving the smooth silkiness of her skin. "What did Jared do to piss you off?"

Erin shrugged. "It really doesn't matter now, does it?"

He squeezed her hand warningly. "What did Jared do to piss you off?"

Erin blew out a frustrated breath. "He told me that I wasn't allowed to go outside. He told me I had to learn the *rules* and that I had to *obey* him!"

"Jared!"

Duncan winced at his mother's tone, but Jared just stared at her.

His father Cord, wrapped an arm around his wife's shoulders. "Come on, sweetheart. Let them work it out. You know the rules of Desire as well as anyone."

"But—"

Duncan grimaced at the look on his mother's face as she came to kiss him goodbye. She kissed his brothers and then Erin, whispering something in her ear.

No one spoke until his parents and Ace walked out, leaving them alone.

Erin pulled out of his grasp and stood with her hands on her hips looking at each of them. "If this is going to work you're going to have to learn that you can't order me around! I will not *obey* anyone!"

Duncan narrowed his eyes. "You'll soon learn just how wrong you are about that. Now I see why our married friends get so frustrated with their women. Our job is to protect you and to take care of you in all ways. And we'll do it no matter what you say. Get used to it, baby."

"Damn it, Duncan. I won't stay where I'm going to be bullied!"

Jared pulled her close and leaned over her, his nose almost touching hers. "We're not going to put up with you thinking you can disobey us and get away with it."

Erin didn't back off. Duncan hid a grin as she poked Jared in the chest. "You'd better not even think about spanking me. I'll leave so fast your head would spin."

Jared's face tightened. "You're not going anywhere, love. Not ever. Don't start threatening us with leaving or I *will* paddle your ass."

Erin gasped, clearly outraged and Duncan thought this might be a good time to intervene. He threw back the covers and gingerly stood. "Get my boots. I want to get the hell out of here." He'd deal with Erin as soon as he got rid of this headache.

* * * *

When they got back home—damn, she'd started to think of this as home more and more—she heated the soup Isabella brought over. Isabella and her husbands stayed long enough to satisfy themselves that Duncan was okay before leaving.

Isabella drew her aside as they said their goodbyes. "My sons love you. I know you've been through a lot lately, but I'm asking you as their mother not to break their hearts. I know the way we live in Desire must seem so different to you but it works wonderfully for all of us. You're a strong woman, Erin, strong and caring, the kind of woman I'd always hoped my sons would fall in love with. They're domineering, but they'll always put you first. But if you don't think it'll work with my sons, please tell them before they fall any harder."

Erin thought about Isabella's words all day. Several of the town residents came by to visit and Erin kept the coffee pot going all day. Isabella, along with her husbands Ben, Wade, and Cord all came back after checking some things at the store, bringing cookies and cakes for all the company. Erin couldn't believe the amount of visitors they had, Rachel, Boone, and Chase included.

Reese was retelling the story of what had happened to Boone and Chase. "So when we walked in, it was already over. Erin had taken care of Jim. You should have seen it. The knife he pulled on her was stuck in the ceiling. Ace had to use a ladder to get it down."

Warmth spread through Erin at the pride in Reese's voice. It felt nice to be with men who could appreciate her ability to defend herself and not feel threatened by it. "I told you I took self-defenses classes in

Houston. One of the women in our office was attacked and our boss sent us to take them. I liked it so much I kept going. I was their star pupil."

Jared kissed her forehead. "That's my girl. But you're not going to have to worry about anything like this happening again. We've been too soft with you, something that was brought home to us rather abruptly this afternoon. We're going to do what we have to do to make sure something like this never happens again."

"Yeah." Reese moved closer and caressed her leg. "We've let you get away with a lot because of the danger that's been around you. That was our big mistake. Once you learn the rules you'll be expected to follow, everything should be fine."

"Excuse me?"

Jared brushed her hair back from her face and looked down at her, his eyes glittering in warning. "Oh, yes, love. If you hadn't disobeyed me today, you never would have been in danger. Once you learn to obey us, you'll be fine."

Erin blinked in disbelief as Clay, Rio, and her brothers-in-law nodded in agreement.

Chase grinned at her. "She has to learn that you're serious about taking care of her. A red bottom ought to show her you mean business."

When both Erin and Rachel started to speak, Boone held up a hand. "You knew the rules when you came here. They're not changing for either of you. I told you that when you first got here, Erin."

Clay, who'd just come through the door, heard the last part of the conversation and nodded. "Nothing's worse than when your woman's hurt or in danger. We had to learn fast to get Jesse under control for her own safety. Erin has to learn the same lesson."

"What a minute! Are you telling me that you actually *spank* Jesse?"

Clay frowned at her. "We do whatever we have to do to keep her safe. She has rules she has to obey for her own well being. She knows we'd never do anything to hurt her or allow her to be hurt."

"You spank Jesse, and she hasn't killed you yet?"

Clay's lips twitched. "I didn't say we never had to sleep on the sofa."

Chapter Ten

It had been three days since the incident with Jim.

Erin was a nervous wreck.

She and Duncan had just come back to the house from their visit with Dr. Hansen, who'd wanted to make sure Duncan didn't have any lingering effects from being knocked unconscious and had wanted to make sure that her arm had healed properly. Duncan hadn't wanted to go, but Erin had been insistent. It surprised her that he'd actually listened to her.

The men had been nothing but polite, too polite, since they'd brought Duncan home from the hospital. But the look in their eyes worried her. They hadn't made love to her since then, but all three looked at her hungrily. That didn't worry her.

It was the look of determination and the sense that they had been waiting for something that made her uneasy. She didn't know what, but she knew them well enough to be wary.

She and Duncan went into the house, finding both Jared and Reese in the kitchen drinking coffee. They both looked up when she and Duncan walked in.

Reese put his cup down and turned. "What did the doctor say?"

He and Jared had been furious when they'd seen the bruises on her and had handled her with kid gloves ever since. Her assurances that she'd had worse while training had been ignored.

Remembering what Isabella had told her that night, she tried hard to walk away. She'd worked on several speeches to tell them she was leaving and why she could never be what they wanted.

She'd never spoken the words. It would be like cutting off her own arm to leave them now. But she'd never be able to get entirely comfortable with them, always concerned that she would offend one of them or make someone jealous.

How the hell could she get over that?

"I'm fine." Duncan shot Erin a look. He'd been overly polite ever since they'd finished at the doctor's.

Jared and Reese both came to their feet. "You're sure?"

She eyed them suspiciously, actually taking a step back as Jared approached. She planted her feet, determined not to let them see any weakness. "Everybody's in tip top shape."

Jared moved toward her. "It's about time. We have some things to take care of."

Erin didn't get the chance to run before Jared threw her over his shoulder and headed for the bedroom, both Duncan and Reese following them. She trembled just thinking about the pleasure to come. When he threw her onto the bed and started undressing her, she reached for the hem of his t-shirt only to have him slap her hands away. "Hey!"

Reese came down beside her and lowered his mouth to hers, cupping her head and holding it in place. He nipped at her lips, making them sting, forcing her mouth open and plundering inside. His mouth felt so hot and firm on hers and she kissed him back hungrily. She'd missed this so much.

Her head spun as he explored her mouth with his as though for the first time. His hair felt soft and silky beneath her hands as she tried to pull him even closer.

She felt her jeans being pulled down her legs and then off. As always, having the attention of all three of them at once made her arousal grow like wildfire. Reese lifted his mouth from hers just long enough to pull her sweater over her head, before reclaiming her lips with his. She hated even that small break of contact. Her breath caught as she heard her bra and panties rip in their haste to remove them. Writhing, she struggled to get closer to Reese, growling her frustration when the others held her down flat. Her breasts begged for attention, her nipples throbbing. The ache at her center had her rubbing her thighs together in defense.

Reese lifted his head and moved away, eyeing her with an air of superiority. Erin cried out in surprise when Jared lifted her from the bed and flipped her effortlessly over his lap.

"What are you doing?" Erin yelped as she struggled. Staring down at the bedroom carpet, she heard and felt the men move all around her and knew they all looked at her now vulnerable bottom.

"We've all waited patiently until you and Duncan completely healed, but now that you have, it's time to show you how serious we are. The reason that you got hurt is because you disobeyed me. You've been warned of the consequences of that, haven't you?"

"Damn it, Jared! If you spank me, I'm leaving."

"Now you threaten me. You, my love, aren't going anywhere. You're our woman. We've claimed you and will do whatever is necessary to keep you and keep you safe. But you're going to be punished for disobeying me and putting yourself in danger. Also for saying you don't belong here and for not trusting us to believe you about Jim. *And* for walking around on eggshells with us because you're scared you'll make one of us jealous when we already told you it wouldn't happen. Maybe this'll make you think twice before you do any of it again."

Erin shivered as fear and lust battled within her. No one had ever dared do something like this before. Indignation warred with respect that they would actually have the balls to do this to her. The first sharp slap of Jared's hand on her ass startled a squeal from her, which really pissed her off. She never squealed. She struggled uselessly as the slaps continued, extremely aware that both Duncan and Reese watched. She struggled, she cursed, she threatened, but nothing stopped the slaps on her bottom. He anticipated every movement and she couldn't shift enough to get any leverage.

"The next time I tell you to stay put, you'd better do it. Do you hear me?" Jared's cold, deliberate tone sent another shiver through her and she knew he had to have felt it.

Infuriated at them for doing this and at herself for getting turned on by it, Erin decided to take the wind out of his sails by giving in to the pleasure. Once Jared knew he could get his way by spanking her, he'd always threaten it. She would show him he couldn't control her this way. Besides, there was no way she could outmuscle him and she'd be damned before she gave in. "Come on, Jared. You've got me all hot now. How long are you going to make me wait?"

Silence fell over the room for several long moments before Jared slapped her ass again. "You smartass. Do you think I'm stupid? You think I don't know what you're doing? You think you can play me? Do you really think we don't know you?" Jared slapped her ass again, making it burn. The heat he ignited between her thighs inflamed her. "You don't work tomorrow, love. I think this is a nice time to enforce some rules and to teach you not to underestimate us again. We won't stop until you see the error of your ways."

She would kill all three of them the very first chance she got. "Rules? Jared, I don't care about your rules. Let's just have some fun."

Another slap landed, making her ass burn. "Fun? You think that's all this is to us? Fun? I ought to paddle your ass so hard you won't sit for a week."

Duncan knelt next to her, pushing her hair out of her eyes. "You're really in for it now, baby. The women in Desire have invisible leashes around their necks. Consider your leash tugged."

Incensed, Erin glared at him. "Leash? Leash? I'm not a fucking dog. If you think for one minute you're going to get away with this, then you've underestimated me!"

Duncan laughed. "And there she is."

Jared slapped her ass again. "She's trying to hide her arousal from us. She's scared we'll see how much she likes this. Get the butt plug, the new big one we bought for punishment."

A chill went through her. Both anticipation and fear made her tremble. She'd be damned before she would let any of them see either.

Reese leaned down next to her as Duncan moved away. "You have to learn that we'll do whatever we have to do to keep you safe. There's been a lot of trouble lately in Desire. The women that come here are getting hurt and we can't allow that. You could have been hurt or even killed when Jim came at you with that knife, all because you disobeyed. I understand you don't want to be told what to do. But we have an obligation, a *need* to protect you. That's the way we were raised. That's the way this town runs. You're just going to have to learn to live with it. And us."

Duncan came back, his bare feet once again in her line of vision. "You knew what you were getting into with us, baby. Now you're going to have to deal with it. You're not going to wimp out now are you?"

"Fuck you!"

Reese turned to Jared. "I really don't like that mouth of hers."

Jared slapped her bottom again. "No more swearing."

His coldly issued order only pissed her off more. "Fuck you, too!"

Another slap landed, harder than the others, and she bit her lips to hold back a groan. She couldn't believe how hot this had made her and she tightened her thighs together to ease the ache. The helplessness and vulnerability of being in this position should have scared her. Instead it only heated her blood and made her hotter than she had ever thought possible.

Lust combined with anger and became more. More powerful. More intoxicating. More violent.

Panicked, she tried to tamp it down, tuning out their erotic words and trying not to think about what they did to her. Hands and mouths touched her everywhere. Instead of the soft caresses they normally used, the sharp nips and pinches only served to inflame her even more.

The need that continued to build astounded her.

Knowing that if she let her passion free it would give them a weapon to use against her, she fought it like mad. If she gave in to the dark hunger inside her, she'd be defenseless. She squeezed her eyes closed and tried to think of something else.

Her bottom burned. She'd never in her life been spanked and she had never imagined it could be such an erotic experience. She could never let them find out just how much this affected her. She was mortified and stunned at just how much the combination of heat and the feeling of vulnerability excited her.

Several more sharp slaps landed in rapid succession before she saw Duncan move down towards her legs.

Reese pushed her hair aside so he could meet her eyes. "You're fighting it, sweetheart. We won't let you. Jared's going to open up that ass while Duncan shoves a really big butt plug inside your tight little hole. Let's see if you can fight what that's going to feel like."

"Why don't you just fuck me and be done with it?" She struggled even harder but it was like trying to move a mountain.

"Be done with it? You really are turned on, aren't you? Don't tell me this is more than you can handle."

Duncan ran a hand over the burning cheeks of her bottom. "Maybe you'll think twice about disobeying us next time."

Erin balled her hands into tight fists, her nails digging into her palms, clenching her jaw against the heat as Jared placed both hands over her hot bottom. "Maybe you'll think twice about doing this to me again when you find out it's more than *you* can handle."

Jared spread her thighs even as she fought to keep them closed and separated the cheeks of her bottom. "You're going to see just how wrong you are about that, my love. We can handle your passion, together and separately. You're trying to hold back from us. We can't move forward in this relationship until you trust us enough to let go. You might as well give in. We're not going to stop until we have it all."

As Jared keep her bottom cheeks spread, she knew it was Duncan who worked the cold lube into her. Moisture coated her thighs as Duncan pushed his fingers into her clenching anus and she struggled in vain against her arousal. She tightened on him no matter how hard she tried not to. She would definitely get them for this.

Reese nibbled at her neck. "I'm going to watch them shove the plug into that tight little ass of yours, darlin'. Watch while it fills your bottom and then we can begin."

Reese's teeth scraped that ultra sensitive spot on her neck and made her shiver. Damn it, they'd learned every erogenous zone on her body and used that knowledge without remorse. Bastards.

Erin whimpered when the plug touched her sensitive hole as fingers traced her folds. "Oh, God!"

Duncan chuckled wickedly. "Your spanking made you nice and wet, didn't it, baby? You like your punishment, don't you?"

"Fuck you!"

She moaned freely now, unable to stop as the plug pressed firmly against her puckered opening. Oh, God! She needed her ass to be filled, but she didn't want them to know it. Having never experienced anything in her ass until she met them, she couldn't believe how quickly she'd come to crave it. She would die if they knew. Panting, she squeezed her bottom closed as much as her position would allow it. Already wild with need, she wouldn't be able to hide it much longer if they continued this way.

The plug pressed harder until the tight ring of muscle gave way for its invasion. Erin panted as a chill went through her and her bottom clenched at the plug repeatedly despite her struggle not to. It widened and stretched her tight opening and she gasped, whimpering in her throat as it continued to stretch her.

Jared ran a hand over her back. "Look at this nice tight little hole stretch." His voice didn't sound as cool and calm as it did before. Now it sounded tight with need, thrilling her.

She groaned as the stretching continued, her bottom on fire from the spanking and the stretching of her anus, and she had to bite her lip to keep from demanding more. The plug pushed relentlessly into her and she cried out as it widened even more before narrowing sharply. She groaned at the fullness as the base of the plug pushed against her opening. Oh, God, she felt so full. Impossibly full.

Oh, no. The first shudders began as incredible waves of pleasure washed over her. She couldn't come now! Oh, God, she couldn't stop it.

Erin bit her lip harder to keep from crying out but couldn't control her body. She tightened impossibly making the burn in her bottom even hotter, swallowing the screams and holding her body as stiffly as possible, praying they didn't notice.

Hands slid over her back and bottom. Duncan chuckled. "That's one. Look how she tries to hold it in. Do you think we don't know when you come, baby? Look at you, naked and over Jared's lap. Your ass is nice and warm and pink, and filled with a plug. You're a naughty girl, huh? Just the way we like you. But for some reason you think you can hide it from us. Tsk. Tsk. Bad girl."

Jared pushed her hair away and turned her to face him. "We're going to make you beg for the next one. All you have to do to come is to admit we were right and that you've learned your lesson."

Erin clenched her teeth. "I don't obey anyone." One of them ran rough fingers over her slit and she couldn't help but tighten on the large plug in her bottom. It took every ounce of self control she had just to speak coherently. "You should know that by now. I'm not about to let anyone boss me around."

Duncan slapped her ass just hard enough to get her attention. "My turn." She found herself lifted and transferred to his lap, all her struggles useless against them.

Once again the slaps started and she raged at them even as she fought her own impending orgasm. How in the hell could a spanking turn her on so much? She hissed as fingers ran through her slit again and into her and she couldn't keep from thrusting on them.

"Does our baby want to come?" Duncan crooned, chuckling.

"Go fuck yourself." She couldn't stop rocking her hips.

Duncan laughed. "No, baby. I'm going to fuck you. We're all going to fuck your ass hard and deep just as soon as you apologize to Jared for disobeying him and promise all of us that you'll obey us from now on."

She felt the plug being shifted in her ass and worked herself even harder on the fingers inside her pussy. "Oh! You're going to be ahhh!…an old man before that happens!"

Jared moved to kneel beside her and turned her head toward him. "I don't think so, love." When his lips twitched, she wanted to smack him. "I think a few more minutes should do it. Especially when I start spanking your sweet pussy. I have a feeling you're going to *love* that."

She tightened on the fingers and the plug invading her. "You wouldn't dare." Oh, God, please let him be bluffing.

Jared lifted a brow. "Where you're concerned, my love, I would dare anything."

Duncan delivered several more slaps to her bottom, spacing them over every inch of her buttocks. "Your bottom is so nice and pink. And hot." He put his hot hand over her and she squirmed at the heat.

The fingers in her pussy withdrew suddenly, and she whimpered at the loss. "I hate you. Put them back."

Her arousal had grown alarming, taking her over. With her legs held wide, she could feel her juices flow and tried to rub her clit against Duncan's jean-clad thigh.

He held her in place and chuckled again. "You can come any time you want to. You know what you have to do, baby. Just tell us what we want to hear and we'll make you come nice and hard."

Without warning, she found herself flipped to her back on the bed. Jared grabbed her wrists and held her hands high over her head as Duncan settled himself between her thighs, keeping them spread wide. He laid a hand over each of them, pushing them even further apart as he looked over to where Reese approached the bed.

Erin followed his gaze, panting and moaning and saw Reese move toward her with something in his hands. It looked like some kind of chain, and the look on his face as he approached with it made her struggle again.

"What is that? What are you going to do to me?"

Reese smiled and said nothing as he approached and leaned down to take a nipple into his mouth. He didn't play or tease, just sucked it hard, using his tongue to press it to the roof of his mouth, making her gasp at the exquisite pleasure-pain. He released her nipple and before she could even take a breath, attached something to it.

The sharp bite of pleasure nearly made her come on the spot. "What is that?"

Reese smiled faintly. "Your nipple clamps." He adjusted it to his satisfaction, earning a groan from her. "They'll remain on your nipples until we're through."

Erin tried to squirm but every time she moved, she felt a pull on her nipple and gasped.

"They have pretty little weights attached to them. It'll feel like they're being pinched and when you struggle, the pressure will increase."

"Oh, God!"

When he took the other into his hot mouth, Erin fought to remain still. She lost the battle when Jared leaned over her and began to kiss her leisurely, running his tongue over the seam of her lips until helplessly, she parted them.

Once inside, he used his tongue and lips to drive her insane with need as Reese adjusted the other clamp. Once the other clamp had been put into place, she felt the folds of her slit being parted.

With Jared taking her mouth, her hands held over her head, clamps on her nipples pulling with every movement and her thighs spread high and wide, her folds spread, and a huge plug up her ass, Erin thought she couldn't feel any more helpless or vulnerable.

She'd been wrong.

She gasped and screamed into Jared's mouth when she felt her clit sucked sharply once and then released. She still felt pressure on it and she struggled, only to feel it being pulled.

When Jared lifted his head and looked down at her slit, she looked up to see Duncan and Reese both smiling as they all stared down at her slit.

"What did you do? There's something on my clit!"

Duncan chuckled. "Yes, baby. A clit clip."

"A clit clip? What's that?" She couldn't take any more. She felt the warning signs of an impending orgasm and tried to move so she could come, but they held her still.

"It's a little weighted ring attached to your clit. It'll hold the hood of your clit back so that your pretty little clit can't hide from us. That will make the spanking on your pussy a lot more effective."

"Oh, God! You can't do this!" Erin couldn't imagine feeling any more helpless than she did at that moment, but she knew deep down that the men would never cause her any more than erotic pain.

She forced herself to lie still, hoping to ease the torment. "Please, I can't do this. You don't know."

They all froze, staring down at her. Reese leaned over her, nuzzling her jaw before moving back to watch her face. "Don't know what, sweetheart?"

"I c-can't stop it."

Reese caressed her cheek as Jared and Duncan tugged at the clamps on her nipples. "Stop what, sweetheart. Stop what you're feeling. Why would you want to stop it?"

Erin squeezed her eyes closed, gulping in air, no longer able to lie still. The tugs on her nipples and the tug on her clit as she moved undid her again. Her cries sounded hoarse and nearly animalistic to her own ears, even though she'd turned her face to muffle them against her arm. She could only imagine what they thought of her.

Duncan gripped her jaw and turned her to face him, his eyes

fierce. "You don't want us to see you this way, do you? Open your damned eyes."

Struggling to breathe, Erin squeezed her eyes closed even harder. A slap on her slit had them popping open. It burned hotly, becoming a heated sizzle, a sensation she'd never even imagined. She whimpered. "You can't."

Duncan grinned wickedly. "I can. I will. You're trying to hide from us again, Erin, and I don't like it."

Jared tugged her nipple. "None of us do. So why are you afraid to let go?"

Erin's face burned as she looked at each of them. All three regarded her intently and it didn't look like they had any plans to move until she answered them. Closing her eyes against the distaste she knew she would see on their faces, she blurted it out. "It's too much. I like it too much. There. Are you happy? You know my secret. Now let go of me."

"Open your eyes." Jared's tone brooked no argument. Instead of the distaste she thought she'd see, his eyes held gentleness and compassion. "Did you think we didn't know that a woman as strong as you are had strong passions? We love that about you. We always knew it would take a strong woman to deal with the three of us. When you came along we knew we'd found her."

Duncan grinned. "Did you think it would scare us off? Did you think we would think you were kinky for liking your ass spanked, your ass filled. In case you've forgotten, we're the ones doing the paddling and filling your ass. We've been afraid of going too far. But you can take it, can't you, baby?"

"So you'll let me go whenever I want?"

Jared sank his teeth into her shoulder, before looking back at her. "Not if you're creaming the way you are now. I don't care what you say, you're not getting away until I get my promise and make you come some more. We'll have to explore your limits, love. Won't that be fun?"

"Oh, God."

Reese leaned down from where he straddled her and kissed her hard. "But don't for one minute think you're getting away with trying to hide from us and for not obeying Jared when he told you to stay put. Any more secrets?"

Erin nearly went over again at the love and lust on their faces. "Maybe. I'll think about it later."

Reese chuckled. "You do that. We're going to get them all out of you. Now about that promise to behave…"

Erin's heart melted along with the rest of her. She'd never before found a man strong enough to stand up to her and now she had three of them. Her temper, her passion didn't intimidate them at all. They would win this and she knew it. But she wouldn't make their victory an easy one.

Reese and Duncan moved between her legs, each of them holding a thigh high and wide.

Reese ran his fingers toward her center. "Last chance, sweetheart. Apologize to Jared and promise to obey us like a good little girl."

"Fuck. You."

Duncan slapped her between her legs and she cried out hoarsely as her folds and clit stung.

She couldn't breathe, couldn't stop rocking her hips as the heat swirled around, touching her slit everywhere. Her inner folds stung, then tingled, along with her clit. She'd never felt anything like it. The tingling went on and on, small tremors going through her as she had several mini orgasms in rapid succession.

The heat from her buttocks made it even worse and the whole area between her legs burned. "Oh! Oh, God. Please. Ohhhh! It won't stop!"

Another light slap made it even worse. Her clit felt as if it had swollen to ten times its normal size and she could actually feel it throb in time to her heartbeat. The tingling went on and on, and she screamed over and over as the mini orgasms continued.

The pleasure far outweighed the pain but it wouldn't stop, and she couldn't come hard enough to get satisfaction. "Please, I need to come." She panted, groaning as her struggles pulled on her nipples and her clit.

Jared raised a brow. "Apologize for being a bad girl."

"Never! I swear you'll pay for this."

"I look forward to it, my love."

She found herself flipped to her knees and the plug in her rear being slowly removed. She moaned and whimpered deep in her throat as it twisted and moved inside her. Fisting her hands in the bedding, she growled her frustration as they kept her legs parted, and she had nothing to rub her clit on. Calling them every name she could think of, her voice harsh but weak, she fought, stilling when the movement of the clips on her nipples and clit set her off on another series of little orgasms. "Oh, no! Not again. I can't stand it."

Three condoms landed on the bed beside her. A large brown hand reached for one, making her shake even harder.

She heard the shuffling of clothing being removed behind her and she felt a cock push at her bottom hole, even as the fluttering continued. Pushing back, she growled, needing to be filled again. She distantly heard chuckles but no longer cared. Needing to come more than she needed to draw another breath, she groaned as a thick cock began to press into her anus.

"Ohhh! Ahhhh!" Erin couldn't help the primal sounds of need and hunger that came from her. She didn't care if they knew how much she needed them. When she felt another thick cock press insistently against her cheek, she turned and latched onto it greedily. Sucking it as deeply as she could to her throat, she groaned as the cock in her ass slid deep.

She heard a harsh groan. Duncan. With his cock thrusting into her bottom, she sucked the cock in her mouth even harder and heard another groan. Jared. She hadn't even cared or paid attention.

Overloaded on sensation, she moaned and whimpered in her

throat as she clamped down on the cock in her bottom while sucking the one in her mouth greedily.

Reese's hands moved over her. "Christ, she's beautiful."

"Perfect." Jared groaned, then hissed as she used her tongue, gathering his flavor.

Tears filled her eyes as the pleasure crested. Without warning, she began coming, waves and waves of pleasure that continued to wash over her. Tightening on the cock in her anus, she groaned at the burn as the pull on her clit and nipples got even worse. Hearing Duncan's harsh growl, she felt his hands tighten on her hips as he plunged deep inside her bottom. Erin felt the orgasm gain in intensity and she came even harder.

The tight muscles in her bottom milked Duncan, and she heard his deep growls of pleasure as he came deep inside her. Her clit throbbed in time to her heartbeat as her body tightened. Sublime pleasure raced through her, stunning her with its intensity.

Jared's hands tightened on her hair as he slid from her mouth. Duncan slid from her ass, leaving her clenching uselessly. Struggling to catch her breath, she moaned and cried out, and then screamed as another slap struck her pussy.

Her clit throbbed and stung, tingled and swelled, and she felt as if her whole being revolved around the sensations between her legs. Her bottom and pussy clenched desperately, empty and needing to be filled. "Oh, God. Please. Fuck me, damn you! Don't spank my slit anymore."

"Are you going to be a good girl and obey us?" Jared's deep voice rumbled in her ear.

"You, ahhh! Don't, oh, God, understand—"

Reese moved close on her other side. "No, honey. You don't understand."

Another light slap landed on her clit and sent her over again. It seemed that she never finished coming, only the level of the orgasm changed. She'd never known pleasure could last this long. She didn't know how much more of it she could bear. She never wanted it to end.

Another thick cock pressed at her anus and slid inside in one smooth, firm thrust, making her cry out hoarsely once again. Hands in her hair turned her head and she found Reese beside her, his cock pushing at her lips.

"Take me into your mouth. I want to feel your tongue on my cock, honey."

Whimpering and moaning, she took him inside and used her tongue on him the way she had with Jared. When she felt the bed shift, she knew Duncan had moved close beside her and felt his hands move to her breasts. He began to pull at the clips on her nipples, making her whimper in her throat. The cock in her ass thrust relentlessly, accompanied by slaps to her already hot ass cheeks.

Duncan bit her shoulder. "Are you ready to apologize?"

Erin didn't answer, just continued to suck Reese deeply as more slaps landed, each harder than the last. On the verge of coming once again, Erin growled around the cock in her mouth when Jared plunged deep inside her ass and held her still as he pulsed inside the tight walls of her anus.

If she could just move, the pull on her clit would give her the release she needed. But they wouldn't let her. The men seemed to know just how close she'd come as they teased her, trying to coax her into apologizing.

Jared slid from her bottom hard and fast, leaving her gaping. The muscles spasmed at the abrupt emptiness and she whimpered pitifully. Reese withdrew abruptly from her mouth, leaving her completely empty as they flipped her to her back.

Reese reached for the last condom and rolled it on, watching her face the entire time. Lifting her legs high and wide, Reese pressed his cock into her ass, making her scream.

"Please! Oh! More, please. I'm begging."

She tried to reach for her clit, so close to another orgasm that her mind had shut out everything else. She found her hands gathered in a strong grip before she could reach her destination and cried in anguish. Her cheeks soon became as soaked as her thighs as she cried helplessly. The delay of the strong orgasm she knew loomed just below the surface and the teasing fluttering of mini ones became too painful to bear.

Reese's cock pressed inside but he didn't move. Jared and Duncan had moved to either side of her and held her immobile, playing with the clips on her nipples but not touching her clit at all.

Her bottom burned where it touched Reese's thighs, increasing the level of heat. Her clit throbbed, ached, and tingled, feeling huge as it begged for the attention the men denied. The pull on her nipples only made it worse. She couldn't go over. They just kept pushing her higher and higher toward the edge, but kept a strong grip on her, not allowing her to plunge until she thought she would die of it.

"PleasePleasePleasePlease. Fuck me hard. Touch my clit. I have to come."

Jared's lips touched her ear. "Say you're sorry you were a bad girl."

"I'm sorry. Let me come."

"No, love. Tell us that you're sorry that you were a bad girl."

"I'm sorry that I was a bad girl. Now let me come."

Duncan pinched a nipple, sending one of those mini orgasms racing through her system again. "Say that you'll obey us from now on."

"Damn you! Let me come."

Both Duncan and Jared pulled at the clips on her nipples while Reese ran his fingers through her slit, avoiding her clit.

"Oh, God! Ahhh! Pleeease!"

Duncan slapped her pussy again. "Say it."

"I'll obey you. Damn you. Let me come!"

Reese began to thrust into her as rough fingers stroked her clit and Erin flew. Screaming hoarsely, she came and came as Reese's thrusts got harder and faster as he held her legs high and wide. The strokes on her clit continued and she just kept coming, harder and longer than ever. Reese groaned loudly and thrust hard, holding himself deep as he came, his cock pulsing inside her.

And still it continued. Her screams of pleasure turned into hoarse moans until finally small whimpers became all she could manage.

She barely felt the clips being removed as the men stroked her soothingly. Her whole body trembled so hard she didn't think she'd ever recover. Not quite sure just how many times she'd come, they all seemed to have blended together, she lay completely spent. Erin didn't even have the energy to open her eyes as she felt lips on her cheek, kissing her tears away.

She didn't even open her eyes when Jared's low rumble sounded in her ear. "I love you very much, Erin. But if you ever do anything to jeopardize your safety again, I won't go so easy on you."

Warmth at his declaration of love washed over her before the rest of what he'd said sank in. *That* had been easy? She couldn't even imagine what else they could do. She couldn't think about it right now. Her eyes wouldn't open.

* * * *

Jared swept the hair back from the face of the woman he'd come to love more than he ever thought possible. He smiled indulgently as she frowned and grumbled in her sleep. He didn't believe for one minute that she would ever be the type of woman to obey them. Knowing she'd been trained in self-defense eased his mind in some ways and worried him in others. She might be a little too self-confident and willing to take on more than she could handle.

Erin would always be a strong woman, strong enough to keep them on their toes. He now couldn't imagine a future without her in it. She moaned as he lifted her and a fierce wave of protectiveness washed over him. She always appeared so strong and determined but moments like this reminded him just how little she was. He grimaced as he thought about what could have happened to her only days before and vowed that he would do whatever he had to in order to keep anything like that from ever happening again. If a spanking would keep her safe and let her know how serious he and the others took her safety, then she would get spanked as often as he and his brothers deemed necessary.

Duncan had already gotten into the shower and Jared joined him, carrying Erin in his arms. Reese came in behind him and between the three of them managed to wash her, propping her against Duncan. Jared could see how much his brothers loved her, cuddling with her and washing and rinsing her tenderly, smiling indulgently as she frowned and groaned grouchily as they took care of her.

Afterward, they dried her and slipped her naked form into the bed, tucking the covers around her securely before leaving the room. They still left a light on for her, knowing she may wake in the middle of the night and still be confused about her surroundings. It wouldn't be long before she got used to living here.

Walking into the kitchen with his brothers, he sighed. "I can't wait until she finally admits she belongs with us and we can finally start our lives together."

Reese sat at the table. "When we were sitting together at the Christmas party, I kept thinking that by next Christmas we may have already had a baby with her."

Duncan turned from the refrigerator, throwing a beer to each of his brothers before opening his own. "Damn. Wouldn't that be something?"

Jared chuckled as a wave of love for their woman washed over him. "Mom and the dads would be over the moon. Did you see how they were with her when we ate over there the other night?"

Reese grinned and took a sip of his beer. "Yeah. They love her almost as much as we do. When Mom realized that Rachel's baby wouldn't have a grandmother, she appointed herself grandma of her baby, too."

Duncan sighed as he joined his brothers at the table. "It seems to finally be coming together for us. Now if we can only get Erin past this fear of upsetting one of us or making us jealous, we can finally get married and start our lives together. She won't agree to marry us until she believes we can do it."

Reese nodded. "Yeah, it pisses me off the way she walks into a room and won't approach any of us until one of us calls her over. She's so afraid of hurting our feelings that she can't get comfortable."

"Yeah, but what the hell are we supposed to do about it?" Duncan asked, running his hand through his hair in frustration.

Jared looked at each of his brothers in turn. "I think I might have an idea. We're going to have to show her. Words don't convince Erin of anything. She has to see it for herself."

Chapter Eleven

Erin sat on the deck at Rachel, Boone, and Chase's house, watching the way her sister interacted with her husbands. Rachel walked out onto the deck and without hesitation went to sit on the swing next to Boone and put her feet in his lap. Boone covered her legs with the light blanket and started rubbing her feet as Erin knew they'd done many times before.

She looked over to see Chase smile at Rachel before turning back to talk to Reese. Frowning, she watched him, looking for jealousy. Finding none, she turned to find Rachel watching her questioningly. Erin smiled at her reassuringly before looking away and back to the men again.

She loved all three of them. She couldn't deny it even to herself any longer. If she walked away from them now, her heart would be in tatters.

All three of them proved to be good men. Kind, loving, faithful, and strong. So strong. The kind of men she never thought really existed. They kept her on her toes, witty and sharp and didn't fear her temper at all. Sometimes they actually seemed to revel in it.

It had been a week since they'd delivered their own brand of punishment, forcing her to agree to obey the rules they set in place for her. Since then, they'd been nothing but loving and showered her with affection and attention. True to their word, at least one of them made themselves available to her at all times. Not used to such attention and used to pretty much taking cares of things for herself, she'd been surprised that their skirmishes had only been minor.

She found that she not only loved them, she also *liked* them and respected them more than she had ever thought possible. They spent evenings together making love and talking and she found they had a lot more in common than she had at first believed. They had the same set of values, including family, and the men had spent more and more time with Rachel and her husbands, talking excitedly about the new baby. Although the men had been friends for years, they'd become even closer. She got the feeling they were bonding as future brothers-in-law.

More than one reference had been made that this would be their niece or nephew and Isabella and her husbands talked about having a baby in the family to spoil.

When Jared brought up marriage and having their own children, Erin had changed the subject. He'd let it go but she knew by the looks in the men's eyes that they wouldn't let it drop. They'd been hurt by her avoidance and she knew she'd have to make a decision soon.

As much as she loved them, or maybe because of *how much* she loved them, Erin hadn't been able to commit to marriage. She still worried about the jealousy and had been unable to walk into a room and approach any of them without worrying about how the others would take it. She didn't understand why they couldn't just go on the way they had been.

But the men wouldn't have it. They wanted all or nothing and it appeared their patience with it had come to an end.

No longer did she find herself pulled onto a lap for a kiss and a cuddle. No longer did any of them find their way into her bubble baths. When they made love to her, they did it together. Not once did one or even two of them approach her alone.

She hadn't realized just how much she needed the time alone with each of them until she no longer had it.

But she'd been too afraid to make the first move.

More than once she'd been on the verge of saying something or wanting a hug and a kiss so badly she ached with it, only to pull back at the last minute. The looks of disappointment on their faces when she did only made her feel worse.

Something had to give. And soon. It had to be her.

She couldn't go on this way. More than that, she infuriated herself by being afraid.

All night, she watched her men, her need for them mounting. She wanted to be held, cuddled, kissed. Knowing she could have all of those things just by going to any one of them only made her ache worse.

They looked at her often, sometimes tenderly, sometimes with amusement, often with a longing that pulled at her.

Her hands itched to touch them, knowing how hot and firm they would feel as she stroked them. The smiles on their faces when she reached out to them filled her with a sense of love and well being she'd never experienced at anyone else's hands.

Whenever she'd spent time alone with Jared, she always loved how adored she felt in his arms. Strong and masculine, he always made her feel so feminine and protected, as though nothing could happen to her while she lay in his arms. It surprised her how much she had come to yearn for such a feeling. He took her to the peak over and over, holding onto his formidable control as he saw to her pleasure before giving in to his, and she fought each time to make him lose it.

Her time alone with Duncan made her feel wild and wanton, desired and needed like never before. He would spend time relearning each part of her as though they hadn't been together in months and it never failed to drive her wild. He told her over and over how much he loved her and made love to her with an intensity that would shatter her, holding her afterward until the trembling stopped.

The time spent with Reese alone always seemed different. Sometimes playful, sometimes more intense, almost always gentle, their lovemaking filled her with a deep sense of well-being as if she'd come home.

Riding home that night, she felt cold despite the heater being on. Sitting in the back seat with Reese, she looked over and caught him watching her. He looked so strong and masculine sitting there in his shearling jacket, the night sky a stark backdrop, making the interior of the truck feel more intimate.

The faint light from the dashboard and the streetlights they passed allowed her to see his eyes and her breath caught at the look in them.

Love.

So intense, so fierce, so compelling she couldn't have mistaken it for anything else. A sob broke free and she struggled out of her seatbelt and flung herself in his arms, needing to be held more than she needed her next breath.

"Hey! What's all this?" Reese asked softly, pulling her close.

Erin gripped his shoulders desperately as his arms came around her. His hold tightened when she turned her face into his neck, overcome with emotion. He felt so warm, so big and strong, strong enough to take all she had to give.

"Baby?" She could hear the concern in Duncan's voice from where he sat in the front seat.

"What's wrong, Reese?" Jared's voice sounded tense.

Erin leaned back and looked up at Reese, the tears in her eyes blurring her vision. "I love you. I do." She saw the flash of Reese's smile before she turned to face the others. "I love all of you. So much." She took a shuddering breath, turning back to Reese. "I don't know if this will work, but I want to try. I don't think I can be without you."

She touched her lips to Reese's. "I miss you so much. Will you make love to me tonight?"

His eyes blazed as he lowered his head. "I can't think of anything I want more."

The heat from his body seeped into her until she no longer felt cold at all. Wrapped in his arms with his mouth covering hers, she felt as though she'd never be cold again.

Dimly aware of the low voices from the front, she slumped in relief when she heard their soft chuckles.

When they got to the house, Reese carried her inside, his mouth never leaving hers. They went straight to the bedroom and began undressing each other hurriedly, falling onto the bed as the last of their clothing had been discarded. The only light in the room came from the low light on the nightstand.

When Reese opened the drawer of the nightstand, Erin put her hand over his.

"No. No condom this time." She smiled at his confused look. "You want to start a family, don't you?"

He grinned, his eyes flaring. "Absolutely."

More than ready for him, Erin wrapped her legs around his hips when he moved over her. He surged into her with one smooth thrust and stilled, holding himself deep inside her.

With his hard body over hers, surrounding her with his heat and strength, filling her with it, she looked up at him. She saw the same look on his face that had brought tears to her eyes earlier. Her breath caught again, just as it had before.

Her hand trembled when she reached out to touch his face and her heart melted when he turned his lips to her palm.

He smoothed her hair back, his eyes intense as they regarded her. "I love you so much, honey. I don't think I could live without you now."

She couldn't help but tighten on him where he filled her, feeling his cock jump in response. "I love you, too. I'm just afraid—"

"No, honey. There's nothing to be afraid of. It'll all work out. You'll see."

When he withdrew and thrust back into her, she moaned helplessly. "I don't think I have a choice. I need all of you too much."

"I need you, too. Let me show you."

He made love to her slowly, a combination of long drugging kisses, intertwined with soft caresses and murmured endearments.

She loved it, and took her own time exploring his muscular body and finding spots that drove him wild. Filing the information away for another time, she continued to run her hands and lips over every inch of him she could reach.

Long minutes later, the slow rise to the edge had her gripping his shoulders frantically. "Oh, God, Reese. It feels so good. So good."

He reached a hand between their bodies and stroked her sensitive nub. "Come for me, Erin. Let me feel you fall apart in my arms."

The choice had been taken away from her and Erin flew. Digging her nails into Reese's shoulder, she cried out her pleasure, his words spurring her to greater heights.

"That's it, sweetheart. I've got you. Christ, you feel incredible."

His harsh groan as he found his own pleasure had her tightening on him even more as she dug her heels into his taut buttocks to pull him even closer. Her arms tightened around his neck, holding him tightly as their breathing slowed.

When he lifted his head and kissed her again, she felt loved and desired beyond measure. They kissed and nuzzled, murmuring softly to each other for several minutes before he withdrew and lay beside her, propping himself on an elbow.

The look on his face as he eyed her naked form made her feel wanton and beautiful, and she didn't attempt to cover herself. Instead she lay proudly under his gaze as his eyes roamed over her.

When he finally looked back at her face, his lips firmed. "My brothers and I are going to fight. We always have. We've already fought about you and will probably do it all our lives." He reached down to stroke her cheek. "We all love you very much but sometimes have different ideas about what is best for you. You stay out of our fights. We'll work it out and do what we think is best."

Erin scrambled up, pulling the sheet over her. "I don't want you to fight about me!"

Reese chuckled. "Jared, Duncan, and I fight about a lot of things. Hell, we've had fights over orange juice. I want you to stay out of it, and I don't want you to think that you cause the fights. My brothers and I love you very much and also love each other."

He laughed. "Do you think we're not going to fight with you, too? We're all going to fight, honey. But as long as we all love each other it will all work out. You'll see."

Erin eyed him warily, not at all sure about all of this. She had no choice but to try. She needed to have them in her life.

Believing in starting as you mean to go on, she narrowed her eyes at him. "Just as long as you and your brothers don't think you're going to boss me around."

Reese ripped the sheet off of her and pulled her against him, slapping her bottom sharply, and chuckling at her expression. "We're going to have a hell of a lot of fun keeping up with you."

Sticking her tongue out at him, she scrambled from his arms, rose from the bed and walked toward the bathroom. A sudden idea had her pausing in the doorway. Turning to Reese, she asked. "Would you mind asking Duncan to come in here?"

Sharp relief went through her at his quick grin and she let out a breath she hadn't realized she'd been holding.

"Sure thing, honey. I'm sure Duncan will be right in."

Erin had started her bubble bath, the water still running in the giant tub, when Duncan walked into the bathroom, closing the door behind him.

"Reese said you wanted to see me?"

Naked as the day she was born, Erin approached him, noting with amusement the bulge in his jeans. Approaching him, she slid her hands over his chest, unbuttoning his shirt as she went.

"I wanted to know if you'd take a bubble bath with me."

Now that she had several buttons undone, she ran her hands over his naked chest, leaning in to caress him with her tongue. Licking a hard male nipple, she heard him gasp and smiled against his chest. "Sometimes I get lonely in there all by myself and I want some company."

She looked up in time to see Duncan's wicked grin as his hands moved over her hips and bottom.

"Well, we can't have you getting lonely, can we?"

He undressed hurriedly, lifted her high in his arms, and strode toward the tub. "Shit. I forgot a condom. There's one in my pocket."

Erin tugged his bottom lip with her teeth. "You don't need it. We're making a baby."

Duncan whooped. "Hot damn!"

Giggling, Erin wrapped her arms around his neck as he lowered them both into the scented bubbles, holding her on his lap. She moved until she sat astride him and cupped his face in her hands. "I love you so much. Sometimes I think I could die of wanting you the way I do."

His hands firmed as he pulled her close, lifting her and lowering her onto his length. "I love you, too, baby. More than I thought I could ever love a woman. I never wanted anything in my life as much as I want you."

She nibbled along his strong jaw line as he moved her slowly up and down on his cock. She tried to hurry his movement, but firm hands on her hips prevented it.

"Please, Duncan. Faster."

"No, baby. This time I want to take you nice and slow." He pulled her down until his cock pressed deep inside her and began to run his hands over her. The level of the water had continued to rise and he reached out a long arm to turn it off.

Now that the sound of the water was gone, only the sounds of their lovemaking and splashing water filled the room.

Duncan ran his hands over her breasts, covering them with bubbles, before wiping them away, only to do it again. "You have the most beautiful breasts, baby." Thumbs flicked over her slippery nipples, making her gasp. "I can't wait to see our baby at your breast. Just the thought of it tears me up every time."

Erin felt her own eyes mist. "I can't believe you really want to have babies with me."

Duncan frowned. "Of course we do, Erin. Jared, Reese, and I want it all with you. Marriage, kids, the works. That's why we needed you to believe that we can do this."

Erin raised and lowered herself on Duncan's thick cock and shuddered. "Reese said we would fight and that you and your brothers already fight about me."

Duncan gripped her buttocks, sliding a finger down her crease and making her shudder again. "We do and we will. It doesn't mean we don't love each other or you. We just disagree." He grinned. "Hell, sometimes I fight just for the fun of it."

Erin moved on his cock, her thrusts coming faster as Duncan's finger stroked her bottom hole. "You and your brothers better learn that you can't boss me around." She gasped and cried out as his sneaky finger slid into her bottom with one smooth thrust.

"You'd better learn that you have men who aren't intimidated by your temper, baby."

Erin could feel the telltale tremors begin. "You don't scare me." She groaned as she inadvertently tightened on both the cock in her pussy and the finger invading her most private opening. "I can handle you."

Duncan pulled her down for a kiss. "Show me."

Water splashed everywhere as Duncan thrust into her in total abandon, both of them far beyond finesse. Erin screamed as she began coming, clamping down on Duncan hard as her entire body sizzled. Duncan forced her down on his length, his face contorted as he roared his completion.

He leaned back against the side, breathing heavily, his arms coming around her as she slumped on top of him. "I love your bubble baths."

Erin smiled against his chest. "I know you do. You all do. Why do you think I take so many now? I'm used to just jumping in the shower."

"I have an idea, baby."

Erin sat up and eyed him warily. "Whenever you get an idea, I get nervous."

Duncan grinned. "It's a surprise for Jared, but we'll all love it."

* * * *

They had to take a shower after the bubble bath and as Erin dried off, she looked down at herself yet again and eyed Duncan worriedly. "Are you sure Jared and Reese are going to like this?"

"Positive." Duncan nodded, grinning. He knew damned well he did.

Erin frowned. "They won't be mad that you did this to me?"

Duncan slapped her ass, making her jump. "When are you going to understand, baby? You belong to *all* of us and *each* of us." He rubbed his hand over her bottom where he'd just slapped her. "You get in bed. I'll go tell Jared you're waiting for him."

"No." Erin shook her head. "I want to go to him." She donned her robe and started out, stopping at the doorway. "It feels so much more sensitive like this. I'm already aroused."

Duncan moved forward to kiss her lightly. "That's the point, baby. Plus it lets us see and feel you a hell of a lot better. Wait until you see what it feels like when one of us gets our mouth on you. Jared's going to want to."

She started to turn, only to stop and face him again, frowning. "You got me ready for Jared."

Duncan nodded. "Yeah, so? He would do the same for me."

When she only stared at him in confusion, he turned her and slapped her bottom again, sending her out of the room. "You don't have to understand it, baby. You just have to enjoy it. Now go cuddle with Jared."

His smile fell when she left the room. It would take a lot of patience and understanding before they would be able to make her see that all of this would work out. But giving up wasn't an option. None of them would be able to live without her now.

* * * *

She found Jared in his office, sitting at his desk and looking over some papers.

He looked up at her entrance, and she warmed at the smile that immediately curved his lips. "Hi, love. Did you have a good time with Reese and Duncan?"

Closing the door behind her, she looked for signs of jealousy, grateful that she found none. Smiling at the surprise she had in store for him, she walked slowly toward him. The look in his eyes as he watched her cross the room heated her blood even more. She'd left the robe loose and it slipped off of one shoulder, immediately catching his attention. "Yes. But I have a problem and I'd hoped maybe you could help me with it."

He swiveled in his chair as she walked around the desk, turning to face her. He frowned his concern. "Of course, love. What's wrong?"

Erin bit the inside of her mouth to hide her grin at his look of surprise as she sat on the edge of his desk, moving his papers aside. She untied her robe and opened it. "Look what Duncan did to me. Now I'm cold."

His eyes blazed as he looked over her naked form, stopping when he got to her mound. "He shaved you?"

Erin pouted and fought to hide her grin at his incredulous tone. He stared at her mound, his smile growing, which had her juices flowing even more. She'd never played this way with any other man and loved it. "Now I'm cold. Do you think you could help me warm up?"

Jared's smile stole her breath. "Oh, yeah. I promise I'll do my best to get you nice and warm, hot even."

He pulled her down to straddle him, his lips covering hers. He pushed his tongue inside, where it swirled against hers before exploring hungrily. His hands covered her breasts, tugging at her nipples and she leaned into him, already needing to have him fill her.

His mouth left hers and moved to her neck, attacking the

vulnerable spot ruthlessly. Her head fell back in abandon as his mouth moved down to her breasts. Nipping and licking every inch of them, he sensitized them so much that even the feel of his breath on them felt like a stroke.

She moaned as he helped her lie back on the big wooden desk. Lifting and spreading her thighs, he positioned her to his liking by placing each of her feet onto one of the arms of his chair.

Trembling, she gasped as his hand moved over her mound. "Oh, Jared! It's so sensitive."

"Just lay back and enjoy, my love. I'm going to make a meal of this soft pussy." He swiped a tongue through her folds.

"Oh, God, Jared. It's incredible."

Strong hands under her bottom lifted her to his mouth.

"Jared! I…Ohhh!"

His tongue speared inside her, causing even more moisture to flow from her. Her flesh felt too sensitive, too naked to bear this. She felt exposed like never before as he opened her completely, with nothing to hide her from his eyes or his touch.

"Damn, I love the taste of you." Jared groaned, his breath hot on her folds a second before his tongue scorched her with its heat.

"Jaaaared!" Erin screamed his name as her orgasm washed over her, the touch of his mouth on her bare folds far too devastating for her to resist. Her mind went blank as his mouth moved over her, licking her tender flesh, and sucking it gently.

"I love your pussy bare." Jared kissed his way up her body. Looming over her, he slid his hand slid between her legs as his mouth hovered over hers. "Say it."

Erin opened her eyes and looked directly into his. "I love you, Jared. I love you so much. No condoms. We're making a baby."

His eyes flared as his cock jumped against her. He ate at her lips, his lips firm and demanding as they moved over hers. He pulled her impossibly close and yet not close enough. With his arms wrapped around her, he began to fill her. No matter how many times they made love to her, their initial surge into her never failed to take her breath away.

He filled her completely, not only her body but her heart as well. With his love and strength wrapped around her, she found herself letting go more than ever, finally at peace with her emotions. As Jared moved inside her, she could actually feel the last of her defenses crumbling around her.

She felt him everywhere, his body thrusting into hers deliberately, crooning to her softly as he pulled her closer. Quivers of sensation ran through her until her body became nothing but one trembling mass of need. With it came love so overpowering it scared her.

Jared must have felt her instinctive stiffening. "It's okay, love. I've got you. You can let go."

Looking up at him, the surge of love nearly overwhelmed her. "I know."

The look of surprise and love on his face took her breath away. "I love you, Erin. Come for me. Let me have it all."

Jared's beloved face filled her vision as he dug at the sensitive spot inside her. Her breath caught when his fingers moved over her clit. She came hard and fast, screaming and tightening on him everywhere. When he surged deep, growling in his throat, she tightened even more.

Her pussy clenched his thick cock as her hands tightened their grip on him, fisting them on his back. "Jared. Oh, Jared. Oh, God!"

He continued to stroke her, crooning to her as tears blurred her vision. "It's okay, love. I've got you." He smiled at her so tenderly it brought a lump to her throat.

Smiling through her tears, Erin wrapped her arms around his neck as he lifted her, sitting in his chair and settling her on his lap. Held against his chest, she stroked it, thrilling at the quiver of muscles beneath her hand.

She looked up to find him watching her searchingly. "I do love you, you know."

He smiled indulgently and ran a hand over her hair. "I know you do, love. My brothers and I have known it for a while. We knew you'd finally realize you have the courage to take what we want to give you."

Erin frowned. "I still worry that I'm going to do something to hurt one of you."

Jared tilted her face with a finger under her chin. "Isn't that true of any relationship, love?"

She shook her head. "You and your brothers make it sound so simple."

"And you make it sound so impossible. If you love us and we love you, everything else will fall into place. Just let it happen, Erin. Duncan, Reese, and I will take good care of you."

His hands stroked soothingly as he spoke, and then he helped her up and into her robe, smiling in amusement. "I wouldn't want you to get chilled again."

She watched him dress, thinking it a crime to cover that gorgeous body. Knowing she could have it naked again any time she wanted made it easier to bear. "If I do, I'll bet I can get warmed up again."

Jared laughed, stroking her bottom. "That's true, love. Come on. Duncan and Reese are probably anxiously waiting for us."

She frowned in confusion. "Why?"

Jared led her out of the room with an arm around her waist. "Some things we all need to be together for. Like the fact that you're ready to agree to marry us."

They walked out of the office and into the living room where Duncan and Reese looked up, smiling expectantly.

Erin stopped and put a hand over her stomach as the enormity of all of this finally sank in. "Oh, God. I'm going to marry three men, spend the rest of my life with three domineering, overbearing, and totally irresistible men." She looked at each of their beloved faces in turn and couldn't prevent a smile. "It seems I have no choice. I love all of you too much."

Jared kissed her hair as Duncan and Reese moved toward them. Duncan's grin flashed before he picked her up and spun her around.

"Welcome to Desire, baby."

THE END

www.leahbrooke.net

ABOUT THE AUTHOR

When Leah's not writing, she enjoys her time with family and friends and plotting new stories.

Also by Leah Brooke

Desire, Oklahoma 1: *Desire for Three*
Desire, Oklahoma 2: *Blade's Desire*
Desire, Oklahoma 3: *Creation of Desire*
Dakota Heat 1: *Her Dakota Men*
Dakota Heat 2: *Dakota Ranch Crude*
Dakota Heat 3: *Dakota's Cowboys*
Dakota Heat 4: *Dakota Springs*
Alphas' Mate
Tasty Treats Anthology, Volume 2: *Back in Her Bed*

Available at
BOOKSTRAND.COM

Siren Publishing, Inc.
www.SirenPublishing.com